I0714575

# MARSHAL IN PETTICOATS

The Halsey Brothers Series

By
## Paty Jager

Windtree Press
Hillsboro, OR

This is a work of fiction. Names, characters, places, and incidents either are the product of the author's imagination or are used fictitiously, and any resemblance to actual persons living or dead, business establishments, events, or locales, is entirely coincidental.

MARSHAL IN PETTICOATS


Contact Information: info@windtreepress.com
Cover Art by Karen Ronan
Windtree Press
Visit us at http://windtreepress.com
Publishing History
First Edition
Marshal in Petticoats  2006 (Ebook & Print)

Second Edition
Marshal in Petticoats  2011 (Ebook & Print)

Third Edition
Marshal in Petticoats 2014 (Ebook & Print)

Fourth Edition
Marshal in Petticoats 2022 (Ebook & Print)

Published in the United States of America
ISBN 978-1-957638-26-3

Foreword

The town depicted in this story was an actual mining town on the John Day River in Oregon. At the time the story takes place, the town was called Susanville. But when the miners stole the post office (yes, they really did) thus taking the name of the town with them, Susanville became Galena after an ore found with silver.

If you travel to Galena, you will find a few buildings. And up the canyon at Susanville you can find remnants of a small community and the footings of a stamp mill.

Acknowledgements

Special thanks to my friend, mentor, and editor, Nicole, who believed in my storytelling and honed my writing.

To my mom, Regina Norman, who believed in me and told me I could do anything if I set my mind to it.

# Chapter 1

Galena, Oregon
1886

"What kind of bullets does this take?" Darcy Duncan cradled a shiny, new rifle in her arms.

The merchant on the other side of the counter cleared his throat. She turned her thoughts and gaze from the gun to the merchant's bald head. Both the glass counter and his head shone glossy in the sunlight streaming through the large window. Did he spend hours polishing both?

The man plunked a box of .45-70 shells on the counter. Darcy picked one up. The bullet was nearly the same size as her pointer finger. Something this size was sure to bring down food, keep claim jumpers away, and scare their uncle should he find them. She shivered. So far they'd not been dogged by him, however, she knew it was only a matter of time before he caught up to her and Jeremy. He held deep grudges. Ones her pa hadn't known or he wouldn't have left them in his brother's care.

"I'd like to take a look down the sight outside," she said, setting the stock of the gun against her shoulder.

"Just bring the gun back and pay for it. I don't take kindly to people walking off with what they ain't paid for." The man scowled at Jeremy, who fingered a knife small enough to get lost in the pocket of a pair of trousers.

"If I like it, I'll pay for it," she said and knocked Jeremy's hand away from the knife before walking to the door.

The bullet in her hand made gripping the gun awkward. She slid the cumbersome ammunition into the chamber of the rifle. Slipping the bullet in her pocket wouldn't work. The man would think she was stealing. Neither she nor Jeremy, her twelve-year-old brother, had stooped that low even when their bellies went empty more than a day.

She stepped out of the store onto the hastily thrown down plank walkway. The board wobbled under her feet, causing her to lose balance. Darcy grabbed Jeremy's shoulder to keep from making a spectacle and clutched the rifle against her body. With her luck she'd drop the dang thing and have to pay top dollar for a scuffed up rifle. They didn't have enough money to waste on her clumsiness.

When her legs steadied, she raised the butt of the gun to her shoulder and sighted down the barrel. Squinting one eye, she tipped her head, and held the sight on a man walking across the street. Then another man appeared between the gun and her prey. She moved the gun, following him as he walked. Just like a deer in the woods. Only these deer weren't nearly as agile.

A cry rang out. Two men burst from a building across the street. Darcy trained the sights on a man with a bandana over his face, carrying a saddlebag. He vaulted onto the saddle of a horse tied to a rail. His movements resembled a leaping deer. This was more like hunting. The horse whirled around.

"Look!" Jeremy slapped her on the arm. "A bank robbery!"

BANG! The rifle rammed against her shoulder, a spasm of pain shot up her neck. Black smoke curled from the end of the gun and rolled back along the barrel. The caustic smell of burnt gunpowder burned her eyes and stung her nose. Through her tears, a blurry object fell forward over the neck of the horse and landed with a thud on the ground.

"Oh, blazes!" Her stomach convulsed as she stared at the motionless body beside the horse's nervous hooves. Darcy pushed the rifle at Jeremy. He shook his head and shoved it back at her. She scanned the storefronts and cringed as every person along the street, save the man lying face down in the dirt, stared at her. This was worse than the last town. At least there she'd only knocked the mayor's wife into a pile of cow manure.

Killing a man was serious.

"Darce?" Jeremy touched her arm and pointed to a rotund man headed their direction. The cigar hanging from his mouth puffed like locomotive.

"Let me do all the talking." She swallowed the lump of fear bobbing in her throat. Thrown in jail or being hung would leave Jeremy all alone. She'd do whatever it took, short of killing another person, to keep her brother from living alone or worse, back at their uncle's.

"What a shot!" exclaimed the man from a few yards away. He waddled up to Darcy and whacked her on the back. The momentum of the swat knocked her forward.

"Blazes!" she sputtered, regaining her footing. She scowled at the man. He didn't appear to be upset, but rather congratulating her. Darcy looked him over closer. Yep, he didn't seem angry. A shiver slithered down her back. Something wasn't right. She'd never been congratulated for being clumsy before.

"Young man you just saved the people of Galena from having to round up a posse and reclaim their money."

Darcy stared, opened-mouthed. She couldn't have shot the bank robber if she'd tried. Sure she could usually bring down a deer, but after a few shots. Her Pa had always called her an accident looking for a place to happen. Only this time her clumsiness killed a man. Her gut knotted as a foul taste rose in her throat.

"Yep, Darce is a crack shot with a rifle," boasted Jeremy.

The pot-bellied man stared at Darcy. It was the first time her appearance befuddled anyone. Her uncle had told her she was ugly, gangly, and nothing but trouble. She hoped the man didn't think someone this uncomely could be a girl. Hiding behind the male clothing gave her opportunities not afforded other women. She liked the independence and not having to fend off men. She'd had enough of that at the brothel.

She watched the man's gaze start at her faded black, short-brimmed hat that held her auburn, fuzzy braid curled atop her head. He skipped her face. His gaze traveled down her body hidden under a shapeless, large chambray shirt tucked into over-large, denim trousers held up with suspenders. Her pa's old boots were two sizes too big, but they kept her feet covered and hid the Bowie knife she used for protection.

"How old are you boy?" The man squinted at her. His perusal made her skin crawl. There was something about his beady eyes she didn't like.

"Fifteen."

The man nodded his head as though confirming his own thoughts. "What's your name?"

"D-Darcy Duncan." She squeezed her hands around the rifle in an attempt to stop their trembling. Shooting a deer didn't feel like this. Then her hands trembled with the excitement of a good meal. The gnawing in her belly had nothing to do with hunger. It was disgust at taking a life.

"I'm Tobias Craven." The man extended his hand. "You're new to these parts, I can tell." He winked and smiled, showing a row of straight, even teeth with two large incisors under a tobacco stained, gray mustache. "We could use someone of your talents in this town."

Darcy's stomach twisted with revulsion as her slender hand was enveloped in his smooth, fleshy one. Pa always said a man with a smooth hand ain't did a lick of work. She looked at Mr. Craven's shiny, blue vest and fancy suit with a gold watch fob and wondered how he made his living in an upstart mining town like Galena. And why he was so danged honored to meet a scrawny kid like her. He reminded her of their uncle. She jerked her hand out of his as the crowd of townsfolk pressed in on them.

"Who got him?" someone called out.

"Must be some crack shot," said another.

Jeremy puffed up his chest and climbed onto a sack of corn.

"It was Darcy Duncan, best shot this side of the Snake River," he said, making his young voice carry to the far reaches of the crowd.

"Jeremy! Come down from there." Darcy tugged on his shirt, dragging him off his perch. She pulled him through the crowd.

"You know as well as I do it was just an accident," she hissed through clenched teeth.

"Yeah, but they don't know that. Maybe we can get some money out of it." He rubbed his stomach. "I ain't eaten all day, and you said the last of the money was for mining supplies and that gun." He pointed to the rifle she still clutched in her hands.

"Blazes." Her throat constricted as she forced the words out. "They're gonna think I stole this." She didn't need stealing added to the other list of things she was sure would be drummed up against her. She spun around to head back to the mercantile. The crowd moved in unison toward them.

"Criminy! They're coming to get me already." Her pa didn't teach her to be a coward. She stood where she was; ready to be thrown in jail for stealing and killing a man. Course it wouldn't be the first time she'd tried to talk her way out of trouble. Seemed like everywhere she and Jeremy went, they ended up talking to the local officials. Then have to hightail it and hope their uncle didn't get wind of where they'd been.

The crowd stopped a few feet in front of them. Mr. Craven stepped forward.

"Darcy Duncan, I think the town is behind me when I say we would like to hire you on as our marshal." The man straightened his spine, tipped back his head, and waved his lit cigar, adding the nauseating fumes to the air around him.

"Our town has sprung up out of the great necessity to fulfill the requirements of the many gold seekers flocking to the Blue Mountains in search of their fortunes. With this great influx of people we have a need for some law."

"Yeah, especially since the post office disappeared!" yelled a man. A rumble of agreement came from the crowd.

Darcy had been in town when the gap between the livery and mercantile appeared one morning. The miners of Upper Creek had become tired of walking down to Galena for their mail and decided to move the post office to their camp.

Being accident-prone, her heart and sympathies went out to the town.

"What makes you think I could keep order in a town buzzing with gold?" She wondered at his sanity asking what he presumed was a young man, whose head barely came to the middle of most men's chests, to be a marshal.

Sure, she'd run away from the whore house her uncle sold her to after their parents died of diphtheria and helped Jeremy escape the cruelty of their uncle. Getting them back together hadn't been easy, but they were together and she'd fight anyone who tried to separate them either by good intentions or force. She'd bumbled through the best she could, keeping them fed and clothed, however, she wasn't one to take the welfare of a town into her hands.

In the few days they'd been in town, houses and tents had popped up along the middle fork of the Day River overnight. Freight wagons and pack trains pulled through the town several times a day, unloading and loading to move on to the next mining town.

"The way this young man can handle a gun, I say he's the perfect person for the job." Craven smiled and pointed to the gun she had yet to pay for.

Jeremy winked at Mr. Craven. "Darce is bashful about his shooting abilities and we," Jeremy cleared his throat, "he'd be honored to become a lawman." He stretched to his full height of five feet and placed a hand on the man's shoulder. "How much does it pay?"

"Jeremy!" Darcy grabbed hold of his ear and dragged him down the street. "We'll discuss it and get back to you," she hollered to the crowd over her brother's screeching.

She pulled him down an alley between the assayer's office and the livery. Building debris, packing crates, and piles of soiled animal bedding littered the alley. The smell of horses, wet hay, and dung permeated the air. Darcy kicked at wood shavings beside a crate and stubbed her toe. Pain shot through her foot. Frustrated, she plopped her backside down on a wooden box and grabbed her foot as she glared at her dimwitted brother.

"You know I can't shoot! That guy just got in the way." She rubbed her foot and glanced out toward the street. "I can't be a marshal of any town let alone one with bank robbers popping out of banks."

A hand rested on her shoulder. Darcy looked up at her brother's solemn face.

"I'll help you," he said with such conviction, she didn't laugh at his childish innocence. They'd done everything together. Faced their parent's death, faced their vengeful uncle, and survived on their own. Why shouldn't he think the two of them could face down outlaws?

"And I'm hungry." His young eyes beseeched her. "Maybe the town provides meals to the marshal. They did in Wilsonville. Remember?" He rubbed his stomach. His was as empty as hers and she was ready to do just about anything for a piece of bread.

"Please, Darce, I haven't had anything decent to eat in a week."

She cringed. He did need a stable place to live for a while and food in his belly at night when he went to bed. She looked at Jeremy's pants riding low on his hips, still not touching the tops of his shoes.

"The mayor gives me the willies. He's not what he seems." She hoped to prey on her brother's distrust of males in authority.

"You weren't too honest telling him you were only fifteen." Her brother's arched eyebrow reminded her of their father. Her face heated with shame. She had lied.

"Do I look like a nineteen year-old-male?" She stared him in the face. "I don't have any whiskers, I'm too thin. It's easier to pass myself off as younger."

"Why don't you stop hiding behind them clothes? You're old enough now to be taken serious as a woman."

"You remember what he said. 'Girl you're so gangly and uncoordinated no man'll ever want you for a wife'. Then he sold me to that woman." Her stomach curdled thinking how her uncle had taken their money and promised her parents he would take care of them only to sell her and enslave Jeremy. Then the bastard had starved his nephew.

"What he done wasn't right. But he was wrong about you, too." Jeremy's stomach growled. He looked apologetically at her and shrugged.

"You need food. We need a place to stay." She mulled the facts over in her mind.

The town called to her heart from the first day they arrived. She was tired of moving from place to place. Galena felt like home. She sighed. Maybe they could do the job. If anything came up, she'd send out a posse and stay in town. They shouldn't question her wanting to stay and protect the town while a posse went off after outlaws.

"I guess it can't hurt to give it a try. If it don't work, we can always cut out during the night with no harm to anyone," she said, reluctantly accepting the idea.

Jeremy pivoted on one foot and bolted back down the alley yelling at the top of his lungs, "We accept! We accept!"

Darcy ran a hand over her face. She looked

toward the street where Jeremy disappeared. A man a few years older than herself leaned against the corner of the building. He wasn't dressed like a miner. A long, heavy coat hung open, revealing a lean body and a holstered gun slung low on narrow hips. Dark curls stuck out from under a gray cavalry hat. A red bandana hung loose around his neck. He stared straight at her, his face expressionless, his dark eyes probing.

Her cheeks warmed under his gaze. She ducked her head, hiding behind her narrow brim. No man or boy, other than the mayor, had ever looked so closely at her. She dressed like a boy to make traveling about easier. She'd never let anyone know she was a woman. There seemed to be only one place for someone of her gender and young years to end up and she'd been there. She would never set foot in a bordello again. She'd been lucky to escape before having to submit her body to a man.

Her fists clenched and unclenched. She couldn't trust any male other than Jeremy knowing her truth. Persuading people she could be a marshal shouldn't be that hard.

She snorted. Blazes, she'd been pretending her whole life. Pretending she was tough, pretending she knew everything. She'd fooled Jeremy so far, so it shouldn't be too hard to fool a town that didn't know her.

The man still stood at the corner, watching. A shiver shook her body. Why wasn't he moving on? She wasn't that interesting. The only way to get to the main street was to go by him. God only knew what Jeremy was telling Mr. Craven. She ducked her head and hurried past the stranger, refusing to look at him.

Gil Halsey had followed the shooter and young boy to the alley. The boy had hurried out like his britches were on fire, yelling at the top of his lungs. He'd looked down right pleased with himself. But the shooter looked less than happy with the outcome. He watched the young man stand up and hurry past him to join the crowd gathered around Tobias Craven.

The shooting was too convenient.

Gil had heard the cries and hurried out of the saloon in time to see the robber fall. The expression on the shooter's face told it all. The young man hadn't meant to hit the robber. Gil settled his hat tighter on his head and ambled along to see about the hubbub around Craven.

The shooter and boy were in the middle of the crowd. The youngest had a smile stretched from ear to ear. The older boy looked out of place. Like he wanted to be down at the creek fishing or tossing rocks at the outhouse behind the saloon. But as Craven talked, the older boy started to take on a more confident stance, though he kept his face shadowed by his hat brim.

Craven raised his hands. He jabbed at the air with a stub of a cigar between his short, fat fingers.

"I'm proud to announce we have a new marshal," Craven bellowed to the crowd and pulled the young man forward. "I'd like you all to meet Marshal Duncan."

Gil frowned. The shooter raised his arms and ducked his head enough to allow the brim of his cap to hide all of his face but a confident smile.

"What we need a lawman for?" someone in the crowd hollered. "The last one didn't stick around."

"He got gold fever." Craven patted the new marshal on the back. "I don't think we have to worry about that with this one."

"I still sez we can handle our own problems," a short, stocky man said, pushing his way to the front of the crowd.

"Now Bill," Craven smiled at the man, "aren't you forgetting the fact them thieving miners from Upper Creek slithered down here and stole our post office?"

The crowd shuffled and murmured.

"By employing a law officer, he can go up to those scoundrels and get our post office back. They had no right to come stealing in here under the dark of night and take our building. If we'd had a marshal, they wouldn't have had the guts to do it."

Gil watched Craven puff up and scan the crowd. He smiled and thrust his arms out as though to embrace everyone gathered around. "Do this for your post office!"

The crowd applauded and cheered.

The new marshal stood in the shadow of the man speaking, his slender body nearly hidden from view behind the older man. The top of his head barely came to Craven's shoulder, and the mayor wasn't a tall man. Nope, the marshal wasn't built like any Gil had come across. He didn't look like a very good prospect for a law enforcer. Why had Craven hired on such a young man for marshal?

Shaking his head at the situation, Gil headed to the saloon where he'd struck up a conversation with a pretty dance hall girl before all the commotion took place.

He stopped and looked toward the man crumpled in the street by the bank. The body looked bigger than the man he followed to this town. It wouldn't surprise him to find Pete had been with the gang who attempted the robbery.

Gil pushed his hat back on his head and looked at the body. The boss wouldn't take kindly to hearing his son was gunned down by a boy. Would bringing back Pete's body cost him his job?

He ambled over to the man sprawled in the dirt. Gil lifted the head and looked him over. It wasn't Pete. Relief flowed through his body like a shot of good whiskey. But the man looked a little like the guy he'd seen Pete with before he disappeared.

The man groaned.

Gil rolled him over. The bullet had only gone through his shoulder. The fall from the horse must have knocked him out.

"Is there a doctor in this town?" Gil called, untying the bandana from around his throat and pressing it to the robber's wound to stop the flow of blood. A few of the merchants wandered out and stared down at the man.

"Aren't any of you going to help?" Gil asked as they all headed back to their businesses.

"He tried to steal our money, why should we help him?"

One of the merchants narrowed his eyes. "He a friend of yours?" They all glared at him, waiting for his answer.

"No, but you can't let him lay here and bleed

to death. He needs patched up and thrown in jail." Gil hooked the robber's arm around his neck. "Where can I take him for medical help?"

A couple of men pointed. Gil followed their pointing hands and groaned. A large house sat on the hill north of town.

He carried the man up the side street. After the robber got patched up and locked in jail, he'd hang around and wait for the rest of the gang to come get him. Then he'd get Pete. Save him the time of following every trail to a dead end.

Gil dropped the unconscious man off at the house of Mrs. Danforth and headed to the saloon. A messenger would be sent to inform him when the robber was ready to go to jail.

He entered the saloon and leaned against the bar, wrapping his hand around the glass of whiskey the bartender put in front of him.

Miners and merchants filed back into the saloon to discuss the new marshal and wonder at the hasty decision of Tobias Craven. But no one would go against the biggest landowner in Galena. Gil shook his head and wondered if Craven knew what he'd done hiring a greenhorn young man like the marshal.

Darcy followed Mr. Craven up the street to the jail. Jeremy skipped as he walked alongside of her, his eyes danced with excitement. She smiled at him and straightened her back. Mr. Craven had given her the rifle. He said they could stay in the quarters over the jail and get their meals at the hotel. It had turned out to be the best job they'd ever had. She grinned, three meals a day and a place to sleep, just to sit in a chair and look important. Maybe being a marshal wasn't that tough.

Entering the jail, a shiver of doubt snaked down her backbone. A large, wooden door with a small window made of metal bars stood open. She had a good look at the small room with two hard, wood beds. Gulping, she looked around at the sparsely furnished office. How would she throw grown men into the musty cell and lock them up? She looked at the rotund, flabby man beside her. *I couldn't even roll him in and lock the door.*

Dread began to gnaw at her euphoria of having a place to live and food to eat. She scanned the wood walls. Her gaze stopped at the wanted posters on the wall beside the window. Her heart jumped into her throat. Could she do this job? Could she act like a marshal?

Jeremy scampered inside the building. He jumped on the cots in the cell and ran his hands over the rifles on a rack along the wall. He appeared delighted with their surroundings. She tried to let his enthusiasm seep through her doubts. Craven had to go. She and Jeremy needed to talk.

"Thank you, sir. We'll settle in now." Darcy shoved Craven out the door and sat down in the chair behind the desk. She stared at Jeremy.

"What have you gotten me into?" It was easier to put all the blame on Jeremy than admit she wanted food and a place to sleep as badly as he did.

"Huh?" Jeremy stopped running and looked at her.

"How am I supposed to lock up grown men in there?" She pointed to the cell. "How am I to keep peace in this town when I'm smaller than most of the women?" She yanked open a desk drawer. The momentum caused something to slide to the front. She pulled out a metal star. It was as big as the palm of her hand and cold. She traced the raised letters with a hesitant finger as her heart hammered in her chest. What man had worn this before? Could she do the job?

"Jeremy, my feet don't even reach the floor when I sit in this chair." She looked at her brother. What had she done?

"You're supposed to lean back and put your feet on the desk. Remember Sheriff Tucker in Wilsonville when we was brought to him after you dumped that barrel of pickles over at the mercantile?"

Her frustration mounted at his memory of the events. "I didn't knock that barrel over. Some little kid was hiding behind the barrel and knocked it over when he ran out after another kid." She swung her feet, heavy boots and all, onto the desk. They landed with a loud thud. The spring on the chair twanged, throwing her forward and shoving the chair against the wall behind the desk. Her chin hit the desktop, clanging her teeth together as her body was thrown into the kneehole of the desk.

Her head started to clear when a soft, deep voice by the door said, "I'd like to speak to the marshal."

## *Chapter 2*

Darcy rubbed her chin and stifled a groan as she stared under the desk to see who belonged to the voice. A pair of dirty, pointed-toed boots with jangling spurs approached. Jeremy scampered around to the front of the desk, stopping the man before he could peek over the top and spy her.

"The marshal just stepped out. Let's talk outside. He don't like visitors when he ain't around," Jeremy said, dragging the man to the front door and onto the wooden planks in front of the building.

Darcy cursed under her breath, then thanked her brother for his quick thinking as she pulled herself off the hard floor. The marshal's badge dropped out of her hand. The metal star clattered on the planking at her feet. Her head and knees throbbed. She rubbed them as she peered out the door to see who asked for the marshal.

Her heart stopped. The profile matched the man from the alley. He leaned close to Jeremy, listening intently.

She bent over, picked up the badge, and pinned it to her shirt before slipping out the back door. The over-sized boots dragged and knocked together as she ran down the alley behind several buildings. Darcy stopped, sucked in air, and walked through the spot where the post office had once stood. She stepped into the street and scanned the wagons lumbering by and the people walking along in front of the buildings.

Most folk appeared to be miners and prostitutes. They all smiled and went about their business in a congenial manner. A few pinch-faced wives' of merchants hurried along the street as though they smelled something bad and wanted to get away from it. Darcy'd met this type of woman before. They weren't a whole lot of fun. She liked to think her mother wouldn't have walked around acting like she was better than others.

She ambled toward the jail in no hurry to get anywhere in particular, even though her curiosity about the man talking with Jeremy had her feet itching to hurry. Darcy stepped onto the planks thrown on the ground in front of the mercantile.

The board tipped up, and her body slanted backwards. She slapped her other foot down halfway up the board to keep it from hitting her in the face. The sound echoed up and down the street. The man with Jeremy looked her way. She smiled sheepishly and stomped on the boards. "Yep, set good 'n' flat," she uttered, to no one in particular.

The man watched her approach from under the brim of his sweat-stained hat. Darcy straightened her back and tried to swagger like she'd seen older men do when they thought people watched.

"Hey, Darce!" Jeremy hollered, swinging his arm like there was an acre between them instead of a building.

"Yeah?" She stopped a few feet from her brother and the man.

Just far enough back she didn't have to tip her head too much to look into his face. She didn't need her hat falling off now.

The man was much taller close up, and his eyes so brown, they were almost black.

"Can I help you?" She forced her voice deeper than usual, crossed her arms, and cocked her hip, putting all her weight on one foot like she was setting to stand and jaw a while.

"This here's Gil Halsey," Jeremy said, patting the man on the arm. "He wants to bring us a prisoner." Jeremy fairly danced as he spouted the last word.

Darcy dropped her arms and stared slack-jawed at her dim-witted brother. They didn't need a prisoner. She liked an empty cell just fine.

"W-w-hat prisoner?" she asked, forgetting to make her voice husky. She hoped the man, staring at her with deeper concentration than a player in a big stakes poker game, didn't see how the idea scared her.

"You didn't kill the man you shot. He's getting patched up. When he's done, I'll bring him over here until the judge comes through and there can be a trial," the man stated flatly. His dark eyes narrowed as they scanned her face.

She cleared her throat and remembered to use her manly voice. "Is he in good enough shape to

stay in the jail? I'd hate to have him die on me."
She didn't like the intensity of his gaze. It made her
skin tingle. His brown eyes finally stopped staring
her in the face, but now they gawked down her
neck, scrutinizing her chest, scanning her trousers
and Pa's boots.

He cleared his throat and looked her straight
in the eyes. "It didn't seem to bother you if he was
dead or not after you shot him."

Dang, it had bothered her. She just hadn't had
time to think on it.

"This is different. He would be under my care,
and I don't want anyone saying I didn't handle
him fair, knowing he's a robber and all." She stood
her ground, staring at his high cheekbones and
long straight nose. He wasn't hard to look at. She
almost sighed, but caught herself.

He pushed his hat back to scratch his head.
His hair was dark brown and curly like new wood
shavings.

"Why did you take this job?" he asked.

Darcy glanced down at the boards under her
feet. Her mind raced to hunt up a good answer to
his question. The truth; she was hungry and needed a place to sleep, wouldn't be the answer this
man wanted to hear.

"Marshal. Marshal Duncan," Tobias Craven
hollered, waddling down the street toward her.

"Yeah, Mr. Craven?" She turned to the man,
sliding her lips into a friendly smile. She didn't like
the mayor, but was happy for the interruption. It
gave her time to sort out an answer for Halsey.

"Could you come with me to my office to
discuss how you're going to go about getting the

post office back?" Mr. Craven looked Halsey up and down. "Do I know you?" he asked, dashing the ashes from his cigar into the street.

"Nope." Gil studied the richly dressed man and wondered what kind of a buffoon he was to have hired this young greenhorn.

Craven dismissed him, dragging the new marshal down the street. Gil watched the two. He got an odd sensation in his gut. There was something wrong about the marshal, and he couldn't figure it out. Maybe the younger boy could answer his questions.

"How old is your brother?" Gil asked. Jeremy started laughing till tears came to his eyes.

"Ain't my brother," he said between snorts of laughter.

Gil thought about that a moment. They had to be brothers. There was too much of a resemblance. Unless they were cousins.

"How old is he?"

Jeremy doubled over as another fit of laughter struck him.

"What's so darn funny?" Exasperated with the boy's attitude, he grabbed Jeremy by the collar of his shirt and pulled him upright. He shook the boy and watched the mischievous eyes turn solemn.

"He's nineteen." Jeremy squirmed out of Gil's grip and stood with his hands tucked defiantly on his hips.

Nineteen? He should be showing some male attributes. Whiskers, muscle. The boy Craven escorted down the street didn't look that old.

"Why did Tobias Craven hire someone so young as marshal?" Gil looked at the innocent face of the boy. "What did your—the new marshal do to get the job?"

"He shot the robber this morning." Jeremy looked at him all seriousness. "Didn't you see it? The whole town saw what a hero Darce is."

Gil scratched his head. There had to be more to it than that. He saw the shooting. It was too damned convenient for Craven. From the word around the saloon, Craven wasn't well-liked or respected, but he had money and liked to use it to get what he wanted. And he seemed to want a compliant marshal.

"How long you been in town?" Gil asked, leaning against the jail doorway.

"We came in on a freight wagon couple a'days ago." Jeremy sat down on the bench by the door.

"Freight wagon?"

"Yeah, Darce said we needed to save every penny we made at the last town so's we had enough money for supplies." He kicked the toe of his boot against the side of the bench.

"What'd you need supplies for?" Gil wondered at the two traveling alone. Figured they must be orphans to be so easily sucked into a scheme with Craven.

"We're going to get us a claim." His young eyes lit up. "Darce says if we work real hard digging gold, we could get enough money to finally build a house and settle somewhere."

"Where's your Ma and Pa?"

"Diphtheria got'em five years ago." The sadness in the boy's eyes told of a tight-knit family.

"You don't have any other relatives to take you in?" Gil didn't miss the hatred that snapped into the boy's eyes.

Jeremy narrowed his eyes and said defensively, "Why're you asking so many questions? We're doing just fine."

"I'm not. Dang, boy, don't get your dander up. The two of you aren't no match for the kind of people that come here looking for gold."

"We'll be fine. We've outsmarted worst." Jeremy threw him a glare and jumped off the bench, heading down the street.

Gil watched him duck into the hotel. There was something in their past. He shook his head. He knew how the boy felt. There were things in his past he didn't want anyone else to know either.

Lifting his hat, he scratched his head and stared at the wanted poster nailed next to the jailhouse door. What was Craven thinking hiring a wet-behind-the-ears boy for a marshal? They had to be up to something. If the brother knew anything, he wasn't talking.

He looked in the jailhouse door. Gentleness and innocence had wavered in the older boy's eyes. That wouldn't help him throw robbers and drunks in a jail cell. Neither one of them boys could jail anyone. He shook his head.

Meeting both the marshal and Jeremy, he also knew they didn't have a clue what they were up against. He should just ride out and look for Pete. But if his gut was right, Pete would come to Galena looking for his buddy. It was best to stay right here and keep an eye on the marshal and the boy. 'Cuz his gut also told him, they were going to need his help.

Darcy sat in the wooden chair across the desk from Tobias Craven. So far he hadn't said much more than he liked the way she could shoot. And she hadn't found a thing she liked about the man. He was full of himself, smelled of stale cigar, and had a calculating stare that reminded her of a mean rooster.

"Did you know the robber is still alive?" she asked. By the raising of his eyebrows and the glint of anger that flashed through his beady eyes, he hadn't known.

"He is?  Where is he?" He leaned back into his chair, his round head sinking into the cushioned back. His plump hands rested on the wooden arms of the chair. The vigorous tapping of one sausage-like finger gave away his irritation at the announcement.

"Being fixed up before he's brought to the jail."

Craven winced ever so slightly. Why didn't he want the man put in jail? It was where a robber belonged. She didn't like the idea of an outlaw in the cell beneath where she slept, but she couldn't let him go. After all, he did try to take the town's money.

"When does the judge come round?" she asked, hoping it was soon and she'd be rid of her unwanted guest. A tremor of fear chilled her. Surely he wouldn't be the judge on this side of the state.

"End of the month," Craven answered, though his mind seemed to be on something else.

"Oh." That was a long time to have someone in the cell. But plenty of time to catch up on eating and sleep if they had to leave in a hurry. "So what do you want me to do about the post office?" she asked, changing the subject to one that appealed to her more. She slid to the front of the chair so her feet would touch the polished wood floor. Her toes scuffed the surface as she swung them back and forth.

Craven looked across the desk. Smiling ruthlessly, he said, "Put a posse together and take your badge up to Upper Creek and get our post office back. Those no-good miners up there had no right stealing the whole damn building!" He slammed his fist on the desk and glared at her like she was the one who stole the rickety structure.

"I'll see what I can do."

He heaved his body up off the chair and leaned across the desk. "You won't see. You will get it back. We can't be an incorporated town without that post office." He sat back down and looked at her through narrowed eyes. "I'll pay you a good wage and feed you and that brother of yours if you do what I say." He stared at her point blank with his dark, beady eyes.

Darcy almost slid back in the seat of the chair to avoid the stare. His hollering and anger reminded her of the uncle they narrowly escaped. She'd stood up to him when she took Jeremy, and she could stand up to this man as well.

She planted her feet firmly on the floor and stared back at him. Squinting, she looked him square in his round face. He looked a lot like an old boar they had when she was a child, kind of jowly and ugly. All Craven needed was a crumpled ear and he could be that old boar's brother.

"Exactly what do you mean?" she asked.

"I mean, you just sit behind that marshal's desk, do what I tell you, throw the drunks in jail, and we'll all be happy." He smiled and slid a bag across the desk.

Darcy eyed the bag a moment before she picked it up. It was heavy for its size. She untied the string wrapped around the top and poured gold nuggets into her hand. The weight was amazing for such small rocks. Her grin spread thinking of all the food she could buy for Jeremy. And new clothes.

She hadn't done a thing to get such a windfall. This was like the time in school when a boy gave her a stick of candy if she'd go behind the schoolhouse with him. She frowned. He'd wanted her to show him her drawers. Nothing good ever came from getting something too easily.

She thought about Mr. Craven words. He'd asked her to do what he said, not what the town said. She knew a marshal worked for the town, not one man. He would pay her more than the job was worth, if she did as he said. It didn't sound like he had the town's best interests in mind.

She'd always done an honest day's work for her money. Ma and Pa raised her that way and that was what she'd taught Jeremy. She weighed the nuggets in her hand.

This was too easy.

She looked up at him. He grinned and waved his fat hand in her direction.

"There's more where that come from, if you do as you're told."

Darcy slowly replaced the gold. She smiled

back and placed the bag in her trouser pocket. He was up to something, and she and Jeremy were going to find out what. Pa raised them to be honest, but you didn't have to be honest with a dishonest person.

She'd take the gold, but she wouldn't use it. She'd keep it as a reminder the man sitting in front of her wasn't honest, and it was her duty as marshal to find out what he had planned.

Standing, she nodded to the man. If she didn't shake or say anything she wouldn't really be lying to him either.

He stood and walked around to the front of the desk. "That's my boy. Remember there's more if you just do as you're told and keep your mouth shut." He slapped her on the back. Her big, heavy boots stayed rooted to the floor as her body flew forward. To keep from falling, she flailed her arms and tried to shuffle her feet. The over-sized boots were her undoing once more as her body headed toward the floor.

Darcy grabbed the closest object—a coat tree. The tall, wooden tree teetered. She thought for a moment she wouldn't fall, but as usual, luck wasn't with her. The coat tree fell to the floor with her underneath. Inhaling the body odor from Mr. Craven's jacket, she choked and gagged. She shoved the coat aside, kicking the wooden rack off her legs.

Mr. Craven stood by his desk. His lips puckered in an attempt not to laugh. She glared at him, stood, and stalked out. The door barely hit the frame before she heard a thunderous belly laugh from the other side.

She stomped off fuming. That hadn't gone well—or had it? She'd just proven to Craven what a clumsy fool she was. If he thought she was a blunderer, he wouldn't take her nosing around seriously. That would give her the time and space to find out why he was worried about the prisoner, and why he didn't want her to do the job of marshal.

Darcy wandered out of the building a smile tugging at her lips at the thought of besting the man. She looked up and down the street. Her heart fluttered with pride. The streets were clean, the buildings small, but ample for the miners who came to town to buy supplies. Only the business people lived in town, so there were few houses as most lived above their stores. The people she met smiled. She smiled back, tipped her hat, and headed to the hotel.

Her stomach rumbled, reminding her she hadn't eaten since the day before when she and Jeremy had split a roll they'd received for carrying wood for the cook at the hotel. The woman had been eager to help them when Darcy had explained they didn't have any money—well none to spend on food. They needed all the money for mining supplies. She rattled the coins in her pocket. They still had the money if things went wrong and they needed to take off for some other town.

Inside the hotel restaurant, fresh baked bread and roasting meat welcomed her as she looked around. The thought of picking up and leaving again, didn't set well with her. She was tired of roaming. At nineteen, she wanted to settle down, preferably with a husband. To find a man who could tolerate her uncomely looks and clumsiness would require a miracle. She sighed. That day may never come. She'd seen women who were hard to look at married, but she also noticed they didn't trip over their own feet, nor have a habit of irritating the men folk.

Every male she'd ever come across other than her pa had brought up her hackles and caused her to argue. Granted they didn't know she was a female, however, she had a feeling she'd feel just as contrary to a man giving her orders. Just like Craven. She'd smiled, but she hated the fact he manipulated her. Or he thought he was manipulating her. She grinned. No man—she remembered the hardened old woman her uncle sold her to—or woman would tell her what to do from now on.

Darcy took a seat at an empty table by the front window. Watching the people walk by on the street, her circumstances flashed through her head. Her curiosity wanted to find out why Craven was leery of the prisoner, and why Halsey had taken an interest in the prisoner. To do that, she would need to be on friendly terms with the town folk.

A girl younger than herself stopped at the table to take her order. Her brown hair was pulled back in one long braid. Buckteeth shone pearly white when she smiled.

"Are you really going to be the marshal?" the waitress asked, batting her eyes like a smitten schoolgirl.

Darcy cringed at the outright flirting before she remembered everyone believed she was a boy. She cleared her throat and said in a deep voice, "Yeah, I'm going to give it a try." Flexing her arm, she winked at the girl and felt the eyes of everyone in the restaurant watching her. She looked around, with her hat tilted down to cover half of her face, and smiled.

"And you hit the robber with one shot." The girl practically swooned. Darcy squirmed in her chair. This was a little more attention than she liked. Usually when everyone watched her it was because she'd just caused a catastrophe. She didn't know how to take this new feeling of someone other than Jeremy looking up to her. She felt like even more of a fake.

"I'll have steak and potatoes," she said gruffly, dismissing the girl.

Her mouth watered at the thought of meat. It had been nearly a year since she'd sunk her teeth into a steak. She remembered the day clearly. She and Jeremy had helped a farmer in Wilsonville. Everything had been fine until they encountered the law. She frowned. It had been the kids playing in the store who caused the problem, but even her own brother hadn't believed her. Who would have thought a whole barrel of pickles could cost every coin they'd saved to that point?

She looked up when the waitress plopped a plate on the table in front of her. Potatoes were piled high alongside a hunk of meat swimming in its juice. Darcy closed her eyes and rubbed her belly. She could already feel it going down. Maybe this job wouldn't be so bad after all. If she could just stay away from trouble and find out what Craven had planned without raising his suspicions, she could eat like this for as long as she liked.

An elderly man with a face that resembled a

dried apple stopped beside her chair. His watery eyes peered at her with a strength she didn't think existed in his frail body.

"Is it true Tobias Craven hired you as marshal?

"Yes." She watched him. "You know much about him?"

"He's been round here since the first gold was assayed. He's got paper on most of the mines." Moving his head slowly he looked around the restaurant. "He owns most of the businesses, though not outright." He leaned on a cane. "If you plan on staying, watch your back. Strange things happen to the people connected to Craven." He tipped his hat and hobbled out of the restaurant.

Darcy stared after the man. Strange things. Strange in what way?  Unusual accidents? A shiver ran down her back. She'll have to be careful deciding how far she planned to follow Craven's orders. Fear gripped her belly. She had to decide to what extent she wanted to put Jeremy in danger while finding out what Craven had planned for the town.

She looked up. Halsey crossed the room and stopped at her table.

"I just dropped the prisoner off at the jail. Jeremy's watching him at the moment, but it isn't a good idea to leave him alone with someone as despicable as a robber." The way his gun hung low on his hip and the way he watched her, she knew he was trouble. What kind, she wasn't sure. She wasn't even sure he wasn't mixed up with the prisoner in some way.

What was his interest in the wounded man? He could even be in with Craven, even though they acted like they didn't know each other in front of the jail. They could have been setting her up. The only person she trusted was Jeremy, and he sat at the jail with a man capable of robbing a bank. She wondered if the prisoner was capable of worse deeds.

"I'll head over there when I finish my dinner," she said in a deep voice. Her gaze drifted over his face. She wasn't sure what he was about, but she'd keep an eye on him. It wouldn't be a hardship to look him over when she saw him.

Smiling thoughtfully, she cut into her steak. No one could ruin her appetite. She'd need all the strength to keep an eye on the prisoner and find out why Craven had hired her.

# *Chapter 3*

Gil had an uneasy feeling about the new marshal. Marshal Duncan had been hesitant about keeping the robber in the jail then took off to Upper Creek by himself and came back with nothing but a smile and a shrug.

"What do you mean, they won't bring it back!" Craven ranted as he confronted the marshal in the middle of the street.

"They said they liked having the post office up there." The marshal turned to walk away.

"I pay you to do what I say. Why didn't you take a posse up there, hook onto our post office, and drag it back?"

"If I go up there with a posse, what do you think those miners are going to do the next time they come to town?" The young man took a defiant stance, but kept the brim of his hat lowered to keep the riled man in front of him from clearly seeing his face.

Gil watched as the marshal spun and walked

to the jail. The mayor huffed and fumed in the street as a freight wagon lumbering through the dirt hid him behind a veil of dust.

It appeared the mayor and the marshal didn't get alone, but that didn't set with the rumor Craven and the marshal ate dinner together in the hotel restaurant every night. Was their arguing in the middle of the street a ruse? Gil shook his head. He was tired of trying to figure out the relationship between the two.

He looked at the jail. A chat alone with the prisoner was where he'd been headed when he spotted the two arguing in the street. The prisoner had been in too much pain to get anything understandable out of him when Gil escorted him to the jail. After a couple of days recuperating in a cell with only two boys to talk with, he figured the prisoner would be itching for some adult company.

Gil walked through the open door of the jailhouse. Jeremy swept the wood floor as the marshal leaned back in the chair polishing his badge.

"Excuse me?" Gil smiled when their heads turned in unison. Both sets of eyes widened with surprise.

"What can we do for you?" Jeremy asked, stepping between him and the marshal. Gil smiled and pushed his hat back. Though the boy was younger, he was obviously protecting the marshal. Gil thought back to the way the older boy never let anyone see his face. There was something about the marshal that made the hair on the back of his neck prickle.

"Just came to talk a spell," Gil said, walking across the freshly swept floor. He pulled up the only other chair in the room and sat down. Gil looked around the room before pushing the brim of his hat up and settled his gaze on the young man behind the desk.

The marshal tipped his head, shadowing his face with his hat.

"You ever look anyone straight in the face?" Gil asked, half-kidding, half-irritated.

The brim of the hat shot up and gray eyes glared back at him. "What's it to you?"

Gil thought the marshal's voice didn't sound as deep. In fact it had a pleasant sound to it—a feminine sound. The younger boy said the marshal wasn't his brother, but there was a definite likeness. Gil smiled a 'genuine from his heart' smile. It worked on the cook at the restaurant down the street when he wanted an extra piece of pie.

"Just seems a marshal shouldn't be afraid to show his face," he said, leaning back in the chair.

The marshal's expression didn't change a lick. He stared hard at Gil like he tried to see right through his skull and into his head to know what he thought.

"I'm not afraid to look anyone in the eye," the marshal finally said.

"Then why do you hide behind that brim all the time?" The marshal flinched. Gil couldn't help but smile. He'd hit a nerve.

"Maybe I don't like people nosing into my business." The brim came down again.

Gil stared at the top of the dusty, faded hat. "Being hospitable, doesn't mean a body is nosing into your business. Might do you well, to be more hospitable to folks. Might make your job a little easier."

The brim came up, and the gray eyes glared at him. "I am hospitable—to respectable people." The marshal's gaze looked him up and down. "I haven't decided whether you're respectable yet." Marshal Duncan didn't smile, but Gil saw a glimmer of whimsy in the gray eyes staring back at him.

"I see. What makes a man respectable?" The marshal had a slender face. Even for his years it appeared more delicate than it should. Having grown up with a passel of brothers, he knew the stages of a male's development.

"Well, being law-abiding." The marshal narrowed his eyes. "I haven't seen you do anything unlawful, yet."

Gil smiled. He didn't know why, but the young upstart tickled him. "What else makes me respectable?" he asked, noticing the younger boy had stopped sweeping and headed up the ladder.

"You aren't dressed like a miner."

"You think miners aren't respectable?" Gil gave no value to a man who spent his life digging for rocks and letting his family suffer, but in the same instance, he didn't think too many of them were lowlifes.

"No! I was just naming the reasons I'm wondering about your respectability."

Gil shook his head. How in tarnation had he gotten himself on this topic of conversation? All he wanted was to talk with the prisoner.

"Darce, maybe he could tell us—" Jeremy came alongside the desk, his hand held out.

The marshal jumped up as if a snake bit his backside. "Jeremy, where'd you get that?" The marshal sprang at the boy and a nugget the size of a grown man's thumb dropped to the floor.

Gil stared at the shiny rock. "Where did you find that?"

The boy snatched it up.

"Give that to me," the marshal growled, ramming his hands on his hips.

"I found it under your mattress, and I want to know where it came from," Jeremy said, dropping the nugget in his trouser pocket.

The marshal crossed the room, grabbing the younger boy about the neck. They struggled as the marshal dug for the nugget in Jeremy's pocket.

Gil leaned back in the chair, watching, wondering about the honesty of a young man who would not tell his friend he had gold. When the arm around the younger boy's neck started to make him turn blue, Gil decided to intervene. With quickness he revealed to few people, he crossed the floor, and scooped the marshal up around the middle.

He weighed less than a saddle, but struggled like a wild cat. The dusty, worn hat fell to the floor and a thick, auburn braid tumbled down the slender back.

The marshal stopped struggling, and Gil stared at the long hair. The marshal was a girl? He loosened his grip, settling his hands on her waist. It curved in like a woman's. He spun her around to get a good look at her face. She squirmed, and his hand slipped, cupping a firm mound under the chambray shirt. He pulled his hand back as if he'd just touched a hot pan. Yep, she was definitely a girl. From the size and of the lump, the marshal was more than a girl—she was a woman.

Marshal Duncan froze, and Gil looked down into her gray eyes. He'd never experienced such a jolt. His eyes scanned the scattering of freckles across the bridge of her nose and watched her tongue flick out to wet rose-colored lips. Why hadn't he noticed those feminine qualities before? 'Cuz, you weren't looking, echoed through his head as he stared down at her.

"Hey!" Jeremy punched him in the side. "Get away from my sister!"

The boy slapped a hand over his mouth and looked at Gil with scared, wide eyes. In a whisper he added, "You ain't going to tell, are you?"

Gil willed himself to look at the boy and not the flushed face of the woman taking a step away from him. The way she'd kept her hat tipped so no one could really see her face made sense. She could hide her body under baggy men's clothes, but a face as angelic as hers would be hard to pass off as a boy if people were allowed to stare overly long.

"Why don't you want people to know your female? Does Craven know?" Gil stared at the marshal. The resemblance to her brother was uncanny, but there were definite womanly attributes that any true-blooded male should have seen.

"Mr. Craven doesn't know." She stepped forward and clutched his shirtfront. "You won't tell will you? This is the best deal we've had since our parents passed."

He gently removed her hands from his shirt and backed up. "I won't tell." Gil knew the two were desperate for food and a place to stay. Letting on the marshal was a woman would only put them back out on the street. He'd rather keep an eye on them and know they were fed and had a place to sleep than tell the town a young, accident-prone woman protected them. He needed to think this through. Had the prisoner heard the truth about the marshal?  Would that complicate things? He swore under his breath and walked out of the building.

What happened? One moment he thought she was a greenhorn boy and the next he fantasized about her soft pink lips. Gil walked into the saloon still in a daze and ordered a whiskey. The dance hall girl he favored sashayed over, but he didn't want to think about her. His hand still tingled from touching Marshal Darcy Duncan.

Darcy crammed her hat on her head as tight as she could get it and sat with her head face down on the desk. Her heart fluttered, remembering his strong hands holding her and his eyes looking at her as though he'd never seen anything like her before. She groaned. It proved her uncle's words about her being uncomely.

Blazes! Halsey knew she was a girl. Would he tell, and she'd lose the badge? They hadn't had such a good job and a place to live in a long time. She could have risked everything by his discovering the truth. All because she'd kept the gold hidden from Jeremy.

She moaned. Halsey hadn't come by just to talk. Had he known she was a girl and came to prove it? She didn't think so. He'd looked genuinely shocked by his discovery. Her cheeks warmed.

No one had touched her so intimately. The waves of shock and heat his touch caused still radiated through her body. How could one touch make her body react so?

What did the man want? Was he a spy for Craven? Everywhere she went Halsey seemed to be there—watching.

Before she cleared things in her mind, a shadow fell across the desk. She tipped her hat forward and looked up. A dark-haired man, about her age, stood in the doorway, staring at the jail cell.

"Boy, you got a friend of mine in there," the man said good-naturedly and walked over to the desk.

"I wouldn't claim him for a friend since he was shot robbing a bank." She watched the corners of his mouth turn into a smile.

"You're sassy for such a young pup." He walked toward the cell.

Darcy grabbed the rifle leaning against the desk and pointed it at him. "Don't go near the prisoner."

Jeremy popped his head in the door and disappeared. She hoped he was headed off to bring reinforcements, the gun felt heavy in her shaking hands. From the glint in the man's eyes, he knew she was bluffing.

"Red. Red, it's me Pete," he called through the cell window.

"Wondered when you'd get me out of here," the prisoner answered from the other side of the door.

Darcy stood, shoving the chair backwards. It hit the wall with a crash. The man named Pete, turned, his hand clutching a gun aimed at her.

"That wasn't smart boy. I could have shot you right where you're standing and you'd never know what hit you."

"And you'd be keeping your friend company in the cell," Gil said, walking through the door, his hand hovering above the grip of his gun.

"I got this handled," Darcy said, walking forward. She didn't want anyone saying she couldn't take care of things.

"Hey, Gil, it's been a while." Pete stepped forward, dropping his pistol into his holster. Darcy eyed the two men. Gil knew the friend of the prisoner? Is that why he'd visited the jail so often? When the other man's hands went in the air, Gil leaned against the doorframe, crossing his arms and watching the man advancing toward him.

He appeared relaxed, but the tension between the men hung in the air as thick and rank as hog stench. They acted like old friends with a strong undercurrent of distrust.

"Came to see if Red, here, is being treated fairly," Pete said, stopping in front of Halsey. "Surprised to see you here."

"He's being treated as fairly as a bank robber can be expected to be treated," Darcy said. Both men looked her direction. There was a trace of annoyance in Gil's eyes, and a glimmer of humor in Pete's.

"You two can reminisce at the saloon. This is my jail, and I don't feel like any visitors at the moment." She waved the gun toward the door in an attempt to get them out. The two men eying each other with an emotion close to hatred, made her edgy. If they were going to draw their guns again, she wanted it out of her sight.

"When ya getting me out of here, Pete?" the prisoner called from the cell.

A smug look crossed Pete's face, and he looked directly at her. "Soon." He motioned to Halsey. "Let's go get a drink and talk about old times."

Gil stepped aside, allowing the man to exit. He leveled a stern look on her and quietly said, "Close and bar the door behind me."

Jeremy popped in the door as Gil stepped out. Darcy hurried across the room, slamming the door and barring it. Nothing made sense. Gil knew an outlaw, yet he did and said things that made her think he was law abiding. He didn't make sense.

"Where'd Pete go?" the prisoner called.

"To get a drink," she answered and turned to Jeremy. "Why did you bring Halsey of all people when you saw I needed help?"

"He has a gun strapped to him, and the man I saw in here looked like he could outgun a miner."

She smiled at his wisdom. It was true, none of the miners would be a match for a man used to living by the quickness of his gun. How fast would Gil be? Her heart fluttered thinking of him in a gunfight. He annoyed her, but she wouldn't want to see any harm come to him. Even if he was in cahoots with an outlaw.

She watched Jeremy climb the ladder to the room where they slept above the jail. It was going to be a long night. She'd need to stay alert in case Pete decided to come back and spring his friend.

Gil followed Pete into the saloon. Out of difference for the friendship they once had, he wanted to know why Pete left the ranch and all he would inherit from his father. Gil hadn't been able to figure out the wild side of the Chandler heir since he started working at the ranch. The young man had thought Gil was as wild as himself when he first hired on. Sure they'd gone to town a couple of times and whooped it up, but Gil didn't believe in causing trouble to have a good time.

He couldn't believe Pete went looking for money by stealing, when he had it falling into his pockets from his father's ranch.

"Why'd you leave?" Gil asked, taking a sip of whiskey.

Pete laughed scornfully. "I'd never get that ranch. Pa told me years ago I was unworthy of it." He pulled a plug of tobacco out of his vest pocket. Tearing a corner off, he looked at Gil. "Why bust my tail for him when I can ride into a town, take what I want, and ride out?"

Gil shook his head. This man had to return to the ranch. He wanted the foreman job. He wanted it more than he'd wanted anything in his life. Ranching set well with him. It wasn't as backbreaking as mining. He took another sip of whiskey and watched Pete stuff the tobacco in his mouth and down a jigger of whiskey.

Gil knew the hours his father had toiled at the mine. That wasn't the life for him. He wondered if his brothers still worked the mine or if they'd moved on. As always when he thought about his family his gut knotted and his throat went dry. He chased thoughts of them out of his head. He didn't need to bring back all the guilt that sent him out into the world.

He flexed his fingers. They stung from the tight grip he had on the glass of whiskey in his hand.

"Pete, your pa asked me to bring you back. I'm going to do it one way or the other." Gil leaned against the bar and stared at his friend.

"He won't be too happy when he hears I killed you." The man's tone had gone void of all emotion.

Gil didn't let his gaze waver. The threat didn't scare him—it made him determined. He knew Pete was handy with a gun. But Pete didn't know the hours Gil spent learning to draw his gun after the death of his parent's and younger brother. It didn't erase the guilt he felt for not being there to help them, but it prepared him to never have to feel guilty for someone else's death he could prevent.

Pete shifted and turned his head. The man was a coward. Instead of staying and fighting for what was rightfully his, he rode around taking from weaker people. Any loyalty he'd once had for the man faded like smoke from a chimney.

Gil couldn't take Pete back until he knew how many were in the gang and how they planned to get their partner out of jail. He didn't want anything to happen to the marshal and her brother. The two were starting to get under his skin, and he couldn't shake it.

Darcy lifted her tired head from the top of the desk. Her body ached from sleeping in the chair. After Gil left with the outlaw, she tried to stay awake. Later that night or was it morning—she shook her groggy head—a runner came to tell her of a drunk who needed to rest the night in the cell. When he was cozy in the cell with the wounded outlaw, she couldn't keep her eyes open any longer. She'd fallen asleep with her head on the desk.

Banging from the occupied cell set her teeth on edge.

"Knock it off!" she hollered, picking up a book and heaving it at the cell door.

"Come make me, lad," taunted the grizzled old man she dragged into the cell the night before. He'd come out of his drunken stupor in a foul mood.

"Who's making all the racket down here?" Jeremy asked, climbing down the ladder from the sleeping area.

"The fool drunk I put in there last night," she said, waving her hand to the cell. She scratched her head. "Go get them and me some food from the restaurant."

Jeremy jumped at the offer. She wished she could have left the noisy building, but she didn't want Jeremy to have to put up with the likes of what she had behind bars.

"Do you want to stay in there longer?" she asked, glaring at the bearded man.

"Old Tobias must be paying you real good to throw people who owes him money in here."

"What do you mean?" She crossed the room, but stood a distance from the man. He smelled sour and a dog would've loved to roll around in his mouth. It smelled like something had died in there.

"The only people other than him," the old

man jerked his thumb toward the robber, "that get thrown in here owe money to Tobias Craven. He held the papers on their claims, and they couldn't pay him back on time 'cuz they was locked up in here."

"Do you owe him money?" Darcy had wondered why a runner had shown up to tell her this man was drunk down at the saloon.

"Need to pay it before the end of the day or I lose my claim."

"To Mr. Craven?"

"Yep."

"Then why'd you go drinking so much the day before you needed to pay him? You got the money to pay or did you spend it all on drink at the saloon?" She couldn't feel sorry for a man who smelled like he did and acted irresponsible. She knew a couple of mules that smelled better and had more sense.

"Old Tobias invited me into the saloon. He wanted to buy me a drink. Then some pretty little thing came over and sat in my lap."

Darcy gagged at the thought of sitting on the man's lap.

"Next thing I know, I'm playing cards with some men and the girl keeps filling my glass." He smiled a nasty, brown smile. "I never turn down free whiskey!"

"It wasn't free if you're losing your claim."

He hung his head. "That's so. That's so."

"Why does Craven want all these mines? Are you getting lots of gold out of them?" Darcy tried to reckon why the wealthiest man in town would want all the small claims.

"It keeps me in whiskey and food. But I wouldn't call it a big strike." The man sat down on the empty cot.

Darcy shot a look at the cot where the wounded outlaw lay. He was on his back, his good arm draped across his face like he wasn't listening, but she could tell he was too still to be sleeping.

The miner's shoulders slumped as his head rested in his hands. "It's all I got. I put everything I owned down on that claim."

"Come here," she said, motioning for the man to walk over to the door.  He just stared at her. "Come on, get over here," she ordered, taking the keys from her pocket and opening the jail door. She pulled the old man out and shut it quickly behind him before the other prisoner could realize the door had opened.

"If I let you go, do you have the money to pay him off? And then take me out to look at your claim and all the other mines Craven stole?" Darcy had an inkling this information would get her to the bottom of Craven's dishonesty.

The old man looked at her like she was crazy. It was a reaction she'd received before. Especially, since taking on the job of marshal.

"If I can get to my claim, I got some more gold stashed." He grinned. "What're you up to?"

"Just trying to figure out what's happening around here, that's all." Darcy crossed the room and looked at the man. "I'll go with you to get the gold. That way I can see what Mr. Craven wants with your claim."

She walked to the door and stuck her head out to see why Jeremy wasn't back yet. He stood by the mercantile yakking to Gil Halsey, the basket of food dangled from his arm forgotten. She frowned in irritation and hollered.

"Jeremy! Bring me that food then get to the livery and get me two horses." Dang kid gets her into this then he goes and hangs out with the enemy.

Jeremy ran over, handed her the basket, and headed off to the livery at a run. Halsey took a step into the street in her direction. She thought about having him stay with the prisoner, but didn't want to leave him alone with Jeremy and the robber. She still wasn't certain what connection he had with the man locked in the cell.

Darcy ducked back in the jail. She handed food to the wounded prisoner and the old miner before sitting down at the desk and stuffing rolled up hotcakes into her empty stomach. When she finished, she and the miner stepped out of the building.

Jeremy charged up the street, pulling two big horses behind him. Darcy hurried out to the hitching post.

"I'm taking Mr. Winthrop to his claim," she said, adjusting the stirrups for her short legs. "We'll be back before supper."

"How come I'm not going with you?" Jeremy asked. His small mouth turned down at the corners as his eyes turned puppy-dog like.

Darcy knew the feeling of being left behind. She patted his shoulder. "I need you to stay here and look after the prisoner. You're the deputy. Bar the door, and don't let anyone into the jail. He's got friends hanging out around here."

Halsey crossed the street, headed directly for

them. "And don't tell him where I'm going." She motioned for Mr. Winthrop to get on the horse as she pulled herself up onto the tall gelding.

Squeezing with her legs, she urged the horse forward and headed out of town without looking back. Halsey would question Jeremy. Hopefully her brother could keep his mouth shut. She didn't need the likes of Gil Halsey following her around when she finally had a clue to Craven's plans.

# Chapter 4

Darcy had never been to a real gold claim before. For all her talk, she knew next to nothing about finding the shiny nuggets. She stared at the lean-to Mr. Winthrop called his shack. Being a miner didn't look appealing. It would be like living behind a stable. Something she and Jeremy knew first hand.

The claim sat on the edge of a babbling, clear stream. The sluice box stood on the embankment, two legs in the water and two legs out. A round, shallow pan leaned against the bucket on the ground next to the wooden box.

Winthrop dismounted and handed Darcy the pan. "You can try your luck up there." He pointed up stream. "I'll be right here digging out my stash."

Darcy took the pan and eyed him doubtfully. Should she leave him alone? The crystal clear water and shiny objects on the bottom of the stream-bed called to her as sure as the scent of a meal.

Dismounting, she tied the two horses to a

bush. To ease her mind the man wasn't trying anything; she glanced back over her shoulder. Mr. Winthrop busily dug beside his lean-to. Elated at the prospect of finally panning for gold, she whistled and continued on up the creek.

Trout darted around the colorful rocks on the bottom of the streambed. Their shiny sides glistened in the sun. Birds twittered in the maroon dogwood brush on the opposite shore. She breathed in the crisp air and looked around. It was a beautiful spot to spend all day searching for gold. The tranquility was almost as good as gold.

Squatting next to the stream, she scooped up dirt and rocks. She'd watched a couple of miners work a stream when they first came to Galena. Swirling the contents in the pan, the water picked up the lightweight objects, sloshing them over the edge. A lot of dirt and rock still remained. She added more water and swirled the pan, again.

The horses snorted. She swung around and found Mr. Winthrop trying to untie the gelding he'd ridden out to the claim.

"Hey! Where're you going?" Darcy dropped the pan and spun to stop the man. Her two-sizes-too-big boots tripped over the rocks, and she fell, face first into the cold water.

Gasping and flailing as the frigid water numbed her knees banging on the rocks, she tried to gain her footing. By the time she had her feet under her, the man had disappeared into the underbrush.

Darcy stood, soaking wet and shivering. She stared at the far side of the lean-to, searching the trees and brush for Mr. Winthrop. There wasn't a bush moving or a snapped twig to be seen. For an old man he moved fast and slick.

"Mr. Winthrop, please, come back here." Darcy stared into the trees where her prisoner disappeared, searching for a flicker of clothing or the sound of movement. The large, sodden trousers clung to her legs and made a slurping sound as she walked to the back of the shack. She stared at a freshly dug hole big enough for a canning jar. He did have more money. That he hadn't lied about.

Blazes! Why had she let a drunken old man get the better of her? She didn't know if he'd been telling the truth about owing Mr. Craven money or if he just used that as a means to get out of jail early.

"Leave it to me to believe some old coot." A light wind came up. She shivered and walked back to the horses. "At least you didn't get the horse," she yelled, grabbing the reins of the horse that carried Mr. Winthrop from town. She struggled to pull her cold body, clad in restrictive clinging clothes, up into the saddle.

She'd learned nothing from this trip, except to not listen to drunks and to watch her step. Defeated and tired, she rode back to town. The hair prickling on the back of her neck told her someone followed. She didn't care. If someone wanted to hurt her, they would have done it by now. She slumped in the saddle and let the horse head for home.

Sitting in the trees on the path from Mr. Winthrop's claim, Gil watched Darcy pass by. She looked sad and lonely. And lovely. For the first time since meeting her, he finally saw the curves of a woman. The wet chambray shirt clung to her body, revealing small, pointed mounds on her chest and a slim waist. He wanted to ride out and join her, but he couldn't let his body make decisions over his good sense. He still didn't know why she rode out to the claim and let the old man get away. It didn't make any sense. Nothing this woman did made sense.

The more he watched her, the more he wanted to know about her. He guessed it was from having been raised with four brothers that he found girls, and as he got older, women so interesting. They were soft in a way no man could be. In their manners, their voice, and their bodies. He could tell a lot about a man within fifteen minutes of meeting him, but a woman–he hadn't found one yet he could truly figure out.

They were a lovely puzzle. He didn't know why one woman's voice could make his teeth grind, while another one could send shivers of warmth through him like a shot of good whiskey.

The marshal had a smooth, gentle voice with a touch of fire. Gil figured it was the heat in her voice and the light in her eyes that wouldn't let him walk away.

He kept his distance in the trees, following her all the way to the edge of town. Before leaving the shelter of the trees, he watched Darcy peel the shirt off over her head and wave it in the air. He knew he shouldn't sit there watching her in her chemise, but he still found it hard to believe there was a woman under the male clothing. Her sitting astride the horse in trousers and chemise proved beyond a doubt she was a woman.

When the shirt appeared dry, she put it on, tucking in the tails and tugging it back out to billow above her trousers. She urged the horse forward, and Gil veered his mount to the left, coming into town from another direction.

He waited until she'd returned the horses and headed to the jail before he rode up to the stable.

"Who owns the claim about three miles out on Buck Creek?" he asked the liveryman as he dismounted.

"That would be Elias Winthrop. I believe the marshal threw him in jail last night for being drunk and disorderly."

"He got any partners?"

"No. You looking to partner up with someone?"

"Nope. Just asking." Gil headed out of the livery and up the street. His feet seemed to have a mind of their own lately. He found himself standing in front of the jail.

Gil took off his hat and combed a hand through his short, curly hair before stepping inside.

"Hey, Gil," Jeremy greeted him and cocked his eyebrow before motioning his hand in a gesture of "what did you find out". Before Gil could say anything, Darcy came down the ladder wearing a new set of men's clothes. Her eyes widened when she saw Gil standing before her with his hat in his hands.

"Ma'am..."

"It's Darcy," Jeremy whispered.

"Darcy, I was wondering if you'd do me the honor of having supper with me at the hotel tonight?" He added a smile that usually charmed a return smile from the ladies. If he had to drag her there she'd have a meal with him. He wanted to see just what she was about. He knew an evening of food and conversation was the way to a woman's heart. They liked to have money spent on them and attention paid to them. He could do that and maybe get her to slip up about why she went out to Winthrop's claim and let the old man get away. He also wondered at her sanity taking on the job of marshal.

Her eyes narrowed and her mouth pursed in an accusatory manner.

"I usually have my meals with Mr. Craven." She looked down at her shirt. "And I don't have anything proper to wear."

"Sure you do, Darce," Jeremy piped in. "You got your Sunday dress you could wear."

"If you remember,"—her eyes shot daggers at her brother—"it was on the small side when I wore it two years ago. And besides I'm not supposed to let people know I'm a girl."

"If you put on a dress and did your hair up, no one would even know it was you," Gil offered, trying to keep her from finding an excuse to not join him.

"I don't have any money for a dress." She looked at him with narrowed eyes.

"What about that gold piece you and Jeremy fought over earlier?" he asked.

"It's not mine to spend."

He wondered about the gold piece. It was just another reason to take her to dinner and get her talking.

Gil tossed a five-dollar gold piece on the desk. It rolled off, landing on the floor, and rolling between her feet.

"Go buy yourself a dress."

Her eyes lit up at the prospect before she looked down at the floor, veiling her gray eyes.

"I can't." She turned and bent over, picking up the coin. Gil nearly groaned as her small backside pressed against the cloth of her trousers.

She straightened and tossed the coin back to him. "It's not proper for me to take money from you." She walked to the back of the desk and sat down.

"It's a gift." He walked around the desk. Spinning the chair, he put a hand on either arm, blocking her in. "I want to eat supper with you at the hotel. You don't want to go looking like the marshal. Take the money and buy a dress." He watched her gaze travel from his lips to his hair to his lips again, then down to his hands holding her chair.

"Why?"

"Why what?"

"Why are you asking me to dinner?"

"You're a woman. I'm a man..." He watched the vein in her neck pulse and wondered what it would be like to feel that spot against his lips.

She sucked in her breath, bringing his mind back to the present. A soft, faintly floral fragrance drifted in the air between them. It didn't go with the person dressed in male clothes, but it definitely fit the picture of her his mind conjured up.

"Well?" With a finger beneath her chin, he tipped her face up to look at him.

"Well what?" A smile teased at the corners of

her mouth.

"Will you take the money and buy a dress and meet me at the hotel at seven?"

She hesitated and his heart hammered in his chest.

"Yes," she finally whispered.

The air whooshed out of her as he spun the chair around. He hurried out the door before he found himself gathering her up in his arms. There was something about the slight build and wide vulnerable eyes that made him say and do things he would never say or do with another woman. Why had he asked her to supper? And why had he offered to buy her clothes?

Groaning, he hurried to the mercantile for a new shirt. After he purchased a new shirt, he'd go to Mrs. Danforth's, the only place in town where a bath could be purchased. He wanted to show Miss Darcy Duncan he wasn't some rounder.

# Chapter 5

Darcy looked at the empty doorway and groaned. What had she done? She'd accepted an invitation to dinner with Gil Halsey.

The shiny coin twinkled at her as though laughing. He'd given her money to buy a dress. She slapped a hand against her forehead and closed her eyes. Why did he ask her? It wasn't her looks, she knew better. He wanted something.

Gil's face appeared in her mind. His dark brown eyes smiled back at her. Small crinkles at the sides told of a man with a lighter disposition than she'd seen so far. Maybe if she went to dinner with him she'd see the real man. Maybe he wasn't the enemy, maybe he could be someone she could trust and lean on. She could sure use another person's opinions about Tobias Craven.

She'd told Jeremy a prospector gave her the gold nuggets for safe keeping. He didn't need to know of the bribe or they were to stay away from any of Mr. Craven's dealings. The people around town had been close-mouthed about Craven. With more digging, she was bound to find someone with enough gumption to give her the low-down on the mayor.

Her eyes popped open. She wanted to walk into dealings with Tobias Craven with her eyes wide open. She didn't trust him. Eating supper with the man hadn't cultivated any new ideas. He just ate and grunted at the other people seated in the restaurant and ignored her questions.

Sharing a meal with Gil should prove to be a little more interesting. If not heart breaking. She knew he only asked her to dinner to get information out of her. No one would ask someone as plain and accident-prone as herself to dinner for any other reason. She sighed. However, it was her first dinner offer, and she wasn't about to pass it up. It could be the only one she ever received.

Sitting here daydreaming wasted time. A trip to the mercantile to buy a dress was in order if she planned to have time to clean up and get changed before seven.

"I'll be back in a bit," she said to Jeremy.

"You really going to eat with him and dress up and all?" Jeremy flashed a crooked smile, and his eyes danced with merriment.

"What? You think I can't look like a girl when I want to?"

"It's that you're wanting to." He jumped up and smacked her shoulder. "You've never wanted to before."

"Maybe I've been thinking it was time I acted like Ma would have wanted instead of hiding behind these trousers." She knew her ma would understand why she'd traipsed around the country dressed like a boy. After her uncle sold her to be a whore at a brothel, she'd bashed the first man who pawed her alongside the head and ran away, leaving a cursing man and madam in her wake. No doubt, if the madam ever caught her, she'd have to pay back the money paid to her uncle.

At nineteen, she was old and homely enough no man would think of her as anything other than a spinster. Even though deep-down she wished a man would look at her with yearning in his eyes. However, it seemed men had a hard time seeing past her clumsiness. Dressed as a boy they laughed and thought it was cute, but she knew the minute she put on a dress they would all have expecta-tions. She would have to act like the ladies she saw walking slow, wearing bonnets and white lacy gloves.

Darcy snorted. She'd rather never have a man than wear them frilly little gloves that didn't protect your hands from barbwire and stickers. She thought of Gil and groaned. He was almost worth wearing the silly gloves. Almost.

"You goin' after that dress or not?" Jeremy chided, jumping into the chair behind the desk. "I'll keep an eye on things while you're gone."

"You do that." Darcy ruffled his hair and headed out the door. She'd never bought a dress before. The only ones she'd ever worn were made by her ma.

She strolled out into the middle of the street. The more she ambled around town, the more it called to her. The lazy river just beyond the south side of town, though strewn with silt boxes and bent over prospectors, was a refreshing sight. The sluggishness of the river made a contrasting backdrop to the sound of hooves pulling heavy loads in and out of town all times of the day and the miners coming in and whooping it up when they hit a big one. Yep, this town was on the verge of losing its innocence, but then again, so was she.

Her cheeks heated thinking of her invitation to dinner. She needed a dress. She also needed to keep her identity a secret. Darcy looked up the side street climbing the hill on the north side of town. A large two-story house stood by itself a short hike up the rise. It resembled one she'd seen in the wealthier part of Portland. The building belonged to Mrs. Danforth. The sign on the side of the establishment read: Baths $1.

Darcy scratched her dusty hair and raised her arm, sniffing. Putting a new dress on a body this dirty would be a shame. She looked at the mercantile and back at the house. If she walked into the mercantile and purchased a dress, then showed up in it at the restaurant someone was bound to take notice. Best to check out Mrs. Danforth. See if she'd be willing to keep her secret and purchase a dress for her. Less chance Craven would put two and two together should someone run off at the mouth about the marshal buying a dress. It also wouldn't hurt to get another woman to buy one since she didn't have a clue about fashion.

She walked up the street and climbed the steps to the wide porch. A large oak door loomed in front of her. Darcy took a step closer and knocked.

"Come in, door's open," crowed a gravely voice.

Darcy pushed the heavy door open and stood in a well-lit hallway leading to a grand, sweeping staircase. A sweet floral scent wafted through the elegant entry.

"To your left!" squawked the voice.

Darcy jumped and looked in the direction of the sound. The head of a large, brightly colored bird bobbed up and down as he danced from one foot to the other on a wooden perch in a wire cage. She'd never seen anything like it. Darcy took a step forward. He ruffled his feathers and squawked again. "To your left!"

Ignoring the urge to inspect the bird, she followed the instructions. And stepped into the fanciest parlor she'd ever seen. The furniture was velvet. Large, ornately framed pictures of women in next to nothing hung on the walls.

Her mouth went dry, and her body began to shake. This wasn't just a bath house. It was what she'd run away from.

"May I help you?" The proper sounding voice jolted her into action.

Darcy turned to the voice, ready to fight to leave the building. A regal-looking woman stood in the doorway, a polite, interested smile on her face. Darcy judged her to be about the same age her ma would have been had she lived. The woman's brown hair had a touch of silver woven in the soft waves pulled back into a braided bun behind her head. She appeared classier than the last woman she'd met in a brothel.

The woman moved so gracefully, she appeared to float into the room. A gown of brilliant blue concealed her body yet showed a well-endowed female. She didn't look a thing like the weathered, alcoholic who ran the brothel Darcy fled.

"Are you Mrs. Danforth?" Darcy gulped and wished she could move like the woman standing in front of her. All her life she'd wanted to enter a room without people expecting her to trip.

"Yes. Why, are you looking for me?"

"This is a brothel." Darcy turned to leave.

"You look like you could use a bath." Mrs. Danforth was beside her so quickly and silently it made Darcy back away for fear she'd be held against her will, again.

"I ain't—"

"You aren't what?" The woman had a motherly look. The kind her own ma would give her when she wasn't quite behaving.

"I'm not here to work."

The woman laughed a soft rumble that made her ample chest bounce. "I wouldn't want you to."

She should have known a woman this classy wouldn't take on any homely girls. A wave of relieve washed over her. She liked the woman, but feared the idea of being in a brothel even for a bath.

"I-I was asked to supper tonight and was wondering..." She pulled her hat off, and her matted braid tumbled down her back.

Surprise sparked in the woman's eyes, before a smile spread across her face. The woman laughed. She took Darcy by the elbow and gently drew her over to the sofa.

"Does Tobias Craven know he has a young woman as his marshal?"

"No ma'am." Darcy replied. "And I'd appreciate

you not telling him."

The woman tilted her head and laughed. "I see where some of the ill-mannered buffoons around here would think you were a young man." She motioned for Darcy to sit. "And why you would want them to. Not too many men like having a woman around whose clearer thinking than they. Sit down and tell me why you came to Mrs. Danforth's."

Darcy sat on the edge of the fuzzy sofa and looked at the woman beside her. She wanted to be like this woman. Full of confidence and looking like she stepped right out of a newspaper advertisement for women's wear.

"A man asked me to dinner tonight." She looked at the woman half expecting her to laugh at the very idea of a man wanting to buy her dinner. When she didn't laugh, it bolstered Darcy's confidence and she continued, "I don't own a dress, well one that fits me, and I was wondering if you could help me buy one at the mercantile." She stumbled on. "I know you don't know me, but I don't know anyone in this town, besides my brother and Mr. Craven." Darcy looked at the woman. "I don't want him knowing I'm a girl. I wouldn't have a job, and me and my brother would have to move on."

Mrs. Danforth laughed softly as though they both had just shared a wonderful secret. "Honey, Tobias Craven is a fool. All he cares about are money and his own satisfactions. If you were to stand in front of him in a dress he wouldn't even know it was his marshal." She eyed Darcy. "What about the man you're having dinner with?"

Darcy stared at the woman. "He knows."

The woman laughed again. "I'm sure he does,

or he wouldn't ask you to have dinner. You must know him pretty well if he's found out you're a girl?"

Darcy blushed, remembering his hands on her body. "Yeah, I guess. I mean I know who he is, and we've talked a couple times." Her fingers touched the coin in her trouser pocket. "He gave me money to buy a dress for tonight."

Mrs. Danforth grinned. "Then we better get you a dress for tonight if he wants you to dine with him that much."

Darcy found herself swooped out of the parlor, up the grand staircase, and into a bedroom. "This isn't going to the mercantile," she protested.

"One of my girls is your size. She won't mind sharing for a good cause and it saves time." Mrs. Danforth opened a cupboard. Her upper body disappeared inside as she searched through the contents of the wardrobe.

Darcy looked around the room. Her mouth dropped open in rapture. Material she could see right through draped a large four-poster bed. Mrs. Danforth's bustle stuck out of a cupboard next to a tall, oval mirror. The floral carpet muffled her footsteps as she crossed to the wall. Darcy traced the smooth design of a flower indented in the fuzzy, maroon wallpaper with her finger. The brothel she'd been sold to was a rundown old house with squeaky beds and mice running amuck.

"You like my wallpaper?" Mrs. Danforth asked.

Darcy spun around, pulling her hand next to her belly as if the wallpaper burned her.

"I've never seen anything like it." Her gaze dropped to the beautiful dark green dress in the woman's hands. The color and sheen drew her across the room. The cool, smooth fabric under her fingers sent shivers of delight up her spine.

"This should fit you." Mrs. Danforth held the dress up to Darcy.

"I can't. This is too fine for me to wear." Backing up, she put distance between herself and the magnificent dress. She longed to feel it on, but knew deep down if she wore the dress it would be ruined, just like everything beautiful in her life had been ruined by her clumsiness.

"With your coloring it will look wonderful and that man won't be able to keep his eyes off you." Mrs. Danforth smiled.

Darcy looked at the dress and thought of Gil. What would his reaction be? She searched the woman's enthusiastic face for any sign of dishonesty. All she saw was a woman's delight in helping.

The dress was gorgeous. Many nights huddled with Jeremy in a barn or livery, she dreamed of wearing fancy clothes and dancing with a handsome man. There wouldn't be any dancing tonight, but her heart fluttered at the idea of seeing what she would look like all fancied up. Maybe she wouldn't look so plain and gangly.

"Go take a bath. I'll set out everything you need for the evening." Mrs. Danforth pushed her down the hall. "Lila! Lila!"

A girl not much older than Darcy with skin the color of newly brewed coffee hurried out of a room at the back of the house.

"See that Miss... What is your name, child?"

"Darcy. Darcy Duncan."

"See that Miss Darcy gets the deep tub and add

some of my special salts to the water."

"Mrs. Danforth that's not necessary." It felt uncomfortable to be beholden to anyone.

"A lady never argues," Mrs. Danforth scolded. "And a bath with salts is definitely necessary."

"I just need to wash the dust off." The idea of taking a bath with salt wasn't appealing.

The woman shoved her down the hall. "And Lila, scrub her tangle of hair and comb it out."

Lila took Darcy by the arm, hauling her into a room no bigger than the jail cell. A large, claw foot tub sat in the middle of the room. A silk screen, decorated with large pastel flowers, partitioned off one corner.

"Step behind there and take off yo clothes," directed Lila. "But don't be stepping your skinny butt out from behind there until I comes back in. George'll be hauling the water in, and he don't like looking at no skinny white girl." She smiled ruthlessly. "It make him do crazy things."

Darcy ducked behind the screen. She'd run into a few crazy men in their travels, and she wasn't about to do anything to set one off now. Especially in the confines of this tiny room. She stayed huddled in the corner watching the shadow of a large man dump many buckets of water in the tub. When he hadn't been back for a while, she crept up to the screen and peeked around. The tub was full and steaming. She'd never had a bath in a big white tub. As a child, her mother bathed her in the round tin tub every Saturday night.

Her fingers shook with anticipation as she unbuttoned her shirt and tossed it to the ground. With the shirt gone, and the suspenders dangling at her sides, the trousers slid off her slim hips. She shucked the chemise and drawers down over her boots before plopping her naked backside on the pile of clothes on the floor. The knotted bootlaces gave her fits before she pulled off Pa's boots.

Darcy walked over to the steaming water. Dragging her fingers through the warm liquid, she sighed. This was a heck of a lot better than washing in cold streams and hard rains. She could come to like being marshal. Food in her belly, a place to sleep, and a good bath now and then.

She stepped over the side. The faint scent of flowers and pine enveloped her. She slid into the tub and sighed, closing her eyes. Nothing had ever felt this good. The warm, scented water flowed over her body, caressing knots in her tense body.

A hand shoved her head under.

She fought her way to the surface and looked at the wicked smile on Lila's face.

"Yer hair would look better chewed off, but the mistress says to wash and comb it." Lila unwound the braid and shoved her under again. Holding her breath, Darcy blew out water when she came back up. Wiping the water from her eyes, she felt something oozing down her head. Darcy put a hand on her head. Something slimy covered the top.

"What's this?" She held her hand out to the merciless young woman.

"It's hair soap. Special made for the mistress." Lila sniffed. "I don't know why she's taking such an interest in a new girl, but I do what I's told."

Her reference to being a working girl caused Darcy to grab the side of the tub and start to stand. Lila knocked her hand off the side and pushed her into the water.

Darcy struggled to sit up and defiantly stated, "I'm not a new girl. I'm here for a bath, nothing more." And the loan of a dress and help dressing. She rolled her eyes. What was she thinking asking a madam to help her dress for dinner?

Lila looked the length of her naked body. "Mrs. Danforth usually takes on ones with more shape to them."

Darcy glared at the girl. "I said. I'm not one of the girls."

"Men likes their women to have more to hold." She smiled knowingly. "They don't like being poked by bony elbows and knees."

"If you keep insisting I'm one of the girls, I might have to put your eye out with one of my bony elbows."

Lila dunked her under again and massaged Darcy's head. The rhythm and skilled fingers lulled her into complacency.

"Yes ma'am. Man wants a woman who is soft to hold."

Darcy closed her eyes and tried to ignore the woman's comments as she imagined Gil with a more buxom woman on his arm. She snorted.

"What's so funny?" Lila asked.

"Nothing. Ow!" Darcy grabbed her hair and slid under the water. A grip on her hair jerked her to the surface.

"Can't get away from me in this thang." Lila laughed gleefully and pulled a comb through the tangled mess Darcy tried to brush every evening.

Tears rolled down her cheeks as Lila pulled and yanked her hair. Her head jerked this way and that, snapping her neck. She didn't know getting dressed up like a lady was so hard on a person. Those women she always thought of as being soft were tougher than they looked.

"Take this here soap and scrub whiles I work on your hair. Lord, you have a mess."

Darcy dutifully scrubbed her body with the scented bar while her head snapped back and forth. She remembered bath times with her mother gently brushing her hair and humming. A lump clogged her throat. Those days were gone. She could only hope to share some with her own daughter some day. Darcy cleared her throat, and Lila stopped combing.

"You okay, missy?"

"I'm fine. Just a little dry." A total stranger didn't need to know how much she missed her mother and father every day. Or how she'd spent the last four years doing whatever it took that was moral to feed her and Jeremy. There were times she'd wanted to sit down and feel sorry for herself.

Thinking of the good times their family had and the good times she planned to make for Jeremy, she'd pushed on. Always looking for a place they could put down roots and live. Galena felt like that place. If she could find out what Craven wanted with the claims along Buck creek.

When her body was raw from scrubbing and the comb moved through her hair with ease, Lila told her to stand. The woman wrapped a large fluffy blanket around her as she stepped from the tub.

Darcy smelled like a meadow full of flowers. Her hair hung damp against her skin, but if felt soft, unlike its usual scratchy texture.

Lila pushed her down the hall to the bedroom where she'd last seen Mrs. Danforth. Two girls a little older than Darcy turned from the bed.

"Hi, I'm Sylvie and this is Rose," said a brunette, pointing to a blonde. They were both dressed in their unmentionables, but they didn't seem to notice.

Darcy cringed and pulled the blanket tighter around her. Their garments were just as skimpy as she remembered, but the girls looked like ones she would have had as friends had she ever stayed in one place long enough.

Rose laughed. "Don't be bashful, Mrs. Dee sent us in here to help you dress." She grabbed the blanket, pulling it out of Darcy's hands.

She stood in front of the two girls. Embarrassment shot heat from her toes to her scalp.

"She was right, you'd make a good addition to the house," Sylvie said, looking her up and down.

"I didn't come here for a job," Darcy said, snatching up the lacy underdrawers on the bed. "I came here for a bath and help picking out a dress."

"I know, but if you ever need a job, she'd hire you on." Sylvie looked at her with sad eyes. "She's decent to work for and takes care of her girls."

"I don't need to be taken care of. And I don't need to work in a place like this."

Both girls looked at her as if she'd just let loose a string of blasphemy.

"We'd be elsewhere if there were more opportunities for us to make a living," Sylvie said.

"I'm sorry. I just want some womanly help getting dressed for dinner." Darcy felt sorry for the two girls. They'd obviously fallen on bad times or they wouldn't be selling their bodies to men. They both weren't hard to look at. She wondered why they hadn't married instead of working for Mrs. Danforth. She also wondered why a lady like Mrs. Danforth ran a house of ill repute.

"We heard you're the marshal. If we could pretend to be a man, we'd have a chance at a job, too." Rose handed her a chemise. Darcy looked at it.

"This is kind of skimpy isn't it?" she asked, thinking the material was mighty thin to keep her nipples from showing through the dress.

"It's what I wear with the dress." Rose looked at her as if she fell out of a tree and hit her head.

"Don't you have something..." Darcy frowned. She didn't know what she meant, but she wanted more clothing between her and Gil Halsey.

Rose and Sylvie exchanged looks and helped her slide the garment over her head and tie the string at the neck opening.

They picked up a funny shaped piece of clothing with strings dangling from it and walked toward her. Darcy backed up.

"What's that for?" She stuck out her hands. "I don't have to wear that do I?"

"It's a corset." Rose wrapped the garment around Darcy and cinched it up.

Darcy remembered hearing and reading about the piece of clothing, but she'd hoped to never have to suffer wearing one. Surprisingly, the garment didn't squeeze her ribs, but shifted her breasts heavenward, making her look more endowed than usual. Her heart thudded in her chest. Hopefully, the dress covered her pushed up breasts.

She stepped into two sets of petticoats, tying them at the waist. "This is more clothing than I've ever worn before, but I feel naked," she mused.

The two women smiled and slipped the beautiful green dress over her head. Rose spun her to button the back. Darcy lifted her gaze from the dress and looked into the full-length mirror. Her eyes just about popped out of her head. Her hair wasn't even finished and she didn't recognize the pretty woman staring back at her in the mirror.

# *Chapter 6*

Gil felt conspicuous all dressed up and smelling good as he sat at his favorite table. He'd seen more than one of the regulars nudge their partners and smile when he walked into the Hotel Restaurant.

He ran a finger under the collar of the new white shirt he'd bought at the mercantile. Eating with the marshal had seemed like a good idea at the time. Now, it seemed foolish. He'd asked a lot of questions around town that might get her in trouble if the wrong person put it all together. Gil frowned and stared out the window.

"May I sit down?" questioned a familiar voice.

"I asked ya to dinner didn't..." The reflection in the window stopped the words from spilling out of his mouth. He turned his head to appreciate the vision standing next to his table. His heart stopped a moment before dancing in his chest. Every person in the place had his or her eyes on his guest.

"Marsh- Darcy, you look great." He stood, all

of a sudden feeling awkward and shy. Pulling out the chair next to his, he inhaled the sweet scent of flowers as she sat down. His gaze traveled over her shiny auburn hair piled on her head, down her long white neck to the small mounds peeking above a lace-trimmed, low-cut neckline. The dark green dress hugged her body in all the right places. Never in his wildest dreams had he thought this woman hid underneath the large chambray shirt and trousers. His heart hammered in his chest so hard he could hardly breathe.

She smiled at him mischievously. "You lose the ability to talk since we last met?"

"I never–You're beautiful." Gil took her hand. He knew every man in the place was envious of his dinner partner. Her hand trembled. "What's wrong?"

"No one's ever said that to me." Tears glistened in her eyes.

He found it hard to believe. She was the most beautiful woman he'd ever had the fortune to lay his eyes upon and even better, she was his dinner companion for the evening.

"Surely, someone's mentioned it before."

She shook her head slowly. "My uncle said I was so uncomely and gangly no man would ever want me."

"He was either blind or dimwitted." His comment brought a smile to her rosy lips.

"I've never managed to walk this far in a dress and kid slippers and not cause something to go wrong."

"It can't be that bad." He continued to hold her hand. The fit was perfect. Her slender fingers fit in the palm of his hand as he gently rubbed his thumb back and forth across the pulse of her wrist. The beat quickened under his touch. He looked up into her gray eyes. They were wet and staring at him with such earnestness he wanted to take her into his arms and hold her forever.

"I have been nothing but a blunderer since the day I was born." She ducked her head, and his heart went out to the awkward girl who had grown into a beautiful woman.

The waitress approached. Gil held Darcy's hand as he ordered steak and eggs for them both. He smiled when the waitress huffed back to the kitchen. She'd been expecting their usual banter over the price or the quality. Tonight, he had interest in no one but the woman at his table.

The other patrons who'd watched Darcy's entrance with interest resumed their meals. They didn't seem to recognize the marshal. Gil breathed a sigh of relief. He wouldn't be putting her in any danger if the rumor he dined with a beautiful woman got back to Craven. He knew Craven wouldn't make the connection. Though he might wonder where the beautiful woman came from in a town scarce of women other than prostitutes.

Gil smiled at his dinner guest. He wanted to know everything there was to know about the contrary creature sitting beside him. "Tell me about your blunders."

Darcy stared at Gil. He was handsome beyond words. His hair shone like a new saddle. A smile unveiled crinkles of mirth around his brown eyes. Eyes that made her feel like she was basking in the warm comfort of sunshine. His fresh shaved face softened his looks. He smelled of shave soap and male. It was unlike anything she'd ever had the pleasure of breathing.

And he actually wanted to hear about her exploits in disaster. She started off with her very first mishap, knocking over Grandma Howard's china cupboard, breaking heirlooms which had come over on the Mayflower. Over apple pie and coffee, she ended with the accidental shooting of the bank robber.

"I knew it," Gil said, sitting up straight and making heads turn in their direction.

"Knew what?" She could sit here looking at him all day. Darcy sighed, resting her chin in her hands.

"I knew you hadn't meant to hit that guy. So how did Craven latch on to you? Did you know him before the incident?"

The hair on the back of Darcy's neck bristled, and her spine snapped straight. "What do you mean? Did I know him before?"

"What is your relationship to Craven? How friendly are you two?"

Her hands clenched in her lap as she stared at Gil. How could he go from being so attentive and wonderful to accusing her of–things!

"Why'd he hire you? Even you pretending, you know," his hands wavered around. She knew what he meant. "I don't get why he wanted you for a lawman."

"You low…" Darcy stood, causing every head in the restaurant to turn to them.

"Darcy, don't cause a scene. I'm just trying to figure things out."

"By being rude?" She swung around and nearly fell when the skirt wrapped around her legs. Her arms flailed in the air as she tried to regain her balance and not topple forward. Gil reached out, grabbing her with strong hands. Her face heated as his touch set off small shocks of awareness throughout her body. She didn't want to feel this way about him.

Not now. Not when he'd made those accusations.

"Don't touch me," she said through clenched teeth. "I got here on my own. I'll find my way back just fine." He took a step back, dropping his hands to his side. With her head held high and her back stiff, she walked across the room and out the door.

Tears trickled down her face as she hurried down the street in the cumbersome dress. She needed to get back to Mrs. Danforth's. She wanted her shirt, boots, and pants back. She wanted to be Darcy. The real Darcy, not some painted up version which made people think things of her that were false.

"What do we have here?" asked a male voice as she passed an alley.

Darcy kept right on walking. She didn't need any trouble in borrowed clothes and no knife.

"Hey, gal, where you headed in such a hurry?" The voice sounded right on her shoulder.

A hand grabbed her arm, and she spun around.

"Home. Please, take your hands off me." Before she could get a good look at the man, he was whipped around, and doubled over.

"Get!" Gil shouted as the man roared to life, running at him with his head down.

Darcy couldn't make her feet move as the two battled in front of her. Her heart bobbed up and down in her throat when the man landed a punch to Gil's stomach, bending him in the middle. The man moved closer. Gil whipped the man's feet out from under him with one swift kick.

The fighting made her nauseous and excited at the same time. Gil moved with speed and accuracy, landing more blows than he took.

Grabbing the man by the shirtfront, Gil held him at arm's length. Darcy watched as he cocked his arm back ready to land another blow. His arm dropped, and he grabbed the man by the chin, turning it this way and that in the dim moonlight.

"Pete?" Gil looked into the squinting eyes of the man he'd spent the last three weeks looking for.

"Gil, you old dog.  What are you beating me up for? This little harlot yours?"

Rage boiled through him. Darcy was far from the kind of woman Pete referred to. Gil twisted the shirtfront and raised his fist. "She's not a harlot. You apologize to the lady."

"Okay, take it easy." Pete raised his hands in submission. "Ma'am, I'm sorry. If Gil says you're a lady, you're a lady, 'cuz he outta know."

Gil groaned when Darcy stepped closer. She peered into Pete's face. "How would Gil know a lady? And how come you know him so well."

"'Cuz, he's never been with one!" Pete slapped his thigh and laughed raucously. The stench of whiskey on his breath told Gil why the man had been so bold. He was liquored up.

"That's enough." Gil landed a blow to the

man's mid-section, folding him into a sitting position against the hitching rail.

"Come on." He grabbed Darcy by the arm,
dragging her down the street to the jailhouse. She
didn't need to ask Pete any more questions. In
his drunken state it was hard to say what all Pete
would have said. Gil didn't want Darcy knowing
what he was really doing in town. With her loyalty
to the badge Craven pinned on her, she'd be following him around thinking he would lead her to
the outlaws.

"How do you know that man?" She stopped in
the middle of the street.

"Keep moving. Every randy man in town is
going to be sniffing at your skirt as soon as Pete
comes around and tells them about the beautiful woman walking the streets alone." Gil draped
his arm over her shoulders, steadily moving her
in the direction of the jail. He needed her out of
that dress and looking like the greenhorn marshal
before Pete decided to look her up.

"You're dodging my question."

He just grinned and pulled her closer. The top
of her head came to his shoulder. His hand slid
down her arm and rested in the curve of her waist.
It felt right to be walking down the street with her
tucked against his side.

They were a building away from the jailhouse
when Darcy pulled out of his grip and stopped in
the middle of the street.

"Not here, I have to get my clothes."

"Where are they? I'll get them and bring them
to you."

"No!"

Her hysterical command had him wondering why he shouldn't get her clothes. There was only one place he could think of that she wouldn't want him going. "Why not? You leave them at Craven's?" He couldn't hide the contempt in his voice. Pete may have been right after all. Maybe she was just a harlot who did men's bidding.

"Are you dimwitted? He'd strip me of my badge if he saw me in this dress." She shoved her fisted hands on her hips. "I left my clothes at Mrs. Danforth's."

He looked her up and down. Someone with a free hand had helped her get fixed up. He hadn't noticed all the little things that now were sticking out like sirens. No wonder Pete had thought what he did.

"You work for Mrs. Danforth, too?" he asked, not hardly believing it since he had more or less dogged her around the last few days and never once saw her enter the big white house on the hill.

She rolled her eyes and tapped her foot. "You sure you never got kicked in the head as a boy? No, I don't work for Mrs. Danforth. You think I'd spend my days as a boy to trot around in my unmention-ables at night?" The spit and fire slowly ebbed in her eyes. "I went there for help."

Gil grinned. "I should have known someone helped you sparkle like a chunk of gold."

The glow of anger sparked in her eyes. "You don't think I could have done this on my own?"

Gil groaned. "I didn't mean it like that."

"Why were you following me?"

He shuffled his feet in the dirt. "Looking the way you were, I knew you were bound to run into trouble." He stepped forward, reaching out to touch a stray curl. "Darcy, stay here and let me collect your clothes from Mrs. Danforth. It's not safe for you on the streets with all these randy men about."

She looked up into his eyes. With her head tilted back, he could see her swallow and wondered what that long creamy neck would taste like.

"What's going on out here?" Jeremy stuck his head out the jailhouse door. "Hey Gil, whatcha doing with this lady when you're supposed to be with my sister?" He stepped out onto the walkway and stopped when Darcy started giggling.

"Darce? Is that you?" Jeremy pulled her into the lamplight of the building and smacked his hat on his thigh. "Whoa you cleaned up nice." He turned to Gil. "Didn't she clean up nice?"

"That she did." Gil couldn't help but look at the woman beside him with admiration. "She's a gem."

Her head jerked up and those gray eyes searched his face. He kept his expression blank. She wouldn't find anything he felt written on his face. She was the first woman to come along and make him feel protective, but that didn't mean he had plans any farther ahead than the present. He wasn't giving any false impressions.

"It was good of you to walk me home, thank you," she turned to enter the building.

Gil grabbed her arm. He didn't want her thinking anything long term, but he wasn't ready to lose her company.

"Jeremy, run down to Mrs. Danforth's bath house and collect you sister's clothes."

Jeremy headed out the door. "Wait." Gil called him back. "Give them this for the dress." Gil flipped a coin at Jeremy. He caught the coin and disappeared out the door.

"I talked about me all night. Tell me about the man you beat up. How you and a robber know so much about each other?" She looked up at him with a determined expression. He wanted to tell her, but it would only make their friendship more difficult.

"There's nothing to tell." He walked over to the window. He'd avoided this conversation all night. It would only make things more complicated to tell her why he was after Pete. For that matter he should have been out there dragging the sorry sod back to the ranch. He couldn't seem to leave Darcy. Something about the way she was dressed tonight made her seem more vulnerable than when she paraded around as the marshal.

"Do you have family?" she asked from close behind him.

"Yeah."

"Who?" She placed a hand on his shoulder. It surprised him she tried so hard to be friendly. He didn't turn around even though he wanted to take her in his arms and tell her his life story. But he would never share with anyone what he'd done as a young boy. He hung his head. The shame of it still ripped at his heart.

"Four brothers." He turned to her, remembering the accusatory looks on their faces the day he left. "We aren't close like you and Jeremy."

"Why?"

He shook his head. "Doesn't matter." He put a hand on her arm, gently rubbing his thumb back and forth across her soft, silky skin. "Why do you care?"

"I like to know my enemies."

His gut twisted. He tightened his grip on her arm.

"Why do you think I'm the enemy?" He wanted to taste her lips and show her what kind of devilish thoughts he had. Tipping his hat up, he slowly lowered his head. He'd make her believe he was the enemy. That would keep her away from him.

"I think it's time for you to leave," Darcy said, taking a step back.

"I'll wait until your brother gets back." Gil gently pulled her to him. He'd held women before, skilled and unskilled in the seduction of men. But he'd never had one that made his tongue feel so thick or his hands itch to touch her.

"Thank you for helping me." She touched a bruise on his cheek. He grimaced. A look of regret crossed her lovely face. Her discomfort softened his resolve to prove himself the enemy.

"It was my pleasure."

"You find beating people pleasurable?"

"No." He touched a sore rib and looked into her concerned face. "It was my pleasure to protect you."

He gazed at the sprinkling of freckles across her nose and stared at her lips. Every nerve in his body told him to kiss her. His arms tightened around her. He used all his control to slowly release her. Now was not the time.

"I-I-I'll be fine by myself." She worried her upper lip with her teeth, and he darn near popped the buttons on his Levis. Her big innocent eyes were all that kept him from dragging her to the floor.

"Maybe you're right." He lowered his hands, feeling the curves of her body as he went. "I'd better get going. I have to head out early in the morning." He walked to the door. With his hand on the latch, he turned back for one more look. "You sure you're going to be alright?"

She nodded her head, and he stepped out into the brisk night air. He needed to find Pete and get back to the ranch before he did something stupid—like kiss that woman.

Chapter 7

Darcy felt more like herself the next day trudging through the ankle-deep mud looking for all the miners thrown in jail on Tobias Craven's word. She looked up at the slow moving clouds which dumped a heavy load of rain during the night. This much rain didn't happen often on this side of the state, but she was used to it from having traveled between Oregon City and Portland more than once in the last few years.

At the mercantile, she knocked the clumps of mud from her feet and entered the building. The walls were stocked with every implement needed to find gold in the Blue Mountains. She eyed the shiny tools thinking about the nuggets tucked under her mattress.

More than once she'd thought about using those nuggets to buy supplies and head out of town. No one would miss her and Jeremy. She didn't think Mr. Craven would come looking for them. He wouldn't waste his time following them for the small bag of gold. Most likely he'd be relieved she was out of his hair.

Craven hadn't hired her on a whim. He wasn't for the good of the town, but rather the good of Tobias Craven. Her friendly feelings toward the people of Galena left the bag under the mattress untouched and hooked the badge on her shirt every morning. She didn't want to see all these good folks come to any harm.

"Morning, Marshal," called Mr. March, the owner of the mercantile. "What'cha looking for today?"

"Information." Darcy walked up to the counter and smiled at the bald-headed man. He was so skinny; his clothes hung on him like he was a stick. But he was kind to both her and Jeremy. She wasn't sure if he'd figured out she wasn't a boy, but he treated her decent and in her book that made him a friend.

"What kind of information?" He handed her a sarsaparilla stick and leaned his elbows on the counter.

"Who would know where I could find these men?" She handed him the list of prisoners.

He looked at the list and squinted at her. "Aren't these the men been jailed over the last few months for being drunk?"

"Yeah. I need to ask them some questions." She squirmed under his stare. "There's paper work that didn't get signed." She smiled sheepishly. "Didn't know it hadn't been taken care of 'til this morning."

He grinned and handed the list back. "I guess since you're new to the job, there'd be things sneak up on you." He pointed down the street. "I'd say the best spot to find what you're looking for would be the assayer's office."

"Thanks, Mr. March." Darcy shoved the stick candy in her mouth and headed out the door. She stepped onto the makeshift walkway. The planking slipped in the muddy ground. Her arms flailed wildly as she tried to keep her balance. Strong hands steadied her. She swung her head around and found Gil smiling down at her.

"That ain't very marshal like," he said, looking at the candy hanging out of her mouth. His hands lingered on her sides. Her body tingled as a wave of heat burned her face. His touch reminded her of the night before. She'd been certain he was going to kiss her before he'd backed off and walked away.

Her feet steadied on the planking, but her knees had gone weak. Cursing her traitorous body, she pulled from his touch.

It still rankled he'd left last night without her drawing him out. She wondered about the man he fought. They seemed friendly. Why would Halsey be friendly with a friend of a bank robber? There were lots of mysteries around the man. The biggest was why she fevered every time he touched her.

He had a silly grin on his face as he continued to stare at the candy in her mouth.

"Don't suppose it is." She frowned at how her body reacted to his touch and wondered how to get rid of the candy. She didn't want to waste it. In all her years of keeping Jeremy and her fed and clothed, she'd learned you never throw anything edible away. She started to shove it in her pocket and thought better of it.

"Here." She poked it in Gil's mouth and headed down the street, veering clear of the assayer's office for fear he'd see where she was headed.

She didn't want Gil to know her actions. If she hung around him too much, she knew her lips would start flapping. She'd always had to work at keeping secrets. Something about the way he looked at her made her want to spill her guts. She shook her head, flinging the thoughts out so she could concentrate on the task ahead.

She ducked down the alley beside the saloon and stopped. Tobias Craven and a man had their heads bent together in conversation at the back of the building.

Darcy dropped down into the mud and crawled to a pile of wooden liquor crates stacked near the back door of the building. Looking between the stacked boxes, she watched the man with Craven look around like something was going to jump out and bite him.

The man was taller and broader than Craven, but he didn't have extra weight. He looked all muscle. Long blond hair curled up at his collar. A big nose shaded his small mouth. The wide hat he wore shadowed his forehead and eyes. Large ears stuck out from his head. He'd be easy to pick out in a crowd.

"I don't care what you and the boys want. I'm paying you, and you'll stay put until I give the word." Craven's voice raised an octave as the man grabbed the front of his coat.

"How do we know you aren't going to fill your saddle bags and leave us sitting here with nothing?"

Craven knocked the man's hands off his coat. "I'll keep the marshal busy with drunks, and you and the boys can ride in and get the money." Craven pulled a cigar out of his jacket pocket. "After I send the marshal off on a wild goose chase, I'll meet up with you and we'll split the money."

The men laughed and Craven slapped the tall man on the back. "By this time next month I'll have started my own enterprise, and you and your friends will be living the high life wherever you wish."

Craven walked to the back door of the saloon, and the man with the large ears headed Darcy's direction.

Her heart pounded clear up in her head making a whooshing noise. She pressed her back against the crates and hoped he wouldn't look back and see her. A box slid behind her as he turned the corner onto the street. She let out her breath and started to stand when the pile tumbled down on top of her.

Darcy screamed and pushed at the falling boxes. One came down and thunked her in the head. She bit her bottom lip and squeezed her eyes shut to stop the tears threatening to spill as the pile covered her.

Gil spied Pete sitting on a horse down the street from the saloon. He pulled the candy from his mouth and headed straight for the man. Pete noticed him when he was a few feet away.

"Where's your lady friend?" A big, welcoming smile spread across his friend's face.

"Where she belongs. I thought you knew better than to bother a woman when she didn't want to be bothered. That what the gang you're riding with teaches you?"

Pete's smile disappear and his face hardened to a glare. "Why are you here bothering me anyway? I thought you'd be back at the ranch belly crawling to my pa."

Gil reached up to grab the sassy mouthed man off his horse and drag him back to the ranch, but the sound of approaching feet made him think better of it.

"Your Pa asked me to bring you back." Gil stepped back and smiled. "And I plan on doing just that."

"Tell him I ain't coming back. I don't like chasing stinkin' cows for long hours and building fence." He looked over Gil's shoulder. "I like the gang I'm riding with. Why don't you join us?"

"It's not for me. I like the ranch. But I can't go back unless I have you with me." Gil stepped forward and dropped his voice to a menacing growl. "I have a lot at risk here, and you're the only one who can help. I will haul you back to the ranch, either with your cooperation or without."

Pete glared down at him. "Don't threaten me."

A scrawny, pockmarked man walked up and stood beside Pete's horse. "You got trouble?" he asked, squinting at Gil and resting his hand on the handle of his pistol.

"No, Gil's an old friend," Pete said with emphasis.

"Remember what I said," Gil knew he'd have to wait until Pete was alone, like last night. He mentally slapped himself for letting his protective instincts make him forget his mission to bring Pete back to the ranch. Then he had nearly kissed the woman. He didn't need her under his skin any more than she already was. She kept getting in the way of his mission.

Pete's body tensed when his gaze traveled over Gil's shoulder.

Gil pivoted in time to see a big-eared man come out of the alley behind the saloon.

"Someone you know?" Gil asked.

Pete glared at Gil and nudged his mount forward, leading another horse. The pockmarked man smiled a tobacco-toothed grin and followed. Pete stopped beside the big-eared man and handed him the reins of the extra horse. The man mounted, and they took off down the street like they were late for dinner.

Putting all he knew together, it appeared to Gil the man had been meeting someone. He hurried to the alley to see if he could catch a glimpse of who it might have been. Moaning echoed through a pile of wooden crates in the alley.

"Is someone in there?" he called, picking up the crates and setting them to the side. He stopped and listened. Nothing. He cocked his head. There had been a noise earlier. A crate moved, and Gil frantically pulled at the crates. Picking up a box, he discovered a large mud-covered boot. His heart raced. He knew the person at the bottom of the pile.

She was covered with mud from her hat sitting to one side of her head, all the way down to the ridiculously big boots. She scowled when she opened her eyes and saw him.

"What are you doing back here?" he asked, grabbing her hand and dragging her to her feet.

"Taking a nap. And thank you for interrupting." She spun as if to walk away and plopped down on a crate.

"You alright?" Gil dropped to a knee to look into her face. Her eyes were large and glassy.

She looked at him, but her pupils didn't focus on him. Gil had seen this before when a mule kicked a cowhand in the head. He slid an arm under her knees and picked her up.

"Don't touch me," she protested before grabbing her head with muddy hands. "Ow! My head feels like someone is stomping in it."

"A box must have hit you on that pretty head. I'll get you to Mrs. Danforth. She's the only one in town that knows anything about doctoring." Gil tucked her head against his shoulder and carried her down the street and up onto Mrs. Danforth's front stoop. He liked the feel of Darcy in his arms. She was light enough to be easy to carry, but enough weight and curves to let a man know he had a woman and not a child in his arms.

He knocked on the door and waited.

"Come in!" called the parrot. Gil ignored the bird, knowing the proprietor wouldn't appreciate him packing the muddy woman in his arms straight into her parlor. He knocked again.

"What you knocking for when the bird—" Lila opened the door and stared at the mud covered woman. "Not her, again. Don't she know how to stay clean?"

"Lila, Mrs. Danforth needs to look at her. She

hit her head, and her eyes don't look right." Gil looked passed the maid. "Should I bring her in the back way?"

"No, just take her straight back to the kitchen."

He headed down the hallway.

"Don't touch the walls. Them's covered with the best wallpaper you can get in this God forsaken country."

Gil smiled as he carefully carried Darcy into the kitchen.

"What is all the racket going on down here?" Mrs. Danforth asked, gliding down the back stairway into the kitchen.

Gil had never been in such a fancy house. It was done in all the best woods and built like a southern plantation he saw in a book. The owner didn't have a southern accent, but you could tell she was a lady of breeding.

"That misfit you took pity on yesterday is back," Lila said, filling a basin with water from the reserve on the cook stove.

Mrs. Danforth looked at Gil and smiled. "You must have been her dinner date last night."

His cheeks heated as the woman appraised him.

"She has good taste." She pushed the muddy hat from Darcy's head and lifted an eyelid. Immediately, she straightened. "You two fill a tub with water. Cold water. We need to wake her up and keep her awake. She's evidently been hit on the head." She scowled at Gil. "Did you do it?"

"No Ma'am. I found her under a pile of wood crates behind the saloon."

Mrs. Danforth sniffed at Darcy. "I didn't take

her for a drinker."

"She hasn't had anything to drink. She tends to have accidents," Gil said, not wanting the woman to think ill of Darcy and not help her.

"What was she doing behind the saloon?"

"I intend to ask her that very question when she's able to answer."

He helped Lila carry buckets of cold water into a bathtub off the kitchen. When it was half full, Mrs. Danforth instructed him to carry Darcy into the room. He stood her on her feet. She swayed into him. Her small, supple body against his wasn't too hard to take. If he hadn't been standing in a room with two other women present he wasn't sure what he would have done.

Mrs. Danforth must have seen the lust in his eyes. She grabbed Darcy by the arm, pulling her away, and ushered him out the door.

Gil sat down on a kitchen chair. Why was this girl—no woman—making him feel things he'd never felt before? The images and thoughts coursing through his head were things he'd associated with being ready to settle down. He figured he'd find a woman that would make him light-headed and his heart race when he was closer to thirty. After the drifting urge had passed. Not now. He didn't want or need someone to tie him down.

Since meeting Darcy, thoughts of settling in one place sounded pretty good. Would Pete's father let him bring a wife to the ranch? As foreman he'd have his own quarters. He ran a hand over his face. He didn't have time for these thoughts. For all he knew, she was no better than Pete. She worked for the biggest crook in Galena. He'd seen one of the outlaws come out of the alley where he'd found her. She could've met with the big-eared man. He may have got rough and knocked her into the pile of boxes.

He knew when the two women placed Darcy in the bathtub. A long rush of curses sailed from the room. A smile spread across his face. He'd never heard those words—or so many—from a woman before. She had a colorful way of shouting her anger.

A while later, Lila pulled Darcy, all wet and wrapped in a wool robe, out into the kitchen. Gil stood. He smiled at the look of surprise in her eyes.

"How come you're sitting in Mrs. Danforth's kitchen?" she asked, looking around the room.

"I'm waiting for you." He stepped toward her. She backed up. Her eyes widened as she stared at him.

"Why?"

"I found you and brought you here. I wanted to make sure you were alright." He reached out and touched her cheek. "How do you feel?"

"Like I was left in a snow drift to die." She closed her eyes. "I just want to lie down and take a nap."

"No!" Lila jumped between them, grabbing Darcy's arm. "Mrs. Dee says you're to keep movin'." Lila shoved Darcy at him. "Take her for a walk around the house. I got better things to do."

Gil moved to Darcy's side, tucking her under his arm. He walked her down the hall, through a doorway, and into the parlor. Two young women, dressed in next to nothing, turned and smiled. He stopped, unsure how to explain the woman tucked against his side. But then, he couldn't be any more shocked than the two women standing, purt near naked, in front of him.

"Excuse me, Lila said to walk around. I didn't know there was anyone else here." He started backing to the door.

"There's a couple of empty rooms upstairs, make her happy use a bed," said the tallest girl. They both giggled.

Gil cringed and looked down at Darcy. She didn't need to hear that kind of talk. From her half-closed eyes and drooping head, he didn't think she'd heard a thing, but he had to keep her moving. He should be following Pete back to his hideout instead of wandering around a bordello with a semi-conscious woman.

"Darcy?" He stopped in the hallway and propped her up against the wall. "Darcy?"

"Yeah?" Her eyes fluttered open. A smile tipped the corners of her small mouth into an inviting sight.

He lowered his head, thinking about kissing those tempting lips.

Her eyes popped open, and she shoved him away. "What are you doing?" She looked at him with an accusing glare.

"Nothing. Just seeing if you were conscious yet. I really need to get going." Gil took a step forward. "What were you doing in that alley?"

She turned her head. "I thought I heard something. The next thing I knew crates were falling on me."

She lied. Her eyes looked everywhere but at him, and he'd seen the outlaw come out of the alley. What was she doing with a man like that?

Why did he even care?

"You need to be more careful." He chucked her under the chin and hollered. "Lila! I'm out of here. She's all yours."

Darcy stared at the door as it closed behind Gil. She vaguely remembered him finding her under the pile of crates. And him carrying her. She looked around. He'd brought her to Mrs. Danforth. Did he think this was where she belonged?  In a brothel?

Lila came down the hall.

"Where's my clothes?" Darcy asked, plucking at the robe covering her naked body

"They're in the yard with the rest of the mud," answered the fresh woman.

"I need some clothes, so I can get back to work." Darcy had planned to follow the man she saw with Craven. Now, she had to keep an eye on Craven and try to talk to the miners at the same time. Her head pounded, sending shards of light piercing through her head and making it hard to think. She'd have to enlist Jeremy to follow Craven while she went out to the mines. The idea didn't set well, but she didn't see any other way.

She had to find out why Craven wanted all the claims. And exactly what the big-eared man and Craven had planned.

# Chapter 8

Dressed in pants and shirt, not nearly as large as her father's, Darcy headed back to the jail to get Jeremy and fill him in on the job she wanted him to do. Gil tipped his hat and rode by smiling as she crossed the street to the jailhouse. She pretended to not see him. His laughter carried over the sound of a passing freight wagon.

"Hey, Gil!" Jeremy called from the jail doorway, nearly swinging his arm off.

"You got better things to do than wave at no-accounts like that man," Darcy said, grabbing him by his ear and dragging him into the building.

"Darce, quit! That hurts. Why you mad at Gil? He bought you dinner last night." Jeremy rubbed his ear and looked at her like her brains had spilled out all over the floor.

"Just because." She sat him in a chair. Placing her hands on the arms on either side of him, she leaned down close to his face.

"I need you to do something real important.

And you need to keep your mouth shut and just listen and watch. Do you understand?"

He nodded his head solemnly.

"If I didn't need to go talk to some of these miners, I'd do it myself, but I can't do both at once."

He swallowed and nodded again.

Darcy looked into her brother's eyes and hoped she wasn't putting her only living blood kin in danger. Her heart ached at the thought of anything happening to him.

"I need you to keep an eye on Mr. Craven. He's up to something. I saw him talking to a man—probably an outlaw—this morning. They were talking about taking something, and I could tell that something wasn't theirs to be taking."

Jeremy's mouth dropped open. "You mean he ain't a good guy?"

"That's right. I've known for some time. But I didn't know he had a plan. I'm getting close to figuring it all out." She smiled. Wouldn't it just wipe that smirk off Halsey's face if she got the goods on Craven?

"Now you just follow and don't let him see you. If he talks to a fella with big ears and yellar hair, try to move in and hear what they're talking about." She looked him straight in the eyes. "He's dangerous. Don't do nothing to get yourself in trouble."

He shook his head. "Where're you gonna be?"

"Talking to some men about land." Darcy waved the list of names she'd salvaged from her muddy pants pocket under his nose and headed for the assayer's office.

She had her doubts about letting Jeremy trail around after Craven, but she didn't trust anyone else. She couldn't let Halsey find out what she was doing. She still didn't know how he fit into all of this. He didn't seem to like Craven, but that could just be a ruse to see how much dirt she'd dug up on the crook.

She knew how her body felt about Gil Halsey. Just thinking of him made her heart race and her body heat. But she wouldn't follow her heart on this. She had to follow her head, and it said to not let anyone know what she found.

At the assayer's office, she located where each of the miners had their mines. They all paralleled one another along Buck Creek. Darcy shoved the paper into her pocket and headed to the livery to get a horse. She smiled. That was one good thing about being marshal. She had the use of any horse she wanted whenever.

Riding had always been one of her favorite things to do, but the last few years she hadn't owned a horse and rarely had the extra money to rent one. She and Jeremy had traveled in the backs of freight wagons across the state. They'd met many nice people along the way, but nowhere had ever felt like home.

She smiled wistfully thinking a quiet ride would help her sort things out. Rounding the corner into the livery, her nose bumped into the leather back of a man as big and wide as the livery door.

"Hey, little man, you need to watch where you're going," the man said, twisting and looking down at her.

Darcy tipped her head back. She clutched at her hat to keep it firmly on her coiled braid and looked up at the man. He was big and solid. Shaggy brown hair stuck out from under a deformed straw hat. He didn't smile just turned back to the person to continue his conversation.

"Sorry," Darcy squeaked and stepped way around the man and his partner. She walked down the aisle looking for the liveryman. The scent of horse, hay, dung, and hot metal hung in the air amid the stomping of hooves and snorts.

"Hey, Marshal!" Ted Haskell called, as he came out from the feed storage room.

"Hi Ted. Who's the big man over there? I've never seen him before." Darcy looked over her shoulder at the two men still deep in conversation at the entrance. Her heart thudded in her chest when the other man turned in the sunlight. He was the man Gil had confronted in the jail and beat up saving her. She'd have to make sure he didn't see her face.

"Ain't seen him around here until today. He keeps to hisself and is real quiet." Ted scratched his head and narrowed his eyes. "Now the other guy, he's been up at the saloon playing cards and doing a fair share of winning. Not sure where he come from either." He scratched his head. "Did see him this morning talking to the guy who rides a big buckskin gelding."

"The guy with the long coat, low slung holster, and gray cavalry hat?" Darcy looked around Ted at the men still standing in the doorway.

"That's the guy."

"Uh-huh." She wondered how much of the

incident last night was staged for her benefit. Had Gil tried to scare her? What was he trying to hide by always dodging her questions about the man in the livery? She'd known all along he wasn't to be trusted. No man had ever treated her like he did. His soft voice and concerned eyes had broken her defenses. She'd be on her toes from now on when he was around.

Darcy looked both men over good so she'd recognize them anywhere, even from a distance. "I'm headed out to Buck creek. You got a horse I could use?"

"Sure, take the gelding you rode the other day. He worked fine didn't he?"

"Yeah, he was great. Thanks." Darcy walked down to the stall housing the gray gelding. She walked slow and deliberate, trying to hear what the men at the entrance visited about.

She talked quietly to the gelding as she brushed and saddled him. A word or two would drift to her between shuffling of horse's hooves, bored sighs, and Ted banging on metal in the back room. She heard the name of one of the prospectors she planned to visit and the "Boss" mentioned frequently.

After saddling the gelding, Darcy led the animal out of the building and headed off toward Buck Creek. The first prospector she planned to talk to was Gustafson. The name the big man mentioned.

Gil smiled every time he thought of the marshal all covered in mud. She'd been a damn pretty sight even with all the filth covering her. But she was up to something. He could feel it. He wanted to follow her out of town, but he'd seen Pete standing in the livery when he brought his horse in to have Ted look at its shoes.

He'd ducked down the alley outside the livery and waited for the man to come out. Eventually he did and Gil popped out onto the street to watch where he went.

Craven came down the walkway across the street. Not far behind, Jeremy followed. Gil forgot Pete as Jeremy whistled his way down the street and bumped into Craven. The man gruffly grabbed Jeremy by the front of his shirt and shoved him backward into a sack of feed standing in front of the mercantile. It looked like clumsiness ran in the Duncan family.

Gil caught a glimpse of his prey crossing the street and entering the saloon. Craven shook his finger at Jeremy and proceeded down the street and down the alley where Gil had found Darcy earlier.

Gil pushed his hat back on his head and scratched. This was interesting. Jeremy followed Craven. At his sister's orders, no doubt. And Craven had tried to get rid of Jeremy. He didn't know who to be angrier with—Darcy for siccing her brother on Craven or Jeremy for being so blatant.

Shoving his hat down low on his head, Gil crossed the street and entered the saloon. He stopped inside the door and scanned the room. The sickening-sweet scent of tobacco spit and stale cigar smoke accosted his nose. Being the middle of the day, the place had sparse customers. Pete stood at the end of the counter alongside the large man with big ears.

Gil walked to the opposite end of the bar and ordered a drink. He turned enough to keep an eye on the door and the men. They didn't talk much just sipped their drinks and stared at the bar.

"Want to play cards?" Ashburn Slaughter asked, patting Gil on the shoulder as he walked by.

"Sure," Gil took a seat where he could watch the men and the door. He knew it wasn't wise to be preoccupied while he played cards, especially with Ashburn, the town gambler. But he needed a reason to hang out in the saloon as long as the two men without them noticing his vigilance. Three other men joined the card game. Two were miners with gold nuggets the size of robin's eggs and the third a salesman for mining equipment.

The game started out amiably. Gil managed to keep his money from dwindling even though his mind wasn't on making any.

A saloon girl walked up to the man with big ears and whispered in his ear. He patted her on the backside and set his glass down on the bar. Without looking around, he wandered out the back door like he needed the privy.

Gil waited to see what Pete intended to do. He ordered another drink. Gil excused himself from the game and headed out the front door of the saloon. He hurried along the walkway and down the alley, keeping to the shadows and ducking behind boxes as he went. He nearly tripped over Jeremy hiding behind a box.

"What are you doing here?" he asked in a whisper, dropping down behind the crate with the boy.

Jeremy looked at him and pressed his lips together. He pointed deeper into the alley and Gil saw Craven approach the man with large ears.

"Has he been standing out here the whole time?" Gil asked, watching the men. He felt Jeremy nod his head. "Did he talk to anyone else?"

"A saloon girl." Jeremy wrinkled his nose. "They was running their hands all over each other and kissin'."

Gil nodded. It had to be the one who brought the message to the man with big ears. "I'm going to try and get closer to hear what they're saying."

Jeremy grabbed his shirt. "I'm supposed to do that. It's my job as deputy."

"No, it isn't. You're too young to be a deputy. You need to be a boy." Gil looked back at the men in the alley.

Jeremy jumped up and ran by him, darting around the two men, disappearing into the privy, and slamming the door behind him.

Gil ran a hand over his face and watched the men look around before continuing their discussion as though a boy hadn't just nearly knocked them over to use the outhouse. He had to smile. Jeremy was a quick thinker, and the men probably didn't even see who he was before he ducked in there.

The men talked for a few minutes more then went back in the saloon. When he was sure they weren't coming back, Gil knocked on the outhouse.

"You can come out now, Jeremy."

No answer. He tried the door. It didn't budge. He pounded on the building.

Nothing.

He walked around. A board had been pried off the back. Jeremy was small enough to have squeezed out the hole and scurried away while Gil made sure the men wouldn't come back.

Damn. The boy heard everything. Gil set out down the alley in search of Jeremy. He knew too much. If Craven even suspected the boy, he'd be dead by morning.

Darcy rode up to the last claim on her list. So far she'd found none of the claims had a great production and most of the miners weren't heartbroken to lose their claims to Craven. What puzzled her more, Craven allowed the miners to continue working the claims for a small percentage. Why would Craven go to such measures to secure land that was petering out of gold then allow the miners to keep digging?

A gunshot set the hair on her arms straight up. Darcy slid off her horse, pulling it behind a tree as she watched the shack in front of her.

"Get off my land!" came a shout from somewhere to the right of the shack.

"Mr. Haines?"

"Maybe."

"Mr. Haines, I'm Darcy Duncan, Marshal of Galena."

"You're working for that shyster Craven. I know all about you."

"You're wrong, Mr. Haines. I'm trying to find out why Craven is buying all the land along this creek." Darcy tied the horse to a low branch and cautiously worked her way through the trees to the back of the shack. She peeked through mountain berry bushes.

Mr. Haines was a small, dried-up, old man who could barely lift the shotgun he'd fired. She stepped out from behind the bush.

"Mr. Haines?"

BOOM!

The shotgun went off scattering birds from the trees around her and sending Darcy flat on the ground at the man's feet.

"Mr. Haines!" Darcy screamed, jumping up and taking the gun away from him. "I'm not here to take your land. Blazes! Will you quit shooting? You're going to hurt someone."

Mr. Haines looked dejected and sat down on a stump used as a chopping block. "He sent you to get the deed didn't he?"

"No," she said emphatically. "I'm not here to get the deed. I'm here to find out why Craven wants the deed and the other claims along this river." Darcy leaned the gun against the shack and pulled up a hunk of wood to sit on. "What is so special about this strip of land along this river?"

"Every man that's worked it has brought up a good amount of gold. But it's getting harder to find. Craven is trying to get the land free and set up a stamp mill here. Then he can make even more money off the miners in the area."

"What's a stamp mill?" Darcy watched the old man pull out a pipe so brown from tobacco it looked like grasshopper spit. He tamped a pinch of tobacco into the bowl and lit it. Taking a big puff, he eyed her.

"You don't know anything about this business do ya?" He blew eye-watering smoke her way and closed his eyes. "I've been at this twice as long as you've been alive I grant ya." He looked out at the creek and then at the mountain behind his shack. "You young bucks think you know everything, but when it comes down to it, none of ya know nothin'."

Darcy settled back. She could tell it would be a long drawn out process to find out anything from this man.

He went on about all the places he'd mined and how he always managed to lose it all to whiskey, women, and cards. He laughed rakishly. "Not always in that order."

"Mr. Haines, what is a mill stamp and why would Craven want one?"

"A mill stamp, Marshal, is a mill that crushes quartz, that's the most common rock gold is found in. It releases the gold from the rock. Then mercury is used to pick up the fine traces of gold. A man can literally squeeze gold out of quartz with a mill stamp. That's what Craven plans to do. Squeeze more gold out of this crick."

"Doesn't it cost a lot to start up one of those places?" Where would Craven get the money for a mill stamp? The land was free since he took it away from the miners, but he couldn't steal a mill. Could he?

"Most mills is started up by big money from back East or Portland." The old man puffed on his pipe. "Why are you so interested in what your boss is doing?"

"He's not my boss. I work for the town and

not a man." Darcy stood. "Thanks for the information." She looked around. "Are you okay here by
yourself?"

"I've stayed alive this long."

"If you need anything just come by the jail.
I'll see if I can help." Darcy walked back to her
horse. She untied the reins and climbed up into the
saddle.

She had a lot to think about on the way back
to town. Mill stamps. Craven. Gil. What Jeremy
may have found out. Her thoughts drifted as well
as her horse.

*Chapter 9*

Darcy noticed the horses surrounding hers too late. She looked up and stared into the eyes of the man with big ears. Sitting alongside of him was the large man she'd bumped into at the livery. Three more men moved in around her. One was tall and skinny with a large mustache, and the other was short and skinny with red hair and a pockmarked face. The third man moved even closer.

It was the man Gil knew. She ducked her head to shield her face from his stare. He rode his horse around her in a circle. She watched him from under her downcast eyelashes. He wasn't hard to look at. His brown hair touched his ears and teased his shirt collar. A smile twitched at the corners of his mouth. She didn't think he was as bad as the bunch he rode with. Or at least she hoped not.

Darcy swallowed and willed him to stop circling. She didn't want him to recognize her as the woman Gil had protected. There was no telling what this group would do to a helpless young woman.

"What we got here?" asked the man with the pockmarked face. He nudged his horse forward and reached out, flicking the badge on her chest. "We got us a Marshal."

A hiss of air eased out between her teeth. She didn't want to aggravate the men. One look told a body they weren't law-abiding miners and were dangerous. But it was downright rude of the man to even touch the badge let alone make fun of her. She was an official after all.

"Kind of scrawny for a marshal." The pockmarked man stopped his horse directly in front of her.

The big-eared man, who appeared to be in charge, walked his horse up alongside the scrawnier man. "Leave him alone," he said gruffly and boxed the scrawny fellow alongside the head.

"Hey!" The smaller man grabbed his ear. "Whatcha do that for?"

Darcy breathed a sigh of relief. If the boss didn't want her hurt, she'd be fine.

"Can't you see the marshal is headed back to town? Let him go." The boss smiled maliciously. "I bet he's looking for some bad men, and they're all in town." The whole bunch laughed loudly and spurred their horses on down the trail.

Darcy sat where she was, waiting to see if they kept going or were playing with her. When she was certain they weren't coming back, she turned her horse and followed.

Her heart beat frantically in her chest as she eased the horse forward, keeping a firm grip on the reins. If she came around a bend or a tree and they'd stopped, she wanted to be ready to run the other way.

She tilted her head and heard the sound of many male voices headed her way. Had she walked into the robber's hideout? Fearful of being caught, she started to slip off her horse and dive for the underbrush.

Her foot caught in the stirrup. She bounced around on one foot trying to untangle her big boot. The sound of footfalls on the path made her look up as a flock of miners came into view.

Her heart slowly resumed its normal beating. She swallowed, reviving her mouth that felt as dry as an old creek bed. Several of the miners she'd talked to earlier in the day came into view.

"You dancing with your horse, Marshal?" one man called out, and they all burst into jovial laughter.

Darcy pulled herself back up onto the saddle and looked down at the men. They ranged in age from gnarled, barely able to lift a shovel and pick, to only a few years older than Jeremy. She didn't know what made a man live by himself and dig in the ground hoping for riches when there were other things in life that took less energy.

"I was checking his hoof and the fool horse decided he'd rather I walk than ride." She smiled, as the group broke into another round of good-natured laughing. She couldn't figure the men out, but she liked them.

"You're headed the wrong direction, Marshal," Mr. Gustafson said, pointing toward town. "There's a dance tonight in the meeting hall."

Another miner said, "We're hoping the ladies

show up so we don't have to dance with each other." A loud roar of laughter echoed through the trees.

What ladies? There was a shortage of women in town. The few respectable ones she'd met were married to the businessmen.

"Mrs. Danforth, she will have her girls there. She is cést magnifique," Pierre La Rouge said, putting his fingers to his mouth and kissing the tips.

The men standing around her horse thought she was a man. Her cheeks warmed at the mention of prostitutes. She ducked her head, so they wouldn't notice how their conversation affected her, and turned the horse back toward town at a trot.

A miner shouted, "Hey marshal, wait for us. You can't have all the girls to yourself." A roar of laughter followed her down the trail.

Darcy kicked the horse into a lope. She would attend the dance, but not as the marshal. She might have a better chance of getting information out of the men if they thought she was one of Mrs. Danforth's girls. She'd heard men tell women things they would never tell another man.

Darcy trotted into Main Street and straight to the livery. The street was quiet for the time of day. Everyone must be resting up for the big doings tonight. She left the horse in the care of Ted and headed to the jail. Her feet thudded on the wood walkway and echoed down the calm street as she made her way to the jail.

"Jeremy. Jeremy!" She walked across the small room and sat down in the chair. Where could she find out more about stamp mills? Rubbing a hand over her face, she wondered if she could get some information out of Craven tonight if he didn't know who she was.

"Jeremy!" She looked around and started to worry. Where could he be? She stared across the street. What if Craven caught Jeremy watching him? She jumped out of the chair and hurried out the door. With determined steps she headed down the street to Craven's office. Relief flowed through her when pot-bellied Craven came out of the saloon laughing with another man.

"Marshal Duncan, where have you been all day?" Craven asked.

"About." Darcy watched him carefully to see if he knew what she'd been up to. He seemed in good spirits. "Have you seen my brother?"

"The little brat ran into me this morning, but I haven't seen him since." Craven pointed a stub of a cigar at her. "You should keep him locked up in that jail."

The other man laughed, and they ambled off down the street.

So Jeremy had blundered. He was probably hiding because he didn't want to tell her he didn't get any information and was caught while trying.

She headed to the restaurant for a meal and mentally ticked off where Jeremy might be hiding.

Gil had spent the better part of the day looking for the boy. He needed to know what Craven and the outlaw talked about. It hadn't looked like a friendly chat; it looked like business. He turned a corner in time to see Darcy walk into the restaurant. She'd been up to something today, and he didn't have a clue what that was either.

Damn. The brother and sister were getting the best of him, and he didn't like it. What really rankled was the fact he shouldn't care about the two and get on with the business of taking Pete back to the ranch. He didn't need to worry about anyone but himself. That was the way he liked it.

He started to cross the street when a group of miners entered town. They were joking and jostling each other. He hadn't seen so many or so lively a group in one spot since his arrival in Galena.

"What are you so excited about? Someone find a gold mine?" Gil asked jokingly.

"We're getting ourselves cleaned up for the dance tonight," one said with a rotten-toothed grin.

"There's going to be a dance?" He'd been so busy trying to find Jeremy, he hadn't talked to anyone.

"Didn't you hear? There's a big dance in the hall tonight. Tobias Craven invited all the miners to attend. Said there'd be girls and whiskey."

Gil looked at all the anxious faces and wondered what was going on. It didn't make sense Craven would start a rumor of a dance and provide the drink.

"Where'd you hear about this?" he asked as a wagonload of woman rolled down the street.

The men began hooting and hollering and ran for the wagon. The women in the wagon stood ramrod straight and stared at the jovial men. A couple of women bent over and urgently said something, but for the most part they looked scared out of their minds.

Gil sauntered over to the wagon. He looked at the driver and recognized a lowlife who hung around Baker City.

"Where'd you get all these girls, Clyde?" Gil asked, motioning to the ten girls standing in the wagon. They didn't look like prostitutes. They were dressed in homespun and shawls. Their hair was tightly wound around their heads and tucked under bonnets.

"I'm making a delivery, so get outta my way." Claude slapped the reins on the mule's backs, jerking the wagon forward. A scream pierced the air as one of the woman toppled over the edge of the wagon bed.

Gil and the miner nearest him caught the woman before she hit the ground. She was about the same age as the marshal. He surveyed the wagon to see if anyone else had fallen out. Out of the corner of his eye, he saw Marshal Duncan hurry out of the restaurant and straight for the wagon load of women.

"Halsey. I should have known it was you causing all the raucous." The marshal looked at the girl in his arms and shook her head. "Did she scream when she looked at you?"

The miners roared with laughter, and the women in the wagon looked at each other.

"No. She screamed when this jug head made the wagon lurch and caused her to fall over the side." Gil couldn't believe he stood in the middle of a street holding a young woman in his arms and defending himself to another. He saw the look of unease in the marshal's eyes before she turned to the driver.

Darcy looked up at the man on the wagon seat.

"Why'd you bring a wagon load of women to this town?"

"I'm just following orders, Marshal. There ain't a law that says I can't give a ride to some ladies if they want it."

"But do they want it?" Darcy turned to the women. "Ladies, are you being hauled around in this wagon of your own will?" She watched as they turned to one another. A rush of gibberish she'd never heard the likes of before came out all at once as each woman opened their mouth.

Darcy looked at Gil, and he shrugged.

Gustafson stepped forward. "They are German." He began an animated discussion with them and smiled at the end. "Mr. Craven has brought these women to us with the prospect of marriage."

A roar went up from the men who had by now gathered around the wagon.

"I want that one!" shouted a man.

"I want the blonde with the big chest," shouted another.

"Halsey, put that woman back in the wagon," Darcy ordered, noticing Gil hadn't relieved himself of the woman in his arms. The woman had become aware of the man holding her and clung to him like a scared child.

"You," Darcy pointed to the driver, "follow me." Grabbing hold of the headstall on the nearest horse, she walked the wagon up the street to Mrs. Danforth's bathhouse. It was illogical to take the women to the brothel, but she didn't know who else had the space. She wasn't about to give them to Craven until she made certain they were here of their own will and not forced to do something they didn't want.

At the bathhouse, she motioned Gil to grab the horse's head so the driver wouldn't decide to tuck tail and run.

She walked up to the door and was about to knock when Lila answered.

"What you all making so much ruckus about?" she asked. When she saw Darcy, she sniffed. "Oh, not you."

"Please get Mrs. Danforth, Lila." Darcy stepped inside and waited for the only person she trusted, even if she did run a brothel.

"What have you brought me today, Marshal?" Mrs. Danforth asked, smiling and floating down the hall.

Some day I'm going to walk as smoothly as that. Darcy smiled. "Well you ain't—"

"Aren't." The woman frowned at her.

"You aren't going to believe this, but I found a wagon load of German woman in the middle of the street."

Mrs. Danforth crossed to a window and looked out. "That you have, Marshal. Why did you bring them to me?"

"I trust you."

The woman turned from the window, and Darcy held her gaze. "Craven brought those women here. I don't know why, and I don't know if they came willingly. Can you keep them until I get to the bottom of this?"

"Tobias Craven ordered German brides for the miners?" She sneered. "How generous of him." She looked at Darcy. "He'd never part with money to bring happiness to others. He's up to something."

"That's my thoughts. I'm hoping to go to this dance he's hosting tonight and see if I can find out what."

Mrs. Danforth looked her up and down. "Like that?"

Darcy's cheeks heated. "No, I was going to wear the dress you gave me."

"Come back about dark. I'll fix you up so Craven won't recognize you." She smiled. "We'll pull one over on him."

A smile spread across Darcy's face. It was nice having Mrs. Danforth on her side. "I'll be back. I'm going to send the women in. Also Mr. Gustafson. He speaks their language."

The woman nodded assent.

Darcy walked across the porch as Craven came waddling up the street. Everyone parted as he neared the wagon.

"Aw, I see my brides have arrived. And right on schedule." He waved a hand. "Take them to the dance hall, Claude."

"No." Darcy grabbed the headstall of the lead horse. "Mr. Gustafson, tell the ladies to get out of the wagon and go in the house. Mrs. Danforth will put them up a night or two." She looked into the reddening face of Craven. "And Gustafson, you stay with them until they are settled since you can talk to them."

The miners looked from Craven to the marshal and back as Gustafson talked to the women. Her stomach rolled over a couple times as Craven's gaze drilled holes right through her.

The woman started to climb out, and Gil stepped forward to assist. When he did, several miners stepped forward to help the women. Gustafson herded the group like a bunch of quail up the steps and into the house.

When the women were in the house, Darcy started down the street. It puzzled her Gil and the other miners accepted her word so quickly over Craven. It surprised and humbled her that the men went against the mayor who seemed to have a hold on everyone in the town. She needed to think about this.

A hand grabbed her arm, spinning her around. The action happened so quickly, she lost her balance and landed on her backside in the street.

"Don't you ever interfere with my business again."

She looked up into the red face of Tobias Craven. He pointed a stubby finger at her.

"Hauling people around against their will is my business." She lifted her badge out of the folds of her shirt. "You made me marshal, and I take my responsibilities serious."

His face puffed up, and his lips squeezed together before he blew out the words. "You're fired! You and your brother better be out of my town by morning or you'll regret ever setting foot here."

He grabbed the badge, ripping it from her shirt.

Darcy clutched the hole in her shirt as he stomped down the street. You may have taken my badge, but I'm still going to find out what you're up to. She stood, dusting the dirt from her pants. Being dirty was getting old. She needed to find

Jeremy and get back to Mrs. Danforth's. She had a lot of work to do in order to attend the dance and not have people recognize her. There were a lot of unanswered questions she intended to investigate.

*Chapter 10*

Darcy climbed the ladder to the room above the jail. Her stomach churned with worry. She'd hunted all over town for Jeremy, and no one had seen him since morning. It had been a stupid idea to have her only kin follow Craven. She shook her head sadly and pulled herself up the last rung.

Before she got her feet under her, a hand snagged her leg. She fell to her knees with a crunch. Tipping her hat up off her eyes, she looked into the scared face of Jeremy. She glared at him and rubbed her smarting knees. When the stinging abated, she turned her full anger on him.

"I've been looking all over town for you." She grabbed his ear and twisted. "If you've been hiding up here all afternoon how come you didn't come down when I called your name earlier?"

"I didn't know if you were alone." He swatted her hand away from his ear and plopped his bottom on the floor "I've been hiding from Gil. He knows I spied on Craven, and he knows I know something."

"Gil saw you spying?" Darcy slapped her head. She had put her only living family member in danger.

"He was spying, too."

"Halsey was spying on Craven? This is all starting to make my head hurt. I thought he worked with Craven."

"I don't think so. He's been asking all kinds of questions about you and Craven. Wanting to know if you knew the mayor before he pinned the marshal's badge on you."

Darcy ran a hand over her face. They both thought the other worked for the crook Craven. She shook her head to clear the thoughts bumping into each other. Now was not the time to figure it all out.

"What did you see?"

"Craven talked with a big-eared man. He said something about a dance and getting everyone in town. And that all the drunk miners and the women he brought in would make a lot of noise to cover. And he'd meet them at the cabin day after tomorrow." Jeremy stared at his boot scraping back and forth on the floor.

"I couldn't hear much more 'cuz they was talking quiet. I pressed my ear to the cracks of the privy, but that's all I could get. As soon as they left, I shimmied out a loose board in the back of the privy and ran so Gil wouldn't find me. 'Cuz, he knew I was in there."

Darcy smiled and rubbed his head. "You did good. We know something is going to happen to-night during the dance." She rested her chin in her hand. The dance was a cover. For what, she didn't know, but she'd be there and watch Craven when he made his move. She definitely needed Mrs. Danforth's help in painting her up, especially now that Craven had threatened her and Jeremy. She didn't want him to recognize her before she knew his plan.

"I want you to find a good spot up on a building tonight where you can see the full length of Main Street. I'm going to the dance to see if I can get some more information out of the miners and Craven."

"But, Darce, you can't ask Craven what he's doing!" Jeremy grabbed her arm in a grip that brought tears to her eyes. She uncurled his fingers and patted his hand.

"I'll be disguised as one of Mrs. Danforth's girls. He won't know who I am."

"Ma wouldn't like it." The disapproval in his voice made her take a good look at her younger sibling. He'd grown up, and she'd not noticed.

"Yes, she would. I'm trying to find out what is going on around here. I won't go off with any of the miners. I got business to attend." She patted his head. "Try to sneak into the restaurant and get some food. Then get up on a roof and keep a look out for the big-eared man. When you see him, come get me at the dance."

He stood. Darcy grabbed his hand.

"And stay away from Craven." She showed him the hole in her shirt. "He took my badge and said we should be out of town by morning."

She hugged Jeremy. He was all she had in the world. "If you don't see me in the morning, go to

Gil and ask him to hide you so Craven doesn't hurt you."

"But I thought you said Gil was the enemy?"

"I don't think so after what you told me. And he likes you. He wouldn't let Craven hurt you."

She hugged him again. "Be careful. I'll be back as soon as I figure out what Craven's doing."

Darcy headed down the stairs. She had a lot on her mind as she ducked down alleys and slipped through the kitchen door of Mrs. Danforth's bath-house.

Gil paced the length of Main Street and fumed. He'd hunted all over town for Jeremy. The boy knew something which could be dangerous to both him and his sister. The longer the boy hid without fessing what he knew, the more danger he made for the two of them. He didn't want to see any harm come to either the boy or the young woman.

Their bond was something he barely remembered having with his brothers. Witnessing it first hand, he didn't want to see it shattered. And he knew good 'n' well Craven wasn't above hurting both of them to get what he wanted. If that happened, he'd hunt Craven down and make him pay. His fingers ached. He looked down at the hand clenching his revolver. He'd shot very few men and all in self-defense, but he wouldn't flinch if it meant saving Darcy or her brother.

After the women were hustled into Mrs. Danforth's, Gil saw Craven with the marshal's badge. That bothered him. Darcy wouldn't have given up the shiny star without a fight. He worried she was somewhere licking her wounds. The fool woman was too stubborn to ask for help.

Going to the dance hadn't crossed his mind as he stood in front of the quiet saloon keeping a vigilant eye up and down the street. Something was sure to break loose with all the distraction of the women and dance. He had a gut feeling Pete and his gang were up to something.

A woman walked down the street from the bathhouse and sashayed toward the dance hall on wobbly legs. Watching her, the thrumming in his chest told him it had to be the accident-prone marshal.

He followed, grinning, as she clutched at the hitching posts and buildings on her way to the hall. Gil shook his head and caught up to the unsteady woman.

"You need an arm to lean on so no one figures out you aren't what you're trying to be?" He smiled when her painted up face went from mad to relieved.

"Oh, it's you." She placed a hand on his arm and smiled.

His gut did a twist. Gratitude shone in her gray eyes. He wanted to pick her up and cart her away from this town and whatever mess she was bound to get herself into.

"Why aren't you shooting me or arguing?" he asked, pulling her closer to his side. He tucked her under his arm and hoped she'd stay there. When the miners saw her, they'd be ogling and drooling. Gil didn't know if he could sit still and not knock a few teeth out. He knew they wouldn't have a clue who she was. His gaze skimmed the length of her. That was what she had in mind with all the paint and low cut dress. As much as he tried to be a gentleman, he couldn't tear his gaze away from her creamy shoulders and white mounds of breast peeking above the silk.

He licked his lips and used all his willpower to raise his gaze to her face. She was oblivious to the hold she had on him.

"I had a talk with Jeremy," she said, lowering her gaze to the board walkway under their feet.

"Is the kid okay?"

"Yeah, he said you were looking for him. He hid from you because I told him you were the enemy." She stopped, then turned and looked at him with her penetrating gray gaze. "Do you work for Tobias Craven?"

"That crook? Hell no!" He stared at her. "Is that what you thought?"

"You were always following me. I thought he had you keeping an eye on me. In case I didn't follow his orders."

"But you work for him," he said, watching her closely.

"No, I work for the town." She lowered her gaze. "Well, not anymore. He took the badge away."

Gil put a finger under her chin and tipped her face up to look at him. "Are you going to back off now? Leave whatever he's doing alone?"

She smiled and started to walk away.

Damn her. She would continue to dig until someone got hurt. His chest ached thinking it would most likely be her.

Gil held her elbow to steady her as she picked up her skirt and stepped up the three steps into the dance hall. The music echoed through the large room. Miners were all decked out in their finest. For some that meant clean clothes. Everyone was in a jubilant mood. Some of the men danced with men while others were lucky enough to get a trip around the dance floor with one of Mrs. Danforth's girls.

The respectable woman of the town stood behind the tables laden with food and drinks, curling their lips at the trollops in bright colored, low-cut dresses. Their gazes roamed to the door as Gil and Darcy entered. By the raised eyebrows and exaggerated frowns, they took the woman on his arm to be one of the fallen women.

Gil looked down at Darcy. She hadn't noticed the looks from the businessman's wives. Her eyes shone bright with excitement. He imagined it was the first time she'd attended a dance as a woman. She was going to be in for a shock when the miners didn't treat her like a lady. He didn't know why most men treated the women who worked in brothels with less consideration than they would any other woman. They didn't all choose the life. Some were thrust into it because of circumstances.

He took her by the hand, swinging her out on the dance floor as a waltz began. Pulling her into his arms, he was surprised at how gracefully she floated around the room.

"You're a good dancer."

"You don't have to sound surprised." Her eyes narrowed.

"It's just you can't walk down the street without getting mud from one end of you to the other."

She looked at him with a sparkle in her eyes.

"Maybe that's what I want people to think."

"You're either a good actor or a good liar." He watched her grin turn into a pout. It took all his restraint to keep from crushing her to him and tasting those pouty lips.

"I don't lie." She sucked in her lip, and he did pull her closer.

"Hey! Don't hog the girl, others of us want a chance to dance with her," said a miner, walking beside them. He looked like he would fight if necessary for a stroll around the wood floor with Darcy.

Gil winked at Darcy and handed her over before she could say a word. He needed to put distance between them, but keep an eye on her. She was up to something, and his head told him it would turn out to be no good. His heart, however, was in serious trouble. Just looking at her made it quicken and his groin ache.

While dancing with him, her steps had been graceful and matched his. With the larger man she bounced around, trying to keep up with his jerky steps. Gil moved his gaze up her curves, and smiled. She chatted away at the miner like a magpie. Her painted red lips tipped in a friendly smile. He walked over to the refreshment table and helped himself to a shot of whiskey. Surprisingly, Craven hadn't held back, it was the good stuff.

Turning to the dance floor, his gaze sought Darcy and found her still in the arms of the big man. He smiled when she spotted him. She rolled her eyes. Someone bumped into his shoulder. When he turned to say something, Craven entered the building.

Gil automatically looked in Darcy's direction. She stood alert, scanning the crowd. He knew who she sought the minute her gaze landed on Craven. Her eyes narrowed, and her brow furrowed. He didn't know what she had in mind, but he knew from prior experience, it would be interesting.

Mrs. Danforth entered the building with the flock of German women. The miners all crowded around the entrance to talk to the women. Gil skirted the crowd, heading in the direction he'd last seen Darcy.

She was deep in conversation with a young miner.

"What would a stamp mill mean to this area?" she asked the man.

He looked at her like she'd slapped him. "Why would a girl like you be interested in such things?"

"I heard Mr. Craven mention it and wondered what it was," she batted her eyelashes and looked innocent, but Gil knew her well enough by now to know she was working the man for information.

"What do I get for me answers?" The miner grinned and pulled her close, grabbing her ample skirts and backside in his hand.

Gil rushed forward. He flung the offending hand aside and pulled Darcy into his arms. "Don't touch her," he said in a low voice.

Darcy looked up. She recognized the strong arms holding her, but the menacing voice didn't fit the man she knew. His eyes glared dark and threatening, his chin set, and his free hand hovered over the gun she'd yet to see him draw.

"I was just haven' a little fun. You don't need to go gettin' yerself all riled up," the miner said, backing away.

"Gil. Gil." Darcy put her hand on his face. The day's growth of whiskers pricked her palm, but she left her hand there, feeling his jaw slowly unclench.

"I'm okay. I can handle myself," she said in a whisper.

She stared into his dark eyes as his scent filled her nostrils. His arm pulled her tight against him then relaxed. She watched as different expressions played across his face, before he tucked them all away and smiled.

"Sorry. He wasn't touching you in a gentlemanly manner." He pulled his arm from around her and leaned against the wall.

Her heart leaped into her throat. He'd been willing to fend the man off with his gun moments before and now he looked at her with such gentleness, it made her shiver.

"I-I said I could handle it." She looked up at him through her downcast lashes to keep him from seeing the emotions whirling around inside of her. She wasn't sure what all of them meant, but she knew he wouldn't like it if she followed him all over like a cow-eyed schoolgirl.

"Sure you could." He chucked her under the chin and started to move away.

Darcy grabbed his shirt, pulling him around to look at her. "I can take care of myself. I have for several years." She didn't know why, but his comment and condescending attitude struck a chord of defiance in her.

"Now, don't go getting all in a fluster. I'm sure you've stayed out of trouble by the skin of your teeth. But you were a kid then. You've become a woman." He put a hand on her cheek. "A beautiful woman." His gaze dropped to her exposed chest.

A scorching wave of heat started at her middle and flared out to her fingers and toes.

"You have no idea what these men around here would do to you if they had the chance." His thumb moved back and forth, caressing her cheek.

"W-w-what would they do to me?" She barely heard herself mumble the sentence over the beating of her heart. His gaze turned dark. Only this time a glimmer of something other than violence flickered in his intense stare.

He stepped closer and wrapped his arms around her, pulling her against his long body. His head dipped, and his lips brushed hers.

Her body pressed against him, yearning to feel his strength. He bent closer, lifting her onto her toes. She wound her arms around his neck to keep from melting into the floor. His lips moved urgently over hers. Waves of sensations rushed through her eager body. He grasped her tighter. His hands moved up and down her back, then down over her hips, tracing the contours.

"That is not proper behavior for one of my girls."

A stinging blow slashed Darcy's bare shoulder, and she turned from Gil, gasping for air.

"Oh?" Mrs. Danforth's angry eyes softened and a smile played at the corners of her lips. "Your dinner date."

Darcy wiped her throbbing lips and looked from the woman to Gil and back.

"Yes, Ma'am." Her stomach churned, thinking

of how she'd just brazenly kissed a man in public.

Gil grasped her hand. "Excuse us Ma'am, but we need to finish our conversation."

"Find some place a little more private." Mrs. Danforth unfurled her fan and moved across the room.

Darcy pulled her hand free. "I'm not going anywhere with you."

"Yes, you are. We need to talk." Gil reached for her hand.

She backed up, staring at him. He looked the same even though only moments before he'd made her body feel on fire. "What do we need to talk about?"

"You. The danger you and Jeremy are in."

"We can talk here." She didn't want to go somewhere dark and quiet with this man. After-shocks from his caresses still sizzled in her body

"No. Someone might overhear and tell Craven." Gil took her hand. They made their way through the crowd of men. She tried not to think about what the men meant by the winks and nods they gave her escort.

Out on the boardwalk, Gil stopped. He looked up and down the street.

"What's wrong?" Darcy followed his actions. The length of the street was still. A few horses were tied to the hitching rail in front of the hall, but farther along the street remained vacant. It seemed unusually quiet for the time of night, but then everyone was at the dance.

"Nothing." He put an arm around her shoulders and headed down the street.

"Where are we going?" She fell in step alongside of him. It seemed natural to have his arm draped across her shoulders. His fingers softly stroked her bare skin.

"You'll see."

She studied his profile in the moonlight. His lean features made her body hum. What was it about him that made her feel things she'd never felt before?

He turned toward the saloon.

Darcy pulled back. "I can't go in there."

"We'll take the back stairs up to my room."

She planted her feet. "I'm definitely not going in there."

# *Chapter 11*

"Are you still scared of me?" Gil pushed his cavalry hat back, allowing the moonlight to reveal his face.

"No. I mean. I've never been scared of you. Only wary." Annoyed by the smirk on his face, she glared at him and folded her arms, nearly popping her breasts above the neckline of the dress. Embarrassed, she yanked up on the front. The shoulders of the garment dropped lower.

"Here. Let me help." Gil stepped forward, running his hands up her arms, scorching her skin as he slid the straps back into place.

Her heart thudded in her chest. The sound of water rushed through her head as he dipped his fingers under the lace of the neckline, shifting the bodice back into place.

She ran her salivating tongue over dry lips and glanced at Gil. His gaze slowly drifted from where he'd settled her dress to her eyes.

"Seriously, we need to talk." He took her hand,

leading her to the base of the stairs on the side of the building.

Darcy gulped. What would her mother think if she were alive to witness her daughter, dressed like a strumpet, sashaying to a room over a saloon? Gil stopped when she didn't follow.

"I swear this is the only place I can think of where we can talk in private." He started up the stairs once more.

Curiosity pushed her forward. She and Jeremy had never had the money to stay in a hotel. And it was Gil's room. She wanted to learn more about the man. Darcy gathered the front of her skirt in her arms and followed his long, lean body up the steps.

The moon ducked behind a cloud. She shivered. Why was she hurrying after a man headed to a hotel room? A man who made her body fevered when he kissed her. The cold shiver of apprehension turned to warm anticipation, causing her to climb faster.

She didn't know near enough about this man. The attraction she had for him unsettled her. They needed to talk. She wanted to learn what he was really doing in Galena.

Her cheeks heated. She also wanted to see his eyes darken and his head bend down. She wanted him to take her in his arms and kiss her like he had at the dance.

At the top of the stairs, he surveyed the alley and street before opening the door and dragging her into the lighted hallway. She dropped her skirt and stumbled from the weight of the billowing fabric which seemed to have a mind of its own. Gil stopped long enough to put a helping arm around her and hurried down the hall. He pulled her into a room on the right.

With his arm still holding her, Gil kicked the door shut, and turned the key sticking out of the keyhole.

"Why are you locking me in?" Darcy asked as fear not for herself, but Jeremy, flashed through her mind. If Gil kept her prisoner to keep her from discovering what Craven had planned tonight, Jeremy could get caught in the mess and come to harm.

"I'm not locking you in. I'm locking other people out."

"Surely, you don't think someone will come looking for us?" Until this moment her evening had been one big game. Plying the miners for information and even flirting with Gil had all been a game of gathering information. Of outsmarting Craven. His comment brought the seriousness of the situation into focus.

"We don't know. Since you aren't marshal anymore who's looking after the prisoner?"

Darcy nearly sunk to the floor as her knees buckled. "I hadn't thought about him."

Gil stared direct and intense. "Is Jeremy alone at the jail?"

"No." She couldn't meet his gaze. "He's hiding from Craven. After taking my badge, Craven told us to stay out of his sight and be out of town by morning."

Gil pulled her into his arms. "I have some unfinished business I'll take care of tomorrow. You and Jeremy head out at first light toward Baker

City. I'll catch up with you there."

"We're not going anywhere." She pulled out of his embrace. His thoughts were noble, but dang, she loved this town and no crooked mayor was going to send her packing.

"You can't stay here if Craven has it out for you." He tossed his hat onto the chair and ran a hand through his hair.

"I'm tired of drifting. I like Galena, and I plan on staking a claim. Me and Jeremy will run it. We'll be fine." Her words held more conviction than her stomach. It twisted with apprehension. What if they didn't figure out what Craven and the big-eared man were plotting? If she couldn't prove his unlawful behavior, she couldn't talk the town into ousting the man.

The look of disbelief on Gil's face challenged her apprehension.

"You don't want to take up gold mining." His statement was firm and final.

"Why not? From what I've seen the miners bring in, Jeremy and I'd be living a life we've not had since our parents passed."

"Mining is hard, relentless work to get any-thing." The look on his face told her he'd had experience.

"Have you mined for gold?" She touched his arm when his expression turned hard and blank.

"I didn't bring you up here to talk about gold mining." He grasped her arms, pulling her to him, and capturing her mouth with his demanding lips. The strength of his embrace, urgency of the kiss, and quickening beat of his heart under her hand, whisked away all thoughts.

Gil held her head in his hands and kissed her. He wanted to keep it soft and light, but her fool-hardiness about staying here and panning for gold, upset him. He didn't want her wasting her life for illusive treasure and the possibility of being killed for a few nuggets.

He shifted his thoughts to the present and breathed in the floral scent on her skin before deepening the kiss. His hands slid through her hair, knocking hairpins to the floor. The soft strands of her silky hair sifted through his fingers, curling around his wrist. Her body pressed against him as she stood on her toes. He seduced her full lips, enticing them to part and let him enter.

When she moaned and opened, his body responded with a surge of heat and need. She tasted sweeter than he'd dreamed. Wrapping his arms around her, Gil picked her up off the ground. He kissed her slender neck and bare chest sprinkled with freckles above the frilly neckline. A throaty sigh slid through her lips as he pushed a dress strap over her shoulder, dropping kisses behind the path of the strap.

Her small hands roamed over his shoulders and down his back. Fever started where her hands touched and built into a raging blaze in his nether regions. He wanted her delicate hands to caress his skin.

"Unbutton my shirt." His voice sounded deeper and huskier as her touch battered at the wall of his self-restraint.

Her eyes twinkled with excitement, and a smile played at the corners of her luscious lips. Her large gray eyes stared into his as her dainty fingers one-by-one unfastened the bone buttons down the front of his shirt.

When the buttons were loose, she pushed the shirt off his shoulders. With reverence, her fingers traced the contours of his muscles, gliding over his skin, tormenting his restraint.

Before he could gather her into an embrace, she leaned in, pressing her breasts against his chest. Her hands roamed over his back, moving as though she memorized every part of him.

Gil couldn't control his need to touch her as she stroked him. He shoved her dress from her shoulders, exposing her breasts. His hands cupped each one, rubbing his thumbs back and forth over taut peaks. Darcy moaned and grabbed fistfuls of his hair, drawing his lips to hers as she pressed against him.

Her bold response to his needs made his body throb. Gil picked her up, kissing her neck and breasts with wet, sweet kisses. The sound she emitted reminded him of a purring cat. She would not leave his arms this night unsoiled. He had to make her his.

Capturing her mouth with his, he laid her on the bed beneath him. He rose up on an elbow to see the emotions on her face. Her grey eyes darkened with desire.

"Darcy, I want you more than I've ever wanted anything or anyone before."

She shivered and smiled. "Me, too."

He touched her lips with a finger and trailed it down her neck and over each breast, stopping at each nipple to circle it several times. She reached up, wrapping her arms around his neck and tried to pull his lips to hers.

"No. No more kisses until you fully understand what I want."

She watched him with questioning eyes. Her body wiggled, and a mischievous smile curved her tempting lips. Lost in her beauty, he didn't notice her hands until he felt a finger skim his skin as she worked at the buttons on his Levis.

"No," Gil said through clenched teeth as he pulled her hands from the task. "You're not touching me there unless you understand once we start again I won't be able to stop until we're done." He looked down at her alabaster skin gleaming in the moonlight. It was so soft and smelled of a spring day. He wanted to take her in his arms and love her until they were both old. But he wasn't going to start something until he was sure she wanted it as well. Her kisses told him she did, but he had a notion she didn't really know what was about to happen.

"Please, touch me more." She looked at him from under lowered lashes. Her cheeks flushed. "I like it."

"Oh, baby, I know you do, but do you know what I'm asking?"

Her eyes opened wide, and she exhaled in a breathy voice, "Yes." She looked up at him. "You. We're loving one another."

"Yes." He kissed her firmly on the lips and let his hands stray to her firm breasts. They were the perfect size for his hands to fondle and caress. "I want to show you how I feel about you."

"Do, please, do." Her hips arched up to him, and he couldn't control himself any longer.

Gil grasped her dress, pulling it down over her hips and revealing her corset, chemise, and drawers. He untied the corset, watching the pushed up breasts take their normal pert shape. The pointed peaks beckoned under the thin fabric of her chemise. He untied the chemise and pushed it down, exposing her nipples. The look in Darcy's eyes as he slowly lowered his mouth nearly burst the buttons on his Levis.

He savored the taste of her as he flicked the nipple with his tongue, causing her to moan and wriggle under him. He untied her pantaloons and pushed the chemise and drawers, sliding them down her body as he rained kisses over her soft skin. From the bottom of the bed, he watched her eyelashes flutter on her cheeks while he removed her shoes and stockings.

"Look at me." He unbuttoned his Levis and dropped his pants and drawers to the floor.

Her eyes widened as his member popped straight out at her. He could tell by the look on her face she'd never seen a naked man before, but the sight didn't repulse her. She crawled across the bed and took him in her hands. He nearly spilled his seed with her curious, innocent touch.

He pulled her up, kissing her until she melted in his arms. He should take it slow. This was her first time. His body didn't listen to his head. He wanted to ravage the small body beckoning him like a butterfly to a beautiful flower. Restraint had never been one of his finer qualities, but he'd take things slow for the woman in his arms.

Darcy wanted him to kiss her and caress her all night. She'd never dreamed being touched this way by a man could be so warm and shocking. His hands burned paths of desire up and down her skin. She'd felt his manhood with her hands and knew when he slipped it in she wouldn't be afraid. Nothing about this man frightened her.

Explosions of white lights went off in her head as his fingers massaged the juncture of her legs, touching the spot that throbbed. She moaned and pulled his head from her breasts to kiss him.

His knee slid her legs apart. She concentrated on the sensations that flowed through her body, pumping her blood and making her breathe in short pants.

He held her breasts in his hands, licking and nibbling on her sensitive nipples. His earnest attention sent vibrations through her body, intensifying the pulse between her legs. Her hips rose toward him of their own accord.

Cradling her head in his hands, he touched her lips with his tongue. Opening to him, she welcomed his kiss. Her body vibrated and pressed toward him. She wanted everything he had to give her. With gentleness, he slid his member between her legs and inside.

She stiffened as her body stretched to accommodate him. He deepened the kiss, reviving the sensations that moments before had her vision blurring. He pressed deeper, rubbing her throbbing core. Her body hummed and warmed.

"Darcy, look at me," his horse voice commanded.

She shook her head, clearing away the haze of euphoria and looked at him.

"This means more...but I don't..." the desire

in his eyes and his furrowed brow reflected her thoughts. Their actions, if her father were alive would lead to marriage.

"I know. I won't hold you to anything." She knew what they were doing made her a soiled woman, just like Sylvie and Rose. But she wouldn't have wanted anyone other than Gil to have deflowered her. She still didn't know his secrets. And until they were out in the open with one another, there could never be a future for them. However, she would forever have this night.

Darcy arched her hips, drawing him deeper. The sensation made her dizzy and a clap of thunder roared through her body. She sucked in her breath, holding onto the feeling for as long as she could. He moved faster and faster inside of her, sending aftershocks of heat and light through her body.

Strong arms banded around her as he thrust deep, pulsed, and stopped. His body went lax, covering her in a warm blanket of male. She grinned, breathed in his scent, and hugged him. Her hands roamed over his small round backside and up his muscular back.

His breathing hitched, and he rose up on his elbows. Kissing her nose, he said, "That was one thing I never dreamed of when I first laid eyes on you."

"What?" She moved her hands around to his front, sliding up his chest and clasping them behind his neck.

"That I would end up in bed with you and live to tell it."

She looked into his eyes and saw the hint of mischief she'd known lurked behind the somber front he showed most people.

"You could still be in danger." She pulled him down and nipped at his lips. "I'm feeling so good, I may need more."

He smiled rakishly, and his eyes lit up, before he frowned.

"We need to talk." He rolled to his side and pulled her into his arms.

"I said this didn't mean we have to get hitched." Darcy didn't like the look in his eyes. He was about to say something she didn't want to hear.

"You need to back off from Craven." The hardness in his voice and direct stare made her cringe. "He's been talking to a band of thieves. They're up to something, and it can't be good. I saw him talking to one of them today when Jeremy hid in the outhouse." He smoothed her hair and kissed the top of her head, completely acting the opposite of his tone. "Did Jeremy tell you what they said?"

"I don't want to talk about this." She slid her hands down his torso, taking his member in her small hands. As a quick learner, she knew how to take his mind off matters she didn't intend to talk about.

"We need to—" He sucked in his breath as she handled his magnificent manhood.

"We need to make love," she said, nipping at his bottom lip and rubbing her body against his. A glint of challenge lit his eyes, before he pushed her onto the mattress. He covered her body with his, kissing her until she struggled for air.

His kisses made her lightheaded. She shivered with delight as he slid down her body kissing every inch as he went. His gentle hands fluttered over her inner thighs just before his tongue touched the spot between her legs that throbbed uncontrollably.

"Oh," she gasped as another volley of sensations shot through her body. "How?" She grabbed Gil by the hair, pulling his face up to hers as she spread her legs inviting him to enter. "Please?" she begged as he touched her then retreated.

"I want to know what Jeremy overheard." He hovered over her, a glint to his eyes as he teased her with his stiff appendage.

She looked at him. How could he stoop so low? Her body quivered with need, and he held back.

She shook her head defiantly.

His hand slid between them and gently kneaded the hair above her throbbing point. She grit her teeth to keep from begging, and his fingers slid in. Her hips rose and he pulled away.

"Tell me, and you can take me," Gil whispered, caressing the rim of her ear with his tongue. She wiggled, raising her hips.

She wound her hands in his hair, dragging his mouth to hers. Two could play the seduction game. She ran her tongue in and out of his mouth, tempting him. She rubbed her breasts against his smooth, hard chest. Her body ached with need, but she continued her seduction until he was worked into such a frenzy he slammed into her, frantically pumping and breathing like a man who'd ran a mile.

Darcy smiled and lifted her hips so he could plunge deeper and deeper, until a roar in her head and a flash of heat scorched her body, leaving her blank and lethargic. She closed her eyes as Gil turned her, embracing her with one arm, his body pressed against her back.

Darcy opened her eyes. The moon was descending in the dark sky. She smiled. Gil lay on his back beside her, breathing in and out; the heavy monotone tempo of deep sleep.

She slid quietly from the bed and retrieved her clothing, all but the corset. There was no way she could get the thing on by herself. She left it on the chair by the door. Gil wouldn't be happy when he woke and found her gone, but Craven had something planned for tonight and from what she could tell the night wasn't over yet. Plus, she couldn't have Jeremy looking for her in the morning and find her curled up in bed with Gil. She'd promised she wouldn't leave the dance with a miner. Grinning, she looked down at Gil. She didn't break her promise. He definitely wasn't a miner.

When she was dressed, all but her shoes, she silently unlocked the door and slipped out into the hallway. She turned the key in the lock and dropped it in her pocket. Gathering her bearings in the dark, she headed to the outside door. At the top of the stairs, she listened to music and laughter drifting down the street from the dance hall.

She looked up at the moon. Its position meant morning was creeping closer. She sat on the top step and put her shoes on, wishing she could go barefoot. But it wouldn't look right her sitting on the walkway below putting on her shoes.

Tiptoeing down the stairs, she made it to the bottom without making a sound or stumbling. She settled her skirt and headed down the street to the jail.

Darcy smiled. Her body tingled all over thinking about what she and Gil had done only hours before. She stopped, ran her hands through her hair, and twirled. Her skirt wrapped around her legs, tipping her forward. She grasped the stirrup of a horse beside a hitching post. She leaned against the horse, one hand on the stirrup, the other patting the warm neck of the animal.

"Do you know what it feels like to be in love?" she asked the horse.

He rubbed his head against her shoulder and stamped a foot.

"It's more complicated than that, I think," she said, lazily rubbing her hand over his warm neck. "This must be what people feel like when they're drunk." Her head spun and a light, carefree attitude she couldn't afford to have the last few years filled her with joy.

She looked up and down the quiet street. The evening had a bit of a chill. The stars faded as the sky began to lighten for the new day. She wanted to shout to the world how she felt, but didn't think anyone would hear. Worse the sound might wake up Gil. She smiled, remembering how he looked sprawled across the bed as she snuck out the door.

Bang!

The window of the building in front of her shattered. Darcy and the horse both jumped as a puff of smoke stung her eyes and halted her breathing.

# Chapter 12

Darcy's hand slid through the stirrup when the horse jumped. Her skirt tangled around her legs as her body twisted with the movement of the animal. Clinging to the stirrup, she worked to release her hand and untangle her legs. The horse dragged her out into the street before she could get her feet back under her.

The long-legged animal sidestepped to get away from her as she tried to free her arm from the stirrup. It was like dancing with a drunk who didn't know the steps to the music. The horse didn't respond to her pulling on the stirrup to stop it, and she couldn't keep her feet under her long enough to dig in and give the horse any resistance.

A man ran out of the building and whistled. The horse jerked his head around, and Darcy glanced up. The big-eared man she'd witnessed talking to Craven dashed toward them. She looked at the building and groaned.

The bank loomed in front of her.

He robbed the bank, and she was attached to his getaway horse.

The outlaw grabbed the horse's reins and swung his foot up to leap in the saddle. He nearly fell over when his foot just missed kicking Darcy in the head. He dropped his foot to the ground and glared at her arm sticking through the stirrup.

The robber leaned forward and sniffed her breath. She didn't know whether to say something or just stand there like a frightened animal. She backed away from the man and her arm slide out of the stirrup easy as you please. Darcy scowled at the horse and saddle as running footsteps echoed on the board walkway behind them.

Before she could even mutter an excuse, the man grabbed her around the waist. He mounted his horse, hauling her up into the saddle with him. The hair on the back of her neck stood up as he tightened his grip and jabbed the animal with his heels. They set off out of town at a lope.

Blazes, her clumsiness got her in a pickle this time. She thought about screaming, but knew the direction they headed no one would even hear. Struggling was out of the question. Her feet dangled alongside the horse as the man's vise-like arm circled her middle, making it hard for her to breathe. Even if she could get the man to let go, there was no way she'd fall from a horse running like its tail was on fire.

Straining to listen beyond the creak of the saddle and snorting of the horse, she heard rapidly approaching horses. The lump, lodged in her throat since her capture, eased as she willed whoever followed to catch up and help. She squeezed her eyes shut and held onto the arm that kept her from dropping into the bushes rushing by in a blur. Mentally, she crossed her fingers and hoped he'd let her go when he'd gone a good distance from town.

He didn't stay to the flat land along the river. The horse climbed steadily up the side of the mountain. Darcy tucked her knees to use her skirt for protection against the tree branches and brush clawing at her legs. They rode at the break-neck pace for hours. At least it felt like hours to her clenched hands and bent legs.

Darcy tried to notice the lay of the land as they rode. The path the robber took, led them up and over a hill. The horse lunged and huffed over the rise. Lights flickered in the trees ahead. Her heart raced with the anticipation of seeing some-one and getting away from the man whose arm clenched around her like a barrel hoop.

The robber kept the horse running along the top of the hill and far enough up from the light no one would see or hear them. She sighed and looked up at the moon slipping behind the mountain. Jer-emy would be frantic with worry.

They rode on until the sun was well up in the sky. Still the man's arm held her tight. Loose strands of hair fluttered across her face, but she refused to let go of the arm for fear of falling.

He pushed the horse through a heavy copse of trees. On the other side she spotted a small log house surrounded by brush and tall pine trees. The man reined the horse to a stop in front of the cabin. She heard another horse, the one she'd long since decided wasn't her savior, stop a short distance behind them.

Darcy didn't have time to look around. The man straightened his arm, and she dropped to the ground, barely landing feet first. The movement jarred all the way up to her teeth and sent prickles of nerves dancing through her cramped leg muscles.

She looked up at him as he dismounted. He looked just as mean in the light of day as he had in the moonlight.

"What'cha got?"

Darcy turned and found the man who'd resided in her jail walking toward her. Her heart rammed into her throat. If he recognized her, she was dead. He had to have heard some of the conversations between her and Jeremy and her and Gil. Would he put all he knew together and figure out who she was?

He walked up to her and stared at her bare shoulders and chest, making her skin crawl. She wanted to run, but stood her ground and even managed to smile back.

"Found her clinging to my horse. Couldn't leave her behind to tell the marshal what we look like," said the big-eared man.

Darcy swung around and looked at him. He didn't know she was the marshal. That would give her time to think up a plan of escape. They didn't look like the type that would let her go alive.

"I wouldn't have told the marshal nothin'. He's a no-account." Darcy smiled and ran a finger down the saddlebag. "You don't look like a no-account."

"Charles, I like this little lady," said Red.

"Red, she ain't a lady. Look at how she's

dressed." Charles flicked one or her shoulder straps down her arm.

Darcy resisted the urge to pull it up and hide. She knew to stay alive long enough to escape, she would have to play the strumpet they thought her to be.

"Don't touch the goods unless asked," she said, playfully pushing his hand away.

Three more horses came thundering up to the cabin.

Charles turned to the horses, and Red sent a lecherous grin her way. She smiled back. I hope they get drunk and fall asleep.

"What took you so long?" Charles asked, walking to the back of their horses and looking out through the trees. "Where's the wagon?"

"Craven took off with the wagon. Said he was going to bury the gold until things cooled down. Then we could dig it up," said the tall skinny man she'd seen with the bunch before. Darcy ducked her head, hoping Pete wouldn't take too much interest in her.

"Skunk," Charles pulled the man out of his saddle and down to the ground. "Didn't I tell you he can't be trusted?"

Darcy stifled a giggle. There wasn't honor among thieves. Charles swung around and looked at her with the coldest eyes she'd ever seen on a man or beast.

"You said his name in front of the girl. Now we have to kill her." He said it like the thought hadn't crossed his mind before, but she could tell by the set of his shoulders and icy stare, he'd already made up his mind.

Darcy started humming. "I didn't hear noth-in'." She walked around looking at the plants and swinging her backside like she'd seen some the prostitutes do when they walked around town.

"Do we have to kill her?" Red asked, following her every move, his eyes bulging and his tongue licking his lips.

"It ain't good to have a woman around," the large, shaggy haired man said, looking at Charles. "You know how they always cause trouble."

"But she is a nice distraction," said Pete, dismounting and walking towards her. She saw the flicker of recognition in his eye as he approached.

Darcy wondered if he was going to be an ally or a problem. His face turned blank the minute she looked back at him.

The leader looked at the young man and then at Darcy. "You're right, Al. We'll get rid of her right before we head out. She might come in handy until then." Charles grabbed her by the arm, dragging her into the cabin. "You know how to cook?" he asked, and shoved her toward the fireplace.

"If I said yes would you let me live?" She batted her eyelashes and nearly vomited when Charles grabbed her breast. His eyes looked cold as a winter storm.

"You won't be shimming up to any of the boys. The first time I see you trying to get them going against one another, I'll shoot you faster than you can blink them gray eyes." He squeezed and let go. She wanted to turn from his vicious touch and glare, but knew to show any kind of weakness, would have them falling on her like coyotes on a rabbit.

Darcy gulped. She was in deep, but she wasn't going to break down. She'd remain calm and form a plan to get away.

Charles thrust a frying pan at her. "There's flour over there. Mix up some food." He turned to the men. "Red and Skunk, get the fire going. Pete, unsaddle the horses. Al show me where you last seen Craven."

Darcy set to work making biscuits and frying venison, while Charles and Al looked at a map drawn of the surrounding area.

"I still can't believe you let him take the gold," Charles said, slamming his fist on the table.

Al sat up to his full height, which dwarfed the other man. "I thought you trusted him. That's why we was working with him instead of doing it by ourselves."

"I was using him." Charles stood. He looked across the table. "I don't trust anyone who comes looking for someone to rob his own bank."

Darcy watched the men's hackles go up and wondered at the closeness of thieves. None of them seemed to trust the other. Pete had returned from taking care of the horses. He sat in the corner watching everyone and smiling at her. Red and Skunk returned. Red leered at her whenever Charles wasn't looking, and Skunk pulled up a chair and started whittling. All the while Al and Charles glared at one another in a silent battle.

She didn't know much about men, and how they interacted, but she felt there would be trouble between them before she got away. And she would get away. Charles was not going to fulfill his threat. She planned on being far from the cabin before he realized she was missing, and he wouldn't have the chance to shoot her.

The others didn't scare her, but they followed Charles. Why? He wasn't that much smarter than the rest. She also couldn't figure out why Craven would rob his own bank and virtually his town. He owned nearly all the real estate in the town and surrounding area—mostly through the way he received the mines from the men he had her throw in jail.

"If you didn't trust Craven why work with him?" she asked, placing a plate of food on the table in front of Charles. He looked at the food then at her.

"What do you care for?"

"I just find this whole thing interesting. Why would he ask you to rob his bank, then take the gold and leave you with the money?" She looked around the cabin at each man. They were definitely not the smartest band of outlaws. Ruthless? Yes. Smart? No.

"So no one would know he'd done it." Red looked at her as if she'd just sprouted horns.

"But it is more or less already his money. He could take it out a little at a time and no one would know."

"He needed a large sum for some investment," Charles said, scratching his head.

"Exactly, he had you risk your lives for what – a fifth of the money.  When he will make thousands from his investment." She saw the thoughts whirling around in the heads of her capturers.

"He's fooling with us!" shouted Pete, looking across the table at Charles.

Charles sat down. "Get them some food and keep your mouth shut," he said, motioning for Darcy to feed the rest.

She handed them each a plate and took a seat on the dirty cot along one wall. Silently she watched them eat.

"Gil! Gil!" Shouts and pounding on the door woke Gil. He smiled and reached across to cover Darcy.

She wasn't there.

He sat straight up. When did she sneak out? Why did she sneak out? Damn, they never really talked about what Jeremy overheard.

"Gil. I can't find her nowhere!"

Gil pulled on his drawers and pants before crossing the room. The key was missing. He tried the knob. It didn't work. The contrary woman locked him in.

"Stand back." With the heel of his foot, Gil kicked just above the doorknob. The door popped open. Jeremy stood against the opposite wall staring.

"Wow. Why'd you do that?"

"Your sister locked me in," he growled, stepping back in the room. He picked up his shirt. As he slipped his arms into the shirt he spied a corset on the chair. He looked at Jeremy, but the boy was so lost in his thoughts he didn't see the undergarment.

"Then you've seen her?"

The look of relief on Jeremy's face made Gil's gut twist.

"Not since last night. Why?"

"The bank was robbed early this morning and no one can find Darcy. Mr. Craven is calling a posse and claiming if the marshal ain't around he's in on it." Jeremy caught his hand. "Gil she ain't in on it. She was going to keep an eye out last night, 'cuz we knew something was happening." He looked up with tears forming in his eyes. "I was up on the mercantile roof watching just like she said, only." He gulped. "I fell asleep."

"It's okay. She shouldn't have asked you to stay up there and watch."

"But I'm the only person she trusted, and I let her down." He wiped at the tears pooling at the corners or his eyes. "You don't think she went after'em do you?  She can't really shoot worth nothin'."

Gil put a hand on the boy's shoulder. Damn. He shouldn't have let the way she looked last night interfere with his finding out what she knew.

"Go to the stable. Get my horse and one for you. We'll go see if we can find her." Gil didn't have a clue where to start, but if Craven was headed out with the posse, chances were he would take it in the opposite direction of the real bank robbers.

If it was the group Pete ran with, he hoped he could talk his old friend into telling him what happened and where he might find Darcy.

Jeremy ran out of the room, and Gil picked up the corset. He held it to his nose and breathed in Darcy's scent. Why did you slip away from me in the middle of the night? He squeezed the corset. How could he have been so naive as to think she would tell him what she had planned? From the first time he laid eyes on her, she held secrets.

He threw the corset back on the chair and jammed his hat on his head. They'd find her. And when he did, she was going to tell him everything and then he'd lock her in her jail until he had this whole thing sorted out. He stomped out of the room and down the stairs.

Jeremy stood out front holding two horses and looking nervous.

"Which way did the posse go?" Gil asked, taking the reins of his horse.

"They went that way." Jeremy pointed down the river.

Gil scratched his head and thought. No one who'd just robbed a bank would stay out in the open by following the river. He looked to the south and then the north. To go south wouldn't take them anywhere to spend the money, not without a long ride. But heading north would get them into some of the larger settlements, where they could blend in and spend the money without rousing suspicions.

"Let's go this way." Gil turned his horse northward. They'd check out the mining towns along the way and see if a group with a woman had rode through. That's assuming she was still dressed as one of Mrs. Danforth's girls. He groaned and hoped the men didn't take liberties with her. Jabbing his heels into his mount, he urged it forward at a lope. He had to catch up to them before it was too late.

# Chapter 13

Darcy woke with a stiff neck. She was thankful nothing else was sore. The robbers had been so busy the evening before bickering over whose fault it was Craven took the gold, they'd ignored her. She'd curled up on the dirty bed and fallen asleep.

It surprised her she could sleep knowing they were robbers and planned on killing her. But she'd had little sleep the night before in Gil's arms. Her heart fluttered. She would either get away from them or Gil would find her. Closing her eyes, she let her mind wander to their loving. She definitely wanted to repeat the experience. Just thinking about him made her warm all over.

She squirmed, imagining his hands on her. The movement started the dull ache of sore muscles. The cot was harder than any ground she'd ever slept on. Darcy rolled over and looked around the cabin. Not a soul slept on the floor or the hard chairs.

She was alone. Her little act must have convinced them she didn't care they were robbers as long as they had money.

Swinging her legs over the edge of the bed, she stood and surveyed the interior of the cabin. The night before the dark corners weren't visible. This morning the sun skimming through a small window, revealed mounds of odds and ends piled in the shadowed corner farthest from the door. She didn't remember seeing the pile earlier, but she'd been hunched over the fireplace cooking before she fell into an exhausted sleep.

Crossing the floor cautiously, she tried not to kick anything and let anyone outside know she was moving around. She picked through the contents of the pile. There were fancy silverware, pocket watches and fobs, and a pearl handled pistol. She checked it for bullets and found none. Pulling up her skirt, she tucked it in the top of her stockings anyway. If a bullet were to be found for it somewhere in the mass of belongings on the floor, it could come in handy. Several tintypes and personal belongings she knew no one would part with willingly were scattered throughout the mound.

She picked up a tintype in a frame the size of her hand. Staring back at her was a man about ten years older than Gil, but no doubt a relation. He sat while a pretty woman stood next to him. Mischief wrinkled the corners of the woman's eyes, and Darcy knew this had to be Gil's parents.

How did a tintype of his parents come to be in the outlaw's hideout? She checked it over carefully. The tintype was made in Baker City. The frame wasn't gold or fancy. Why would they take such an item? Her finger traced the rugged jawline of the man in the picture. Gil would find her or she'd find him. She placed the frame upside down on top of the pile.

Footsteps crunched on the pinecones outside. Darcy ran across to the bed and jumped onto the piece of furniture, landing on her knees. The thin mattress did little to protect her fall and the frame cracked. Landing as she did, pulled the bodice of her dress down nearly popping her breasts over the top of the frilly neckline.

Charles came through the door. His eyes narrowed when he saw her rearranging her dress.

"What're you doing in here?" he growled, crossing the room in three long strides.

"I stood to straighten my skirt, and I fell onto the bed." Darcy smiled up at him. When his eyes lowered to her bare chest and breasts nearly spilling out of her dress, a shiver ran down the length of her back. She didn't want this man or any of the men outside touching her. She needed to get into some decent clothes and out of the dancehall dress.

"When you get yourself straightened, start on some grub for the boys. We're hungry." He reached out a hand and grabbed her dress, yanking the front nearly up to her chin. "I told you last night there'll be no teasing with my men. I don't want them going after each other 'cuz of you."

"Yes, sir." Darcy straightened the front of her bodice, keeping everything well hidden.

"Get some food ready." He stomped out of the cabin.

A long sigh of relief escaped her lips and eased the tension in her shoulders. He didn't seem to like women even though he sure liked to look at her. Darcy wasn't going to worry over his problems; she had enough of her own. The first problem to take care of was her need to use the bushes.

She grabbed a bucket by the door and stepped out into the gentle sunshine. The warmth and friendly glow made her forget she was a prisoner. Raising her face to the golden rays, she breathed deep of fresh air.

"Can I help you, Miss?"

Her eyes opened wide. Red stood only a few feet in front of her. The smell of his unwashed body hit her nostrils the same time Pete hurried over.

"I need some water to start your meal, and I need a trip into the woods." She looked at both men and smiled. "Could you get the water?" She handed the bucket to Red and scanned the trees around the cabin. "Where is the water?"

"Over there behind the cabin." Red pointed to the right of the building.

She nodded her head and started off in the opposite direction.

"Where're you going?" Pete asked, snagging her skirt.

Darcy slapped his hand away and looked at him with as much dignity and haughtiness as she could muster.

"I said I needed a trip into the woods."

"What for?"

She looked down her nose at him like she imagined Mrs. Danforth would if she were in the same situation. "To take care of some womanly business."

The man's face reddened as he grabbed her by the arm.

"We need to talk," he said quietly and with authority. He took her by the arm, guiding her out into the trees.

"What would I have to talk to you about?" she asked, hoping Charles didn't see them wandering off alone. She would rather not find out the relationship between this man and Gil than face the wrath of the gang leader.

When they were out of sight of the cabin, he stopped and looked around.

"Are you spying on me for Gil?" he asked, letting her go and leaning against a large pine tree.

"Gil? Why would I be spying on you for him?" She stepped closer to him. His lips were curved in a smile, but his eyes fixed on her like two hot daggers.

"He's here to take me back to my Pa. I don't want to go back." He leaned forward and cupped her chin in his hand. "If you have any notions of getting away and telling him where I'm at you better get them out of that pretty head of yours." He bent forward and kissed her.

Darcy pulled back and sputtered as she wiped her arm across her mouth. "Don't you ever do anything like that to me again!"

He laughed. "You don't act like no prostitute to me. I figured you wasn't, 'cuz he don't hang around that type of woman. Where'd Gil find you?" He stepped close again.

She backed up and found herself against a tree. He smiled and moved toward her.

"Pete? Pete where'd you and that girl go?" Red

called from a short distance away.

"We're over here, but stay back she ain't through relieving herself yet."

Darcy felt her face heat from embarrassment. She still needed to use the bushes, but with this randy man watching there was no way she'd lift her skirts. And now Red thought Pete was getting an eye full.

She turned and headed in the direction she'd heard Red's voice. Fighting her dress as it caught on the underbrush and wrapped around her legs, she realized she needed different clothes when her chance came to get away from these men.

The first problem was finding someone she trusted to watch out for her while she did what she came to the woods to do. She found Charles over by the horses.

"I can't do my business with these two sniffing after me like male dogs," she said, pointing to Pete and Red who followed her all the way to the boss.

Charles growled and looked at her. After they stared at one another for a few minutes he waved his arm. "You go out there. I'll keep these two busy."

She headed into the trees.

"But if you ain't back in a reasonable time, I'm letting them come looking for you." The glint in his eyes told her they would be allowed to do anything they wanted if she wasn't back in good time.

Darcy gulped and hurried out into the woods. After relieving herself, she hurried back to the cabin, plotting to get her hands on some clothes and get out of there by the same time the following day.

Gil hadn't felt so wound up and eaten with guilt since his parent's death. He'd let his desire take over and not talked to Darcy about what she'd planned. Now she was missing and possibly a captive of robbers.

*I should have stopped her.*

He looked over at Jeremy. The boy had chattered nonstop since they'd left town the following day. Gil had wondered if the boy would shut up long enough for them to both sleep when they bedded down.

He smiled when Jeremy glanced over at him.

"Don't worry, she's alright. You don't know Darcy like I know her. She's tough and she's smart." Jeremy smiled. "I wouldn't be surprised if she jumps right out of the trees at us."

Gil smiled. "I wish I had your confidence. These men find out she's the marshal, there's no telling what they might do to her." The color faded from Jeremy's face, and Gil mentally slapped himself.

"She'd know better than to tell them if they didn't know." He looked over at Gil. "Was she wearing her badge last night?"

Gil thought of the dress that barely covered her shoulders and breasts and groaned. "No, she was dressed like a saloon girl."

Jeremy grimaced then smiled. "She was playing a part, wasn't she? She's done that before. They won't know she's the marshal unless she wants them to. She'll be a saloon girl until she can get away." He laughed.

"She played the part of a preacher's daughter in Astoria.  We didn't have nothing to eat and no money to buy anything. Darce took a dress off a clothesline and went up to this church. She said how she was so and so's daughter from the Baptist church in a small town we'd just passed through and that she'd found me hungry and hurt alongside the road and wondered if they could spare some food for both her and me.

"They took us in and fed us and gave us a place to sleep for a week. We helped them with chores and were eating good until one day the lady said I looked like a boy she'd heard had run away." Jeremy's gaze hardened. "We knew if we hung around any longer he'd find us. So we lit out that night after Darcy put the dress back on the clothesline where she'd found it."

"Who would find you?" This wasn't the first time Gil had wondered at their past.

Jeremy looked straight at him. "Our uncle." His voice seethed with hatred.

"Darcy said you didn't have any living kin." Gil wondered what other things she'd lied about.

"We don't. Kin don't sell their own to a whore house or treat children like rabid animals," he spate the words like venom.

"Your uncle did this to you and Darcy?" Gil had run into some downright ugly people in his life, but not one so low as to do that to kin. "Why?"

"He told our dying parents he'd take care of us, so they wrote up a paper giving him all their money and belongings to care for us." His face reddened as he relived the ordeal. "The first thing he did was sell Darcy to a whore house."

She'd been an innocent last night. He cringed. She'd made it away from a whore house only to have a drifter with nothing to give her take her innocence.

"She knocked a man over the head and ran away. She stole into our uncle's house and took me. I was so hungry, I could barely walk." His eyes lit with pride. "She carried me till we found a wagon that took us far from there. She said nothin' would keep us apart ever again. Nothin'"

Gil looked away. He saw the accusations in the boy's young eyes. Jeremy hadn't said anything, but he knew Darcy and Gil had spent time together the night before. What Jeremy didn't know, were the feelings his sister stirred.

He didn't even know himself what those feelings were. It was something he'd never experienced. He'd bedded a few women, but never had he wanted to make love to them as he had with Darcy. There was something about her that set his whole body on fire when he looked at her, or heard her voice. His groin ached just thinking about her. With luck, this aching he had for her would run its course, and he could move on without yearning for her touch.

He sighed and Jeremy looked at him. His face heated. If the boy knew the thoughts he had about his sister, Jeremy'd have every right to deck him. Looking into a face so much like Darcy's, Gil's heart squeezed. He wanted to be a part of their lives. To be a part of the inseparable feelings they shared. It was something he'd never missed until he witnessed it between the brother and sister.

Since meeting the two, he'd done a lot of thinking about his brothers. What they were like. If they still lived at the mine. If any were married and had kids. He shook his head. No sense thinking about family. They'd made it pretty clear the day he left they didn't care what he did. His stomach knotted. He didn't blame them. They wouldn't want to have a reminder of what had happened to their parents hanging around.

"What you thinking about?" Jeremy broke into his ruminations. The concern in his young voice nearly choked Gil.

"Nothing important." Gil reached over and squeezed the boy's shoulder.  He liked spending time with the boy. And the sister.

He thought of holding Darcy and waking up every morning with her in his arms. It was a pleasant thought. One he'd tried to ignore since he found out she was a girl. If he brought back a wife instead of Pete, he wondered if Pete's father would still consider him for the foreman's job. It would make him more root-bound. He ran a hand over his face and blew air out between his lips.

If the other hands knew what he was thinking they'd be hootin' and hollerin' like a bunch of liquored Indians. Whenever they raised hell in town, he stayed at the ranch and helped them to bed when they came in too drunk to take off their boots. He'd sworn to the whole lot of them he would never get tied up by a woman.

He was still a little shy of the idea. In theory it sounded darn good, but could he actually stay true to one woman and one place?

A flash of gray and red in the trees to his left

caught his attention. He stopped his horse and tapped Jeremy on the arm, motioning for him to be quiet. Listening, he heard the sound of two horses picking their way through the underbrush. Gil turned his horse that direction.

Cautiously, they moved through the trees and brush. At a small clearing, he spotted Craven on a bay gelding. The crook led a black horse with a packsaddle into the trees on the far side.

"How come he ain't with the posse no more?" Jeremy whispered.

"Good question. Let's see where he's heading, especially since this isn't the direction he led the posse." Gil wanted to catch up, but didn't want to be seen. They skirted the edge of the clearing, staying just inside the tree line.

He stopped when he spotted the horse with the saddle standing alone near a thicket. Gil slid off his horse and handed the reins to Jeremy. He whispered, "Stay here while I take a look."

Crouching and using the brush to hide, Gil slipped silently through the underbrush. He approached the sound of digging. A man cursed just a few feet from him, and Gil dropped to the ground. He pushed a limb to the side.

Craven wielded a shovel digging a hole. Sweat drizzled down his jowls as he worked. He wiped at the rivulets with his shirtsleeve and set to scooping more dirt from the hole.

Gil remained on his stomach watching the overweight man slowly make a hole up to his knees and twice as big around as his body.

Craven crawled out of the hole and walked over to the packhorse. He pulled out a canteen and tipped his head back. Water ran down his chin and jowls, darkening his clothing. When it appeared he'd swallowed nearly all the container could hold, he capped it and looped it over a tree branch.

Craven pulled twenty white sacks about the size of a bread loaf out of the packsaddle and piled them on the ground. They appeared to be the kind used by assayers to hold gold. He carried two at a time over to the hole and dropped them in. The way the bags pulled on Craven's arms, they had to be full of gold.

When all the bags were in the hole, Craven covered them over with dirt and stopped to drink the rest of the water in his canteen.

Jeremy had to be getting fidgety as long as Gil'd been gone, but Craven didn't seem to feel he had any reason to hurry. As though he knew the whole town was miles the other direction. Craven finally rolled down his shirtsleeves and put his jacket on. Walking over to the packhorse, he grabbed the lead rope and headed to the saddled horse.

Gil stayed on the ground until Craven mounted and headed through the trees. When the man was out of sight, he approached the hole and scanned the surrounding area. He broke limbs all around the hole, pointing them down to the freshly dug dirt. Then he pulled a small bush and planted it in the hole, to make sure either he or Jeremy could find the spot after they had Darcy safe.

He returned to Jeremy. "Do you know how we got here?" he asked, mounting his horse.

"Yeah."

"Craven buried gold sacks over here." He led

Jeremy to the spot and pointed out the bush and broken limbs. "One of us will need to come back and dig it up after we have Darcy safe and Craven is locked up. Look around good so you can find it if I'm unable to come."

The boy looked at him, but nodded solemnly and looked his surroundings over with a critical eye.

Gil spurred his horse forward. He knew which way Craven headed. The man wasn't getting out of their sight. He had to find Darcy. Bringing Pete back and securing the foreman's job no longer was his single concern. He wanted the feisty woman that agitated him in all the right ways to be safe. It was imperative they find her before Craven saw through her disguise.

*Chapter 14*

Darcy made biscuits and salt pork for the robbers' breakfast. The men became lively from the whiskey they drank with their food.

"How about a little dance," Red said, swatting her on the backside. She jumped and nearly hit him alongside the head with the frying pan in her hand before she remembered her disguise. Slowly, she turned and looked at him with a big smile stretched across her face. It was either that or scream.

"There ain't no music," she said saucily.

Skunk swaggered over to the pile of goods in the corner and pulled a fiddle with only three strings out of the mess. He dug a little deeper and came up with the bow to go with it.

Darcy watched with fascination as he carefully tuned the three remaining strings. In her travels, she'd never had the opportunity to see a musician fine tune an instrument.

"Skunk here'll play, and we can dance," Red

said, grabbing her hand and pulling her toward him.

She looked at Charles. "I'm afraid your boss said I can't do anything to encourage you boys. So I better not dance with any of you." She smiled what she hoped was a disappointed smile and turned back to the fire.

A rough hand swung her around. It was Charles.

"Now you're using my words to turn my boys against me," he said through clenched teeth. "You dance, but you dance with everybody." His glare bore two holes clear through her head. Darcy gulped and nodded.

Skunk tapped his foot three times and slid the bow across the strings, starting a rollicking reel. Red grabbed her around the waist and started bouncing in a circle. The twirling and watching the man across from her bouncing up and down had her stomach churning. Her hands gripped his like a hawk trying not to lose its prey. The only thing she found good about the whole thing was the faster he swung her the farther away from her legs her skirt stayed, making it impossible for her skirt to trip her up.

Red let go of her, and Al grabbed her around the middle picking her up off the floor. She didn't liked being hugged against his body, but at least she didn't have to worry about tripping over her feet or his. She closed her eyes and gulped down the lump creeping up her throat.

Al dropped her unceremoniously on her feet and shoved her to the next partner. She opened her eyes and stared into the grinning face of Pete.

He wrapped his arms tight around her, pulling her body up close to his. The music was still a fast paced reel, but Pete moved slow and deliberate around the floor. His leg pushed against her skirt, invading the space between her legs as they moved around the small confines of the cabin.

She stiffened when his tongue touched her ear. The hair on the back of her neck prickled, and her stomach burned sour. His closeness made her uncomfortable. A different uncomfortable than Gil's touches and caresses.

When the song finished, Pete held onto her. She didn't miss the look in his eyes or the feel of his maleness against her belly. This was exactly what Charles didn't want to happen. Her feet were frozen in place, making Pete think she was enamored of him, when in fact she was scared that at any moment Charles would decide her usefulness had ended.

Her throat constricted, and her chest felt on fire when Charles grabbed her.

"Waltz," he ordered both to her and Skunk. Her body nearly melted in his arms as relief flowed through her like a gentle mountain stream. The tempo of the music slowed, and she found her body floating in measured, rhythmic circles around the small cabin floor. She would have never guessed such a ruthless man could move so smooth and graceful. When the song finished he shoved her to Red, who started prancing around in fast circles again.

"Whoa," Darcy said, trying to keep her stomach still as her head twirled faster than they danced.

"What's the matter?" Red asked, releasing her.

The momentum of the dance sent her twirling toward the fireplace. She grabbed the mantle and stood with her head resting on the wood shelf as her mind continued moving in circles. When her head cleared, she turned back to the room and smiled.

"I'm sorry, all that dancing winded me." She fanned her hand over her face; it was getting warm in the room. She barely had her bearings when Red grabbed her arms and started twirling her around the room once more. After two spins around the cabin, the men yelled, and Darcy smelled smoke.

The pile of goods in the corner was on fire as well as the bed where she had slept. Pete swatted at her dress. Darcy twisted around and found the back hem of her skirt in flames. She screamed, and the men ran out of the burning cabin.

Gil and Jeremy crouched behind a bush watching a cabin. Craven had circled it a couple of times then walked his horse to the back of the building. Gil tipped his head, listening. He could swear there was music coming from inside. His curiosity got the better of him. He started to move forward for a better look when the door burst open. Smoke billowed out followed by five men. They ran and jumped on horses tied to trees. Pete lagged behind. It was the perfect opportunity to separate him from the gang and tie him up to take back to the ranch.

Gil jumped up to mount his horse when Jeremy grabbed his coat.

"Look!"

Flames shot up through the roof of the cabin and a woman stumbled out the door, falling to the ground.

Gil knew that green dress going up in flames. He took a last look at Pete's back as the horse raced through the trees. His heart pumped furiously as he pushed through the brush to get to Darcy.

"Roll, baby, roll!" He shouted, hurrying to cover the distance between him and the woman who meant more to him than the ranch foreman job.

He saw her roll, extinguishing the flames. Her eyes were filled with terror as she clutched something to her chest.

A lump of fear lodged in his throat. He fell to his knees and pulled her up into his arms, batting at the smoldering skirt.

"Are you okay?" He looked at her soot-covered face and disheveled hair and thought he'd never seen anyone so beautiful.

Darcy coughed and looked at him with such sweet innocence it made his gut twist.

"I knew you'd find me."

He wanted to kiss her; instead he pulled her to her feet and inspected the still smoldering skirt.

The thunder of hooves reminded him who they followed. Before he could look up, Darcy was swooped out of his hands. The object she clutched to her chest fell to the ground at his feet. He looked up into the wicked eyes of Tobias Craven.

"I got your girl, so don't try to follow me." The man looked down at Gil with wide, wild eyes. "I know you've been following me. Don't do it anymore or she gets killed." Craven squeezed Darcy around the middle, and she squeaked.

Gil moved to drag her from the horse, but Craven shoved a foot in his chest. "I mean it. Don't follow me or I'll kill this harlot." Craven jabbed his heels into the horse, and they disappeared out of sight through the trees.

"Gil! Gil!  Are you okay?  Where's he taking Darcy?" Jeremy ran out of the trees as Gil bent to pick up the object Darcy dropped.

His eyes misted when he recognized his mother and father. How had she gotten a tintype of his parents? And how had she realized who they were? He looked down at his parents. They appeared happy and full of love. Searching their beloved faces, he tried to find traces of disapproval on their faces. In his dreams, they were always disappointed in him. He'd failed them. Because he'd wanted to catch a frog, he'd left the mine and his parents and younger brother alone. He knew the older boys blamed him for not being there to help when the Indians came through and killed them.

He saw it in their eyes when he came whistling back from the pond, and they all stood there red eyed from crying and thinking he had been taken by the Indians.

He looked down at the tintype and all the old feelings of regret and recrimination flowed through him. He'd let his family down.

Jeremy tugged on his shirt.

"Are we going after Darcy?"

Gil rubbed his coat sleeve under his nose and looked at Jeremy's worried face. Here was a chance to make things right for this family. He wouldn't let Darcy and Jeremy down. Retrieving his horse's reins from the boy, he looked in the direction the scoundrel disappeared with Darcy.

Craven called her a harlot, which meant he still didn't know who she was. That was one thing in Darcy's favor, as long as she kept her mouth closed, he shouldn't figure it out with the dress and the soot all over her face.

He looked at Jeremy and ruffled his hair. "We almost had her."

"We'll get her this time." Jeremy grabbed his hand. "Come on."

"Not so fast, Craven said if we follow he'll kill her. We have to go slow and follow his tracks so we don't get too close too soon." Gil ran his fingers over the tintype. They were so happy together. He looked up at the boy's expectant face.

"Come on. Let's see how easy a trail he's left us to follow."

They led the horses to the edge of the clearing where Craven disappeared. Gil smiled. If the old man held Darcy for long like he carried her when he left, his arm would get tired in a hurry. She may not weigh much, but a man like Craven wasn't use to such work. Especially after digging that hole earlier. Gil led his horse, watching for broken branches and—he reached out plucking a scrap of scorched cloth from a limb. Yep, they would eventually catch up.

Darcy lay limp across the horse's neck. Craven carried her dangling from his arm for a while, then unceremoniously plopped her over the horse's neck. She could tell by the way he patted her backside every now and then he didn't know he patted his marshal. He thought she was a prostitute, giving him the right to put his hands on her anywhere he wanted. She wanted to slap him and tell him to go to hell. But knew she'd be dead if he figured out her true identity. She lay still and dragged her feet through as much brush as she could, hoping if she didn't break branches she at least left something for Gil to follow.

She smiled. Her heart hammered in her chest thinking of the glimmer in Gil's eyes when he looked at her back at the cabin. She'd seen love shining out at her. She may not have seen it a lot, but she remembered her father looking at her mother that way.

The horse stopped. She held her breath and waited. The vulgar man dismounted and pulled her down off the horse. Her numb feet and shaky legs caused her to fall against Craven. Her back pressed against his round belly. Turning her head, she looked up into his pudgy face. His yellow-stained mustache made her stomach churn. She could tell by the look in his eyes, she wouldn't like what was coming.

He pulled her closer, his hands on her breasts. Darcy bit her lip, forcing herself not to say anything. He slipped a hand into her bodice and pulled a breast out. When he bent his head, his mustache poked the delicate skin. She jumped out of his grasp.

"Get back here bitch. You lost me money setting that cabin on fire."

Darcy trembled. She didn't want this man touching her. But she didn't know how to keep him from doing what he wanted. He was a lot bigger than her. Even though he wasn't strong, his sheer size could easily out handle her.

"Your mustache poked me," she said in a breathy whisper.

"Oh, sorry." He smiled apologetically and stepped closer. He grabbed the breast hanging over the bodice and pulled her body to him. His other hand grabbed at the junction of her legs. Darcy squeezed her eyes shut and tried to make believe it was Gil, but that only made her mad. This man had no right to touch her so, even if he did think she was a harlot.

She raised her knee fast and hard connecting with his crotch. A rush of putrid air blew in her face as he bent to clutch his prized manhood. She bent to look at his face contorted in pain. The sight made her smile.

He squinted at her, growled an oath, and slapped her hard across the face.

The act stunned her. No man had ever hit her. Lifting her skirt, she pulled out the pearl handled pistol. His face paled when she pointed the barrel at the spot between his bushy eyebrows.

"Don't you come after me or I'll shoot you where I kicked you." She backed away with the gun aimed at his crotch. When she was a good distance, she turned and ran back the way they'd traveled.

She heard him yelling, "When I catch you bitch, you're dead!"

Darcy ran as hard as she could with the remnants of the dress catching between her legs. If he followed, he'd have no trouble catching her. She had to get back to Gil. He loved her and would protect her.

When her legs collapsed and her lungs burned from sucking air, she clutched the gun to her and collapsed in a heap at the base of a tree. Curling up in a ball, she wished her parents hadn't died, and she hadn't been born with bad luck.

*Chapter 15*

Gil didn't take any chances. He moved cautiously through the trees, noting every broken branch and piece of cloth they found. Darcy had left him a good trail to follow. No one traveling through trees and brush could leave this many clear signals unless on purpose. He smiled. She was smart and brave. Wait till he took her to the ranch, the other hands would fall all over themselves they didn't meet her first.

He chuckled and Jeremy looked at him.

"What's so funny?"

"Nothing, just thinking about the ranch hands where I work."

"Is it your family's ranch?" The wistfulness in the boy's voice matched Gil's own longing to belong to the ranch.

"No. I'm hoping to make foreman when I get back." That was if he brought Pete back.

"You got any family?" Jeremy pulled his horse up alongside Gil.

"I have four brothers. But I don't see them much."

"How come?"

"I haven't lived at home for a long time." Gil hadn't returned since his parents' deaths. He knew he wasn't wanted. "We don't get along like you and Darcy."

"If I had four brothers I'd want to see them all the time. I've always wished for a brother." He looked sheepish. "Don't tell Darce that or she'll knock me six ways to Sunday."

"She's one tough lady, your sister." Gil reached out and ruffled the boy's hair. "We'll find her, and she'll pry be spitting mad when we do."

Jeremy smiled. "Yeah."

Gil rounded a large bush and spied something green piled at the base of a pine. He stopped his horse and motioned for Jeremy to do the same. The green pile didn't move and it had a startling resemblance to the dress he'd last seen Darcy wearing. His chest squeezed with fear. Did being cautious leave Darcy vulnerable? As much as he wanted to race forward and see if it was her, his instincts told him to take his time and view the situation from all sides. He studied the area.

"Jeremy," he whispered, pointing to the object. "Go see what that is. I'll circle around and watch for a trap."

Jeremy nodded, handing his reins to Gil.

Gil flipped the reins of the two horses over a limb. Watching the boy approach the green pile, he snuck through the bushes to the opposite side of the object.

Jeremy knelt by the tree and said something.

Gil's heart pummeled his chest when Darcy sat up and hugged her brother. He watched a little longer from the cover, making sure no one came out from the far side. When he was certain it wasn't an ambush, he made his way to the hugging siblings.

"Darcy, are you all right?" he asked, dropping to his knees beside the woman.

She wrapped her arms around him and wept. He rubbed her back and cooed soft words. He wasn't sure what he said; only she felt right in his arms.

"There, I've got you now and nothing is going to happen to you." He shifted to a sitting position, pulling her onto his lap. She turned, and he saw a handprint on her soot-covered face as well as a breast poking out of her bodice.

The bastard hit his woman. Gil shut his eyes and ground his teeth to control the emotions ricocheting inside. He would hunt Craven down and kill him.

Thankfully, Jeremy was behind Darcy and couldn't see her state of undress. Gil didn't think the boy would understand. The two were close. Riding around with the boy the last two days, he'd learned just how close.

When he could speak in a controlled tone, Gil said, "Jeremy, take the horses about a mile that direction." He nodded with his head. "Make camp, and we'll catch up when Darcy feels up to it."

"Why do I got to go so far off the trail?" Jeremy asked, looking longingly at his sister.

"If Craven comes back looking for Darcy we don't want to be where he can find us easily. Now do as I say and we'll be along." Gil looked down at Darcy's charred dress. "Leave my saddlebags. Your sister is going to need a change of clothes."

Jeremy reluctantly followed the orders. When he was out of sight, Gil took Darcy's head in his hands. He gazed into her wet eyes and gently touched the purple bruise with his thumb. "Why did Craven hit you? What else did he do?"

Darcy avoided looking at him. She gulped and tried to say the words. Her body shook with fear of Carven and fear that Gil would think her the strumpet she pretended. The vile man had put his hands on her—. She felt dirty and unworthy of the concern she saw in Gil's eyes.

"I know he touched you." Gil gently cupped her breast in his hand and pulled the bodice up over both his hand and the breast. His hand remained on her skin, warm and comforting.

"He kept patting my backside when he had me sprawled across the neck of the horse." She looked up into the soothing brown eyes of the only man she ever wanted to touch her.

"What else," he asked quietly, removing his hand from her bodice and picking up her hand. He twined his fingers with hers and kissed the soot-covered knuckles.

"He—he stopped up there." She nodded back the direction she had run. "He pulled me off the horse and started acting randy." She looked into his face. His jaw clenched and unclenched as he stared over her head. She took his face in her hands and made him look at her. "At first I thought, play the part, go along." She gulped as his gaze locked with hers. "But I couldn't." Tears slid down her cheeks.

She wiped at them with the back of her hand.

"When he pulled my bodice down and touched…" She hiccupped and turned away from his penetrating brown eyes. "I kicked him like my pa taught me and ran back this way."

Gil pulled her against his chest and squeezed so hard she could barely breathe, but it didn't matter as long as she was safe in his arms.

"You're never getting out of my sight. Not until we have Craven where he belongs, in his own jail." He hugged her tight before holding her away from his body. "How did your dress catch on fire?"

Darcy told him of the dancing and twirling. She had to smile and laugh as she retold the ordeal.

"Where're those clothes you were talking about?" she asked.

"In my saddlebag. Wouldn't you like to clean up a bit before you put them on?"

"How?"

Gil stood, taking her by the elbow. "About a quarter mile that way there's a lake." He walked over to where Jeremy had unceremoniously dumped his saddlebag. He flung it over his shoulder and escorted her through the trees.

Darcy looked at their surroundings for the first time and found they were in beautiful country. The tall pine and fir trees whispered to one another as birds twittered and called.  The undergrowth wasn't thick and a person could walk with relative ease. Of course it helped half her skirt was gone, so it didn't drag the ground and catch on things.

"Where are we?"

"About half way between Galena and Granite. The lake's called Olive."

They came over a slight rise and stretching before them was a crystal clear lake.

"It's beautiful." She turned to Gil. "How'd you know it was here?"

"Been here a couple times."

"How far is Granite from Baker?"

"A Good day's hard ride. Why?"

Darcy slipped a paper out of the pocket of her skirt. "I think Craven is planning on taking the train out of Baker." She handed Gil a piece of torn newspaper with the train schedule from Baker City. She'd pulled the paper from the man's jacket pocket when she hung by his side. The sound of rustling paper as her body bounced against his had caught her attention. She'd pulled the paper out planning to drop it for Gil to follow. When she saw it was a train schedule, she stuffed it in the pocket of her skirt.

He looked at the piece of paper and up at her. "How?"

"Just lucky, I guess."

He grinned and tried to shove it into his pocket. Frowning, he pulled out the tintype.

"How did you know this was my parents?" he asked, stopping at the edge of the water and staring at the picture.

Darcy saw sadness and regret in his eyes. She wanted to hold him, but instinct told her this wasn't the time. Squatting at the edge of the water, she tested it with her fingers. "You have your mother's mouth and your father's eyes." She looked over at him. "Where are they?"

"Dead." He shoved the tintype back in his pocket.

"When?" She sat down and unbuttoned her shoes.

"I was Jeremy's age. I went down to the pond to look for a frog. I wanted to put it in a lunch pail at school that day.  When I came back my older brothers were running around looking scared. They'd come back with a load of firewood." He frowned. "I was supposed to help them, but begged out saying I had a stomach ache." He picked up a rock and heaved it out into the clear water. "Just 'cuz I wanted to scare a girl."

"What happened while you were gone?" Darcy pulled her shoes off and looked up at his trouble face.

"We thought some renegade Indians came through and killed Ma, Pa, and my younger brother. And took some things." He turned the tintype over in his hands. "But if this was with those outlaws... How'd they get it from Indians?"

"You think that bumbling group killed your family?" She started to stand, but he motioned for her to stay. He came over and squat in front of her.

"I don't know. All I know is my brothers thought I should have been at the house to help protect my mother and younger brother. I saw it in their eyes. Heard it in their voices." He picked up her foot and rolled the stocking down. "I left after a week, and I ain't been back."

"Don't you want to see them? I'm sure after all this time they don't still blame you. They couldn't. It wouldn't be family-like to still have hard feelings." She looked down when his hand slide up her leg, relieving her of the long, black stocking.

"Oh." Darcy sucked in her breath. "I want to

talk about you and your family." His touch ignited small fires of desire. She pulled her foot away. He merely took her other foot.

She looked down at her stockings draped across her shoes and wondered how they both got there.

"I don't want to talk about my brothers. I want to talk about the woman I can't quit thinking about." He reached up, popping the buttons down the front of her bodice.

"This doesn't belong to me," she said, watching the buttons, one by one, disappear in the folds of her scorched skirt.

Gil tipped his head back and laughed. His Adam's apple bobbed up and down as his chin shook.

"I don't think whoever it belongs to will want it back in its condition." He pushed the bodice open with his hands, revealing the lacy chemise underneath. With practiced hands he untied the undergarment and slid both pieces of clothing to her waist, exposing her upper torso to the late afternoon sun.

Darcy wasn't the least shocked to sit beside a lake in the middle of the day with a man staring at her bared skin. It felt right for Gil to touch her and undress her. She willed it to continue.

"Stand," he said, standing beside her and helping her to her feet. He unbuttoned the top of the skirt and untied the petticoat leaving them to fall to the ground around her. She stepped out of the circle of garments.

His hands untied the string of her drawers and gently pushed them to the ground at her feet. She stepped out and stood completely naked before him.

"You're so beautiful." Gil took her in his arms. His head lowered. His soft lips captured hers. Tremors of need shook her as she pressed against him.

He pulled his duster around her, drawing her body into his cocoon of security. His hands stayed on the outside of the coat holding her close as his lips trailed down her neck.

Darcy tipped her head back, allowing him to continue his downward ascent. She knocked his hat to the ground when it hit her in the forehead. Hooking her arms around his neck, she pulled her body up to wrap her legs around his waist.

"When I first laid eyes on you, I'd have never guessed you were a girl." He nipped at her breast. "But now I don't know how I missed it." He grinned and walked to the water's edge.

"What're you doing?" She asked, looking behind her at the crystal clear water.

"I brought you here for a bath."

Darcy looked at his dark eyes and saw mischief brewing, sure as coffee. "You wouldn't?"

He cocked an eyebrow and threw her out into the cold lake.

She came up sputtering and spewing as the cold water bit at her skin like bee stings.

"I'll get you for that!" she screamed, flopping onto her back and kicking vigorously to keep the blood circulating. She remembered Pa telling her one time when they were snowshoeing by a stream that if she fell in to kick off the shoes and keep kicking her legs to keep her blood moving so she didn't freeze before he could pull her out.

Guilt batted the thoughts out of her head. She swam bare naked in a lake while a man stood on shore watching. Her father and mother would be mortified. And what of the night she and Gil shared? Guilt vanished, remembering the long kisses and body heating interludes. Something that good couldn't be wrong.

She cast a glance to the bank. Gil wasn't there. She stopped splashing with her legs, letting them drift to the bottom of the lake and scanned the area.

Her teeth clanked together as they chattered from the body numbing cold. Where could he have gone? The saddlebags were on the sand where he'd dropped them. He must have gone looking for something for them to eat while she got cleaned up. Darcy scrubbed at the soot on her face and worked her fingers through her hair, untangling twigs.

Her legs became tired from staying afloat. She worked her way back to the shore. Just as the muddy bottom squished between her toes something caught her around the waist dragging her back into the lake.

Darcy tried to scream, but the arm around her waist pushed all the air out of her lungs.

"Don't fight me." Gil's voice was soft and seductive.

"You nearly scared me to death," she said through clenched teeth.

"Sorry, I had to make sure no one was around before I took off my gun." He spun her in his arms. The look of adoration in his eyes whisked her irritation away like a leaf in an autumn breeze. He made a path over her face and down her neck with the tips of his fingers. His touch sent delicious shivers through her, culminating at her tingling nipples. Looking down, she found the dark circles peaked.

Gil placed his hands under her arms and raised her out of the water, capturing a nipple with his mouth. He suckled. The warmth of his mouth and nibbling on her sensitive peaks sparked her body to life. She gripped his hair, moving his hungry mouth from one breast to the next. The sensations of the warm and cold drew sighs of wonder from her.

He lowered her, dropping wet open-mouthed kisses up her neck to her mouth. She clung to his neck and wrapped her legs around his waist. In doing so, she rubbed his hardness. The feel of him against her center aroused her even more.

Darcy wasn't cold anymore. The water lapped around her, caressing and cooling as Gil's touch fanned a fire deep within her. She moaned in pleasure when his hands massaged her bottom and his fingers found her hot center. She wiggled and squirmed as his skilled fingers rubbed the spot that sent waves of sensations scorching through her body.

She opened her eyes when he raised her up and slowly lowered her onto his engorged member. This coupling and his touch brought her happiness. Something this right couldn't be wrong. She starred into Gil's eyes as he thrust, deeper and deeper until a burst of white light and spasms of heat rocked her body.

He growled her name and grasped her head in

his hands, kissing her with reverence. Her weary legs shook as she clung to him, savoring the sweet kisses and love making.

Her legs were spent from running and treading the water. When she started slipping from his hold, Gil carried her from the lake. The water ran down their bodies as the evening air brought goose flesh to their skin. She pressed against him, using his body warmth to stave off the cool breeze.

He carried her to the saddlebags and his pile of clothes. Kneeling, he settled her on his duster he had thoughtfully spread out before he joined her in the lake.

The grin he bestowed upon her, before sprawling on the coat beside her, was one tooth short of lecherous, but it made her heart hum.

"Jeremy's going to wonder where we are," she said, trailing a finger down his chest and toying with the hair at the base of his enlarging manhood.

"He'll make camp and wait. He knows you're in good hands." A smile that looked like he'd won a large poker pot lit up his face.

"I'll say." She took him in her hands and massaged.

Gil groaned and studied her, his lips quivered between a smile and not trying to smile. "You could barely hang on in the lake and now you want more?"

"I don't have to hang on here." She moved her hands over his stomach, up his smooth chest, and stopped when she ran her hands through the hair on his head. Clutching his curls, she gently drew his head to her breasts.

Gil smiled mischievously and nipped her rosebud colored areola. Darcy squirmed as the sensations swept through her once more. He suckled until she arched her hips, begging him to enter.

He tipped her onto her back. Darcy welcomed him with spread legs and a smile. His work worn fingers ran through the thatch of hair where her legs joined, touching the spot that sent vibrations humming through her body. She squirmed and arched, wanting him.

Gil knelt between her legs, lifting her hips up to meet him.

"Please," she whispered, seeing in his eyes he wanted to give her as much as she gave him.

Their gazes locked as he entered. His fullness and uncensored emotions filled Darcy with sentiments she'd long ago thought were lost to her.

She shuddered and arched as rivers of warmth and light surged through her body. Peering into the eyes of the man she loved, she knew no matter what happened after today, she would never love another.

When she thought she couldn't withstand any more sensations he plunged, sending his seed deep. His dazed look and sweaty brow made her smile. She reached up, pushing the hair from his eyes.

He was so beautiful. She'd never thought of a man as being beautiful until now. A sheen of sweat accented his muscles and dotted his upper lip. She rose up to him and licked the sweat from his lip before kissing him with all the fervor of her emotions.

Pulling back, she peered into his eyes. They drooped from weariness, but held—was that a spark of love?

"Come here." He ran his fingers through her hair and drew her lips to his. The kiss was long and sweet. Reluctantly, he pulled away.

"When we get done chasing Craven, and I bring Pete back to the ranch, will you come with me?"

Darcy stared at him as the meaning of his words sunk in. Her heart skipped a beat as she looked into his sincere face. There was one thing wrong with his request. He hadn't said what she desperately needed to hear.

Chapter 16

"What about Jeremy?"

"What about him? He can come with us." Gil rolled Darcy onto her back and straddled her body. He held her hands above her head and looked down into her earnest gray eyes. She had to say 'yes'. He'd never met another woman he couldn't get enough of.

"I don't know what you do. How would we live?"

His gaze trailed over her face, drinking in the small nose, frown wrinkles on her forehead and back down to the straight line of her mouth. He'd thought her to be too impetuous for her own good, but now as she contemplated the future with him, she took her time rolling the ideas over. Maybe if he gave her a little more about his past, she'd come around to his way of thinking.

"I'm a cow hand. I've been working a ranch out of Baker City for a little over a year. The owner told me if I brought Pete back to the ranch, I'd have the foreman's job." A brief flicker of apprehension flashed in her eyes.

He hurried to add. "I'm sure the boss wouldn't mind if I brought you and your brother. Jeremy could work the cows with me. You could cook for the hands." Darcy glared at him and struggled to free her hands. He could tell by her contorted face he'd said something wrong.

"Who says I want to be a cook for a bunch of ranch hands? Maybe I want to work with the cows, too."

He looked into her furious face and pressed his lips together. If she even saw him smile, his chances of getting her to come along were over. He couldn't see her dogging a calf twice her size. It just wasn't possible.

"Okay, you don't want to cook. I'm sure the boss could find other work for you. There are lots of things that need done on a big place." He leaned down, kissing her set jaw and working his way up her temple and down the center of her face. His lips touched hers and all sense of place and time fell away. He reveled in her delicate, sweet taste, clean scent, and silky skin. Releasing her hands, he slid his fingers through her hair and held her small head in his hands like a cherished object. He would never get enough of her.

He knew when her anger melted. Her arms wound around his neck, and her breasts pushed against his chest as she rose up to mold her hot body to his. He moaned and pulled away from the kiss.

He wanted her. The hardened length of his manhood ached. He looked into her eyes. They gleamed with knowledge of his excited state.

"We need to talk, not—" He groaned as she took him in her hands. As much as he enjoyed her hands on him, he wasn't going to get side tracked again, like the night Darcy was kidnapped. Just thinking about what could have happened to her at the hands of Craven and the outlaws dampened his ardor.

He grasped her hands, holding them to his lips.

"We really need to talk," he said, looking at her over their entwined fingers. She sighed, and her body relaxed. He pulled her onto his lap and held her.

"Would you and Jeremy go with me to the ranch?"

"What about your brothers?" She turned in his arms and stared into his eyes.

"What about them? They've been out of my life for a long time."

"Where do they live? And when can I meet them?"

What was her interest in his family? "Why do you want to meet them? You'll be living with me not them." He didn't like speaking about his family or even thinking of them. It was a wound he didn't believe could ever be healed.

"They're your family. And if we are married..." Her eyebrow arched.

Gil looked at her. Did she think he meant marriage when he said he wanted her with him? Of course. What an idiot! A girl like Darcy would not stay with him unless it was binding in the eyes of God and the law. He ran a hand over his face.

He wanted her. Was what he felt for her enough to marry her? And he supposed she'd insist his brothers be at the wedding. She believed too much in family. He wasn't even sure where they all were. Two to three could still be working the old mine his pa started.

She pulled away, but he held on hugging her tight. "Where are you going?" he asked, turning her face to look into her eyes. He saw hurt and sadness in the gray orbs.

"You weren't talking about marriage a minute ago were you?" Her mouth twitched. "You thought I was the type of girl to follow you anywhere and slip into your bed when you asked."

"No! You aren't that kind of woman. I know that. I just hadn't thought as far as marriage." He kissed the salty tears sliding down her cheeks. "There are lots of things we need to talk about."

"You can't drag Jeremy and me around with you if you don't get the foreman job. I don't want to travel anymore. I want to stay in one place." She looked at him, disappointment in her eyes. "I can't marry you if you're uncertain where you'll be. Jeremy needs a secure place to grow up." She looked into his eyes. "I need a secure place." Her eyes filled with tears. "I'm tired of always looking for a meal and a place to sleep."

A knot lodged in his gut. She'd been torn out of a loving family and had to battle with her wits to keep she and her brother fed and safe. He knew she was tired of always being strong and dependable. It was time she had someone take care of her.

"Even if I don't get the foreman's job, I could stay on as a hand and still work toward that position." He leaned down and kissed her nose. "I just wasn't ready to take root anywhere, till now."

She smiled and turned her head to wipe her tears on her arm.

"You're sure they'd welcome Jeremy and me?"

"They would welcome my wife." He hugged her tight and kissed her, trying to push away all her insecurities.

Darcy pulled out of the kiss. "I don't know. I've never heard of ranch hands being married. Don't you all sleep in one building?" She didn't like the idea of spending their evenings under the watchful eyes of the other men and her brother.

"I'll worry about that if I don't get Pete back home." He took her head in his hands and captured her lips.

Darcy poured all her longing for the man and her need for security into the kiss. Her doubts, her fears, and her love for the man holding her, all whirled around inside of her. Could he give up the rambling life? Was it something she wanted to risk their happiness on?

His soft lips moved to her cheeks, dropping wet kisses across her face. She melted into his arms, willing her niggling thoughts aside.

"Where do your brothers live?" He stiffened then relaxed.

"Why are you so set on knowing all about my brothers?"

"They are a part of you. If I'm to marry you, I want to know all about your past. They are a part of that." He flinched at the mention of his past. She knew he harbored guilt over the deaths of his parents. She knew it was unfounded and most likely so did his brothers. The only way to prove it to him was to get him and his brothers together.

"I don't know for sure where they are. Some could still be working my pa's mine. It's near Sumpter." He lifted her chin. "We're not that far away. If it means that much to you, we could swing by there on our way to Baker City."

Her stomach fluttered with excitement. He was taking her to see his brothers. It was a start. He cared enough to make her happy and sacrifice his own unease.

"Hey! What!" Jeremy walked out of the bushes to their left.

Gil rolled covering Darcy with the duster and grabbing his gun.

"I've been waiting for you, and you're out here messing with my sister." Her brother stood several feet away his hands fisted at his sides.

"I told you to set up camp," Gil said through clenched teeth.

"I did. Then you two didn't come. I thought Craven may have you again, so I backtracked and followed your trail." He looked at Darcy. Her heart sunk when she saw the look of disgust on his face.

"Jeremy, it ain't what you think. Gil asked me to marry him." Her gaze faltered as she muttered, "sort of." Her brother looked at her like she was vile.

"You think that would matter to Pa, if he'd found you like this?"

"I've done nothing wrong. I love Gil, and we'll marry. Maybe not fast enough for you or Pa, but it will happen." She stood, pulling the duster around her. "You're not my keeper. I'm a grown woman, and I'll do what I want when I want." She stepped toward him, and he backed up.

"Turn around and I'll get dressed. We'll go back to camp with you."

He reluctantly turned then spun back around.

"What about him?" Jeremy pointed to Gil who sat naked on the ground watching them.

Darcy motioned for Gil to turn around. He rolled his eyes, but did as she asked. Darcy tugged on her drawers and opened the saddlebags. She pulled out a pair of Levis and a big shirt which hung to her knees. Tucking the shirt into the Levis helped hold them up. When she was sufficiently covered, she tossed Gil his clothes and smiled.

He smiled back and dressed quickly.

"Let's go." Darcy looked at the charred dress lying on the bank of the lake. Remembering her bath in Olive Lake would always bring good memories. Why she needed a bath made her shudder.

Jeremy scowled at them when Gil flung his saddlebags over his shoulder and took her hand. She indicated for Jeremy to head out.

They walked along in silence. Jeremy in the front, his shoulders slumped and footsteps decidedly heavy. Darcy was sorry he found her and Gil like that, but he had no business bringing up Pa. She'd taken care of the two of them for a long time. What she did was her business and no one else's.

Gil squeezed her hand and raised it to his lips. The familiar tingle started at the point of his kiss and traveled through her body. How could anything that made her feel so alive be wrong? Surely, Pa would understand.

Is this what her parents had felt for one another? She thought hard about the two. What she could remember gave her a warm feeling. They had cared for one another and through their love for one another and made her and Jeremy feel loved. That was what she wanted for her children. She looked at the man holding her hand.

He looked straight ahead, his dark eyes watching Jeremy's back. The hat covering his dark hair rode low on his brow, hiding his eyes from most. Because of her height, she could look under the brim and see the emotions creasing his face. Just looking at him made her heart beat faster. Was this the man she should give her life to? The thought of waking up every morning in his arms made her feet step lighter.

When Craven was in jail, she would make Gil see marrying her would be the best thing to ever happen to him.

At the camp, Jeremy struck his flint together angrily, lighting the dead grass and leaves he'd piled in a ring of rocks. Darcy sat on a nearby rock and waited. She knew when he was ready to talk; he'd give her an earful. He couldn't stay quiet for long. Thinking back, the walk from the lake to the camp was the longest he'd ever gone.

Gil dropped the saddlebag by his saddle. "Need any help?" he asked.

"I can cook." Jeremy said. He looked straight at Darcy. "My parents taught me lots of things I ain't forgot." He shoved a skinned rabbit on a stick and held it over the fire.

"You snare that?" Darcy asked, trying to start up some kind of conversation, before Jeremy exploded from lack of air.

"Yes, while I was waiting for you." He sent her a look that said it would take more than conversation for her to win back his acceptance.

"I thought I saw a berry bush back there a ways." Gil stood.  He nodded towards Jeremy and left the clearing.

She needed to talk with her brother, but she wasn't sure he was ready to listen.

"Jeremy, what you saw –" His eyes remained void of emotion when he looked at her. "Jeremy, blazes, don't make me feel guilty for what you saw." Darcy jumped to her feet and paced between the trees and the fire where Jeremy squatted, twirling the rabbit on the stick.

"Gil makes me feel like I'm special."

"You are. You can do anything you set your mind to. You don't need to go rollin' around bare-assed with a man to feel special." Jeremy stopped turning the stick and looked at her. "Darce, you ain't like other women. You don't need to bed a man to make him give you things."

"Jeremy." She looked at him with disbelief. "Have I hauled you around so much all you've seen is the bad side of people? I don't want anything from Gil—other than his love." She pressed a hand to her stomach to stop the fluttering. "I know he loves me. I can see it in his eyes and feel it when he touches me." She walked to the fire and squat down beside him.

"Can you remember Ma running her hand through your hair or just touching your cheek when you said something clever?"

He watched her with watery eyes and gulped. "Yeah."

"How'd it make you feel?"

"All fluttery and special. I knew she loved me."

"That's what being with Gil does for me." She touched his arm. "I feel the way I did when Ma or Pa praised me. All sqooshy inside and loved."

He wiped at the tears trickling down his face.

"Don't make it something it isn't. I love him, and-and," she faltered. She couldn't say for sure he loved her. He hadn't said so himself. "We'll get married. You and I will live with him on a ranch near Baker City." She hugged him.

Jeremy dropped the rabbit in the fire and hugged her fiercely. "I'm sorry for what I said. I just didn't want to lose you, too."

"You'll never lose me. I won't let you." She kissed his forehead. "You better tend your rabbit or we'll go to sleep hungry tonight."

Jeremy grabbed the stick and blew on the flames climbing the carcass.

Darcy laughed and helped put out the fire.

Gil returned to a scene that made him smile. Darcy laughed as Jeremy told about seeing the men charge out of the cabin with her following in flames.

"I didn't think anything could scare me as bad as seeing you on fire." Gil sat next to Darcy and took her hand in his. He watched Jeremy closely. The boy smiled and pulled a leg from the cooling carcass. Gil smiled back. They must have talked the problem out.

He'd done some thinking while filling his hat with berries.

"If you two are up to it, we need to eat and get moving. Craven has a head start, but he'll stick to the roads. I know a short cut." Gil glanced at Darcy. She looked a lot better than when they found her. He smiled. Their lovemaking could have something to do with her glowing eyes and soft smile. Or the fact she felt safe with him. His chest puffed a little, thinking his presence made her feel safe. He never wanted her to be scared again, or having to handle things on her own.

"If we need to get going to catch Craven, I'm ready." Darcy stood.

"Not so fast." He pulled her down next to him. "I want to tell you the plan." When she put her hand on his leg and softly rubbed back and forth, the words he'd carefully planned to say vanished. She had no idea the sparks it set off inside of him. He put a hand over hers, stopping the caress. When he could think again, he began.

"We know Craven is headed for Baker City, the nearest Railroad. He'll have to purchase a ticket and wait for the next train. I also know the train only leaves Baker City twice a week. He missed Sunday's train and will have to wait for the next one. That will be Thursday. Day after tomorrow." He looked at Jeremy.

"I know a short cut to Baker City, but I want you to take your sister to Sumpter to my brothers. Tell them who you are, and why I sent you."

"Oh, no. I'm not getting stuck in some hole while you chase Craven. I've been after this guy since the day he offered me a bribe." Darcy jumped to her feet and looked down at him, her jaw set.

"I don't want anything to happen to you." He stood up, pulling her into his arms. "I want you safe so we can marry."

The determined look wavered a little as he voiced his marriage proposal for the first time. But he could tell by the set of her shoulders it wasn't enough to stop the indignation his comment spawned.

"If you treat me like I haven't a brain in my head and need to be protected, you better not go out and buy a new suit, 'cuz I won't marry a man who thinks I'm helpless." She jabbed her clenched fists on her narrow hips and glared at him.

"I don't think you're helpless. I want you safe." He rubbed his hands up and down her arms, trying to soothe the hackles he seemed to so easily raise on her.

"I want to be with you," she stated.

How could he leave her behind when she looked at him with those big gray eyes filled with love?

"Okay, we'll all go to Baker." She rose up on her toes to kiss him. He held a hand in front of her puckered lips. "But you have to follow orders."

He cringed when she smiled sweetly. "I'll do whatever you say." Her arms circled his neck, and he was rewarded for giving in with her soft, sweet lips.

Gil forgot where they were and what he'd just given up, when she pulled away. He grabbed her hair, dragging her lips back to his. If they were going to risk their lives for some mining town, he, by God, was going to take every opportunity to taste her sweetness.

"Ahem?" Jeremy cleared his throat, and Gil lifted his head.

He smiled at the dazed look in Darcy's eyes as

her body sagged against him. He knew one way to keep her quiet.

"Let's saddle up and get out of here," he said, setting Darcy on a stump and moving to his saddle. He and Jeremy saddled the horses while Darcy doused the fire.

They mounted, and Darcy swung up behind him. She wrapped her arms around his waist, and they headed east as briskly as they could through the trees and undergrowth. He wanted to leave her in Sumpter, but short of hogtying her, he knew there was no way he could make the woman stay. She would find a way to head after him on her own. It was best to have her with him where he could keep an eye on her.

He patted her clasped hands and smiled. If they could keep up a fast pace, he figured they'd reach pa's mine in Sumpter in a couple hours. They could sleep a few hours and reach Baker City the next day before noon.

## *Chapter 17*

The moon illuminated the night sky when Gil approached the familiar cabin. The building hadn't changed much in ten years. The rapid beating of his heart startled him. It didn't beat from fear, but anticipation.

Through the years, he'd told himself over and over again he didn't need his family. They were better off without him, but he'd longed for their approval. Now, he approached his childhood home and wondered if they would greet him and his future wife with open arms or shun them.

He watched the dark cabin. Did any of his brothers still live here and work the mine? He could be walking into some stranger's home for all he knew. It wouldn't surprise him any to find his brothers had all scattered.

All that remained here for them were bad memories. As he scanned the area around the cabin, happy childhood recollections came flooding back. The day Ethan introduced him to shaving, the way the smells of cooking would float out the open door when they came up from working the mine. The sight of his parents holding hands and talking with their heads bent close after he and his brothers were tucked in bed. Gil gulped down the knot of emotion constricting his throat. Dang, he'd missed his family.

He hadn't realized how much until he saw the cabin. A sob shook his body, and Darcy's arms tightened around him. She placed her head against his back in a quiet gesture of comfort.

Gil squeezed the hands clasped around his middle and eased the horse forward. No light shone in the windows, meaning whoever lived here had retired for the night. He made extra noise, and a light flickered inside.

"Who's out there?" he heard a familiar voice call. Darcy's arms tightened around him, and he felt her heart patter against his back. She was nervous, too.

"Gil." He called back.

Banging and movement could be heard in the cabin. Another light flickered on and a man stood in the doorway holding a lantern. Gil felt like someone poked a fist in his belly. The man standing in front of him had broad shoulders and looked exactly like his father. It had to be Ethan, his oldest brother. Their ma always said he was the spitting image of their pa.

"Whatcha got little brother?" Ethan asked as if they'd seen each other just yesterday instead of ten years earlier. He stepped out of the doorway and another strapping man filled it.

There was no denying the other man was

Hank. His good-humored grin stretched across his face as he slipped his suspenders onto bare shoulders. He looked back over his shoulder and said, "Clay get some clothes on, our little brother's returned, and he's got company."

Gil lowered Darcy to the ground. He needed to do something to keep from jumping out of the saddle and blubbering like a baby. He'd talked himself into believing his brothers had written him off, and here they were acting like he'd only been off on a hunting trip. The relief that flowed through him made his legs weak as water. If he'd known he'd get this kind of reception he would have returned a long time ago.

He watched Darcy tug on her shirt and look across at his oldest brother. Gil smiled. She'd help him through this tough time. He dismounted, motioning for Jeremy to do the same. Taking Darcy by the hand, he led her up to Ethan, who stood a half a head taller and looked formidable standing with his arms crossed over his chest, squinting in the dark at Darcy. Gil figured he wondered why his brother was holding the hand of some boy.

Before he could make introductions, Gil was swept up in Ethan's arms. He hugged him tight and passed him along to Hank, who squeezed him and passed him on to Clay who studied him a moment and slapped him on the back before giving him a hug.

"Where have you been hiding?" Clay asked, keeping an arm around him. "We looked for you when you first left, but no one had seen you."

"I took off for the gold country east of the Snake." He looked up at his brothers and wondered how he could have ever turned tail and run. "Lately, I've been working the Chandler ranch north of Baker City."

"You've been that close, and we haven't run into you?" Hank slapped him on the back and tipped his hat back. "Damn you're still the ugliest of all." They all broke into raucous laughter over the family's standing joke that Gil was the ugliest, when in fact they were all the spitting image of one another.

Ethan stepped forward, holding the lantern up to get a good look at Darcy and Jeremy. "You leave for ten years and come dragging home a couple of kids."

Gil saw the flash in Darcy's eyes. He stepped forward, grasped her hand, and led her up to Ethan. "This is Darcy Duncan and that's her brother Jeremy." He saw the look of amusement in his brother's eyes.

"Welcome, Darcy and Jeremy. I don't know what you did to get this scoundrel to come back home, but I'm much obliged to you." Ethan motioned to them to enter the cabin. Hank stepped aside, but clamped a hand on Gil's shoulder as he went by.

Gil stopped just inside the door and looked around. It had always been a cozy cabin with six boys stacked along the walls in bunks, but the boys had grown to men and they nearly filled the cabin.

"Haven't any of you married and moved out?" he asked, noticing four beds.

"Ain't been lucky enough to find the right woman." Hank smiled at Darcy and offered her a chair.

"Don't be looking at mine," Gil said, moving to Darcy's side.

Laughter rang through the small confines.

"Guess that answers our question," Hank said, taking a seat beside Darcy.

"So how did you two meet?" he asked, drawing all the eyes in the cabin to Darcy.

"I shot a man and became marshal of Galena," Darcy said innocently.

Gil grinned as his brother's jaws dropped, and they stared at the woman he loved with awe and curiosity. He was pretty sure his brothers had never met a woman like her before.

"And you had to throw our rowdy little brother in jail?" Clay asked.

"No, he actually brought me a prisoner I didn't want." Her answer got a chuckle out of the bunch.

Gil took her hand. "I was in Galena looking for Pete Chandler. He's the son of the rancher I work for. Mr. Chandler told me if I brought Pete back, he'd give me the foreman job at the ranch."

"Have you found him?" Hank asked, furrowing his brow in thought.

"I know the gang he's riding with. They kidnapped Darcy." The brothers all looked at her. "She got away, which is a long story." Gil raised her hand to his lips. His brothers raised their eyebrows.

"I've asked Darcy to come with me to the ranch after we catch Craven."

"Who's Craven?" Ethan asked, putting a pot of coffee on the wood stove.

"I haven't said I'd go with you," Darcy said, and the whole lot of them roared with laughter.

"Didn't we teach you the woman has to be

agreeable to marriage? You can't just drag her to a preacher and force her to marry ya," Clay said, slapping his thigh at his own humor.

Gil turned red. She was agreeable to marriage. He hadn't offered to make an honest woman of her. He cleared his throat and looked into her sad eyes.

He had to make a commitment if he wanted to keep her.

"I didn't ask her to marry me." He felt the hard stares of his brothers and Jeremy. "Yet. We've got things to work out first."

A big hand thumped him on the head, knocking his hat to the floor. "You don't drag a woman around and play with her emotions if you aren't prepared to settle down." Ethan stood beside him glaring down. "Is this the kind of behavior you acquired over the last ten years?"

"Little brother," Hank began, "you don't dally with a woman's affections. Either you marry her or you break clean, you don't sully her reputation to make yourself happy."

Gil felt like a schoolboy getting lectured by the teacher. He was a grown man. He knew what he'd asked Darcy wasn't proper. But it had been right at the time. Now looking into the uncensored eyes of his brothers, he knew he'd done Darcy a great injustice.

He faced her. The smattering of freckles he found endearing were faded from the heat of her embarrassment. Her eyes searched his for some comfort.

"I know we discussed this. I do plan to marry you. I'm just not sure when." He saw a flicker of surprise in her gray eyes, before they softened and a smile spread across her face.

"Thank you for asking," she said in a breathy whisper that sent vibrations of need shooting through his body.

"But unless you can provide a stable place for me and Jeremy to live, I'll have to say no." Darcy watched Gil's expression collapse into uncertainty. She wanted to reach out to him and comfort him, but she knew to do that would compromise her position. She had to look out for Jeremy's well being as much as hers.

Darcy glanced around at the men staring at her and Gil. They were all taller and just as handsome.

"Are you old enough to marry my little brother?" Ethan asked, pulling out a chair and sitting beside her.

"I'm nineteen and me and Jeremy have been living on our own for the past five years." She looked at him and wondered if Gil would get that big. Her gaze flitted over all of them. How had so many good-looking men in one family managed to stay unmarried?

Gil squeezed the hand he still held. She peered into his eyes and saw need and fear mingling in the brown depths.

"Can we talk about this after we get Craven and Pete?" he asked, moving his thumb invitingly back and forth across her wrist. The movement sent flashes of heat up her arm and straight to her heart.

"Who's this Craven you keep talking about," Ethan asked, placing his chair in between them.

"We're chasing Mr. Craven. He stole from the

bank, and we're going to bring the money and him back. 'Cuz Darce is the marshal." Jeremy piped up. He sniffed the air and looked at Ethan. "Is that fresh bread I smell?"

Hank slapped Jeremy on the back and roared with laughter. "Yes. I remember being your age, I bet you can't ever get enough to eat?"

Jeremy's eyes opened wide. "Darce keeps me fed."

Darcy looked at the men. They were all just as curious about her and Jeremy as she was about them.

"Jeremy cooked us a rabbit for dinner, but he probably is hungry again. He's going through a growing time." She smiled at Hank, and he cut several slices off a large brown loaf sitting on the table.

Jeremy grabbed one up and stuffed it in his mouth. Darcy wanted to, but waited to see if Gil took one. When he did she picked a piece up also.

"So you're a marshal?" Clay pulled up a chair beside her. "You look might puny to be a marshal, not to mention you're a girl."

Gil squeezed her hand. She smiled. Between the two of them they related how she came to be marshal and why they were after Craven. While they talked, Ethan poured coffee, and Hank placed some blankets on the floor.

"We plan to only sleep a few hours and head to Baker City. We need to be on the train with Craven," Gil looked at each of his brothers. "Where's Zeke?"

"He's off sparking the school teacher," Clay said, wagging his eyebrows.

"It's kind of late?" Darcy looked at the brother's grinning faces and blushed.

"He don't always come home." Clay picked up Darcy's hand. "What do you see in my little brother?"

She smiled at him and pulled her hand out of his grasp. "Love. Safety. Excitement." She knew they hadn't been expecting an answer like that. They all fell silent and looked at Gil as if they hadn't really seen him before.

He cleared his throat. "Darcy and Jeremy need to get some sleep."

Hank stood up and motioned to the bed closest to the stove. "Darcy, you take Zeke's bed. It's over there. Jeremy, you can take the blankets on the floor."

She looked at Gil. "Where are you going to sleep?"

He smiled and squeezed the hand he held. "I'll be fine. Go get some rest while I catch up on what's been happening around here." Gil pulled her to her feet and walked with her to the bed.

She knew everyone watched, but all she saw was his brown eyes filled with desire. He leaned close. "I'll sneak in with you when I finish talking." He placed his hands one on either side of her face and kissed her till her knees melted. She sat on the bed. He knelt and removed the kid slippers borrowed from Mrs. Danforth. With care, Gil lifted her legs onto the bed and placed a last kiss on her cheek before he pulled the covers up to her chin and walked away. Every nerve in her body tingled, but her heart told her she was safe, and she slipped into a blissful dream.

Gil stopped when he turned from the bed. His brothers were all staring at him like he'd grown horns.

"They act like that all the time," Jeremy said, waving it off and flopping down on the blankets on the floor.

"It's strange to see the youngest showing such a tender, loving side," Ethan said, scowling and scratching his thatch of dark hair.

"Get use to it. She means a lot to me, and I plan on giving her a stable place to live." They all looked at him as if he'd spouted blasphemy.

Clay looked at him. "She's got you whipped!"

Gil punched him in the shoulder, and Clay grabbed him around the neck, grinding his knuckles into Gil's head.

"Enough." Ethan grabbed them both and led them outside. They took seats on upturned firewood and watched the stars twinkle in the night sky.

"I'm glad you're back." Ethan's voice cracked with emotion.

"Me, too." Gil looked at each of his brothers. Their eyes mirrored the feelings of sorrow for the lost years.

"Why did you leave?" Hank asked, picking up a stick and peeling the bark.

"I-I felt like you all thought I should have done more when Ma and Pa and Jessie were killed. I shouldn't have been down at the stream trying to catch a frog to put in Laney Wilson's lunch pail."

The day came back to him in achingly vivid detail. The morning had dawned with a beautiful blue sky. The twitter of birds echoed through the tall trees. He remembered the way his mother felt his forehead when he said he didn't feeling well. He'd feigned being sick so he wouldn't have to go with his brothers to gather wood.

When the others had left, and Ma was busy making breakfast, he'd snuck out to the stream. He hunted for a big ugly toad, one with lots of warts or it wouldn't have had the full effect on his prey.

It wasn't until he headed back, he noticed the birds were quiet and the forest didn't feel quite right. Walking into the clearing where the cabin sat, he'd noticed his brothers gathered together. They'd turned in unison and stared at him. He'd walked over and looked down at the bloody bodies of his ma and brother. Unbelieving, he'd followed the bloody trail and found his father. His gut twisted even now at the memory.

A large hand rested on his shoulder, as he shuddered. "I shouldn't have played sick or run off. I could have got a gun to Pa or kept the Indians busy until you all returned. Or, I should have died with them." He looked up into the eyes of his brothers. He didn't find the recrimination he'd believed they harbored all those years ago. Only their sympathy and acceptance. Something he hadn't done for himself.

"We didn't blame you. We were all so stunned by what happened we just didn't know what to say or do. When we finally realized you were gone, we looked all over and couldn't find a clue to where you went." Hank squeezed the hand still resting on his shoulder. "We knew you'd be back some day. I'm glad the day finally came."

"Yeah, we've been wondering when you'd

come back and help out around here," Clay said, slapping him on the back.

"I don't want to work at the mine, I like ranching." Gil looked at Clay and Hank. It was gratifying to know they were ready to take him back in like he'd never been gone.

Always the leader and one to take charge, Ethan interrupted the family togetherness. "How you planning on capturing this man Craven?" he asked.

Gil hadn't got all the particulars figured out, but he knew it would come to him. "I'm not certain. I've been thinking on it and by the time we get to Baker City I'll know."

"That sounds kind of risky." Ethan looked bigger and more imposing sitting on a log in the moonlight than he had in the small confines of the cabin. "You should have a plan made up and maybe take a couple of us along."

"And have Darcy stay here," added Clay.

Gil laughed. "The only way to keep that woman in one place would be to lock her up. I'm not sure even that would work." He turned to Clay. "And don't try none of that sweet talking you did with ma, it won't work on Darcy. She has a mind of her own and when it's made up, nothing can shake her loose of an idea."

"Is this plan going to keep her out of harm's way?" Ethan asked.

Gil's face heated. His plan called for her to sit on the train next to Craven. He knew his brothers would think him a lunatic if he told them that.

"Craven had Darcy as a hostage for awhile today. He didn't know who she was 'cuz she was dressed like a dance hall girl." He thought of her in the low-cut dress and wanted to race back in the cabin and run his hands over her creamy skin. "Craven's only had dealings with her when she pretended to be a young man. He doesn't know it's her when she's all fancied up. I figure on getting her all dressed up, and she and I will be on the train. I'll cause a commotion and get his attention, she'll grab the money, and we'll get out of there. Craven will follow, and we'll take him back to Galena." Gil knew it was a little shaky, but they could do it.

"I think we should come along. He doesn't know us. We could grab him and the money and have Darcy place him under arrest. Then we can all take him back to Galena with the money." Hank rubbed his hands together. "It makes the most sense."

"I don't need your help. We'll be fine." Gil yawned. "What have you all been up to, and why aren't you sharing your beds with a wife?"

Gil listened as they each told how they left the mine for a while and what women they were currently interested in. Exhaustion caught up to him, and he nearly fell off the log.

"Get some sleep, you only got a couple of hours before daylight," Hank tapped him on the shoulder. "Take my bed."

"I got one." Gil stumbled into the cabin, sat down on the edge of the bed where Darcy slept and took off his boots. He shucked down to his under drawers and climbed in next to her. She scooted to him, and he wrapped his arms around her.

They would bring Craven back and get married. He had a few niggling doubts in the back of his mind about settling down, but if anyone could make him want to stay in one place it was the feisty woman sleeping in his arms.

# Chapter 18

Sun filtered through the drab curtains pulled across the windows. Darcy blinked at the ray of light hitting her in the eyes and started to stretch. The warmth of a body next to her, and the weight of an arm draped across her stomach made her smile. Gil had snuck into her bed during the night.

A chorus of snores and heavy breathing reminded her they weren't alone. From the sounds, everyone but her was fast asleep.

She squirmed to her side and watched Gil. The last time they slept together, circumstances had made it necessary for her to leave in a hurry. This time she wasn't in a hurry and could watch him sleep.

His dark eyebrows wiggled up and down as he dreamed. A new growth of whiskers darkened his face. She rubbed a finger over the stubble on his cheek, feeling the scratchiness and listening to the raspy sound. She'd never felt a man's unshaved face before. Anticipation hummed in her mid-section. This wasn't the time or the place for such thoughts, but his closeness fanned flames of desire.

Darcy trailed a finger down his nose and over his lips. She gently rubbed her thumb back and forth across the full lips, while her hand cradled his cheek. Memories of all the kisses they'd shared flowed through her, causing her to tremble. She closed her eyes, savoring the feeling.

When she opened her eyes, Gil watched her. He turned his head, kissing her palm. Her body quivered. By the darkening of his eyes, she could tell he felt her excitement.

She snuggled next to him as his arms came around her. His whiskers scratched when he trailed soft kisses across her face and down her neck. Darcy twined her arms around his neck, kissing him full on the lips. His hands slid down inside her trousers and drawers as he deepened the kiss. He cupped her bottom, pulling it against him.

"That's enough over there," Ethan said, dropping his boots on the floor and waking the rest of the household.

Darcy pulled back. She'd forgotten they weren't alone. What would Jeremy think waking and finding her sleeping with Gil? And his brothers? This wasn't a good example for her younger brother or her future family. Gil pulled her back into his arms. His body shook as he hid his face in her neck and chuckled.

"I don't find this funny," she hissed into his ear.

He kissed her chastely on the cheek and slipped out of bed.

She watched him pull his trousers on over his drawers and walk to the washbasin. He splashed water on his face and toweled off before turning to his oldest brother.

Darcy watched the exchange of glances between the two and wondered if she would ever understand the looks and gestures between them. It seemed Gil sleeping in her bed didn't bother the men, and Jeremy didn't glare at her either.

She scratched her head and looked around. They all looked at her expectantly.

"What?" She threw the covers back and sat up. Her body was fully clothed, and she needed a trip to the outhouse.

"Do you cook?" Clay asked and was hit in the chest by Hank. "What? She's female. I would like something better'n what you cook."

"She cooks real good. Worked in a restaurant once," Jeremy chimed in. They all shot her a big grin and started gathering wood and stoking the cook stove.

"Don't we need to get headed after Craven?" she asked, slipping into the borrowed kid slippers.

"If he's headed for the train, like you think, it only goes through Baker City on Sundays and Thursdays. Today is Wednesday, so I doubt he's doing anything, but cleaning up and resting." Hank smiled at her. "So you got time to make us breakfast.

"I gotta use the outhouse." She stood and headed out to find the necessary.

Gil watched her walk out. She'd tolerated his family better than he'd expected. He'd worried she'd feel awkward around all the men. But she acted like she'd lived her whole life with a pack of heathens.

"I like her," Clay said, patting Gil on the back and setting out ingredients to make biscuits.

"If she cooks as good as she puts you in your place, we should be having one hell of a breakfast," Hank said, hauling out some pheasant eggs.

"Oh, she does. Darcy can do just about anything." Jeremy grabbed the tin plates on a shelf and started setting the table.

Gil grabbed the coffee pot and headed to the door.

"No, you don't." Ethan grabbed a bucket by the door. "I'll get the water. You aren't going out there and detaining our cook."

Gil's face heated, and they all laughed. He'd thought about waiting by the outhouse and escorting Darcy back to the cabin in a round-about way.

Ethan left to get the water, and Darcy returned a few minutes later. She glanced his direction and blushed. Her shyness this morning made his heart hammer in his chest. They worked side by side to make breakfast. She threw together mouthwatering biscuits while he cooked the eggs.

"Where did you find these eggs?" Jeremy asked, scooping a spoonful into his mouth.

"Out by the mine. I heard a pheasant hen making noise and followed her." Hank winked at the others over Jeremy's head. "I found her squatting on a nest made out of dead grass. I picked her up and squeezed her until I popped enough eggs out of her for breakfast."

Jeremy looked up, his eyes wide. "Can you do that with chickens, too?"

The table erupted in laughter.

"He's foolin' with you," Darcy said, patting his

head. Pride surged through Gil. She would make a loving mother. The thought seemed to flow from him to Darcy. She looked up and their gazes met. Blushing cheeks enhanced her shy smile.

She'd blushed twice in one morning. When he first met her, he didn't think there was anything shy about her. He liked this gentle side of Darcy. It made her even more special.

When the meal was over, Ethan ushered them out the door. "Get going so you got time to work on your plan." He gave Darcy a hug. "Listen to what Gil tells you, he's had more experience with unsavory people." He turned to Gil. "If she comes back with any bruises or bumps, you'll answer to me."

"I'll take care of her, don't worry." Gil put an arm around Darcy. "And she'll listen." He glared at her and squeezed. "Right?"

She turned her big gray eyes up to him and said without faltering. "I'll do whatever you say."

It felt like she knocked the wind out of him. Her innocent look and undying devotion put a lump in his throat. He hoped he could live up to all he saw in her eyes.

Gil shook hands with each of his brothers. They in turn gave him a quick hug. They humbled him with their easy acceptance of his return and their statement they didn't blame him for what happened years earlier.

He'd been a fool to run away. That he saw clearly. He mounted his horse and looked down at the gathering. Hank and Clay each hugged Darcy before Ethan placed her behind Gil. Her arms wrapped around his waist and squeezed. Gil put a hand over her clasped hands and looked at his brothers.

"Thank you," he choked out as emotions he'd long suppressed bubbled to his throat.

"You're always welcome here," Ethan said, running a hand through his hair. "As well as any of your family." He shook hands with Jeremy and winked at Darcy.

Gil smiled and turned the horse away from the cabin.

"Don't be a stranger," Hank hollered as they entered the trees on the far side of the clearing.

They traveled a good part of the day through wooded areas and canyons, steadily descending toward the valley below. Gil had many scenarios running through his head on how they'd capture Craven and then retrieve the gold and take both back to Galena. None of them would be favorable to Darcy. He grimaced and urged his horse out into the open valley floor. Ahead of them spread the busy town of Baker City.

Darcy heard the town before she actually saw it. The sound of people and wagons in great quantity reminded her of visits to Portland and Oregon City. She looked around Gil. The railroad station loomed straight ahead. She couldn't believe he rode straight to the station. What if Craven stood around waiting for a train?

"Is it a good idea to ride right up to the station?" She scanned the people on the platform.

"The train doesn't leave until tomorrow. I want to see if he's even been here. He could have changed direction and headed to Pendleton to catch the train. If he plans to head out on tomorrow's train he would have asked about times and tickets. Don't worry, he's probably sleeping and eating until then."

"How do you know so much about the train schedule?" He seemed to have an answer to everything.

"The ranches I worked sent cattle by rail to the east." He took hold of her arm. "Slide down, and we'll see if he's been around."

She slid off the rump of the horse. Her legs wobbled like mush. She took hold of Gil's arm when he swung down to the ground. Together they approached the station agent.

"Was there a bald headed man with a yellow mustache and pot belly here asking about schedules and tickets?" Gil asked when the man looked up from a ledger.

"Yeah, he got a ticket for tomorrow." He looked at Gil and down at Darcy. "You and your little brother need a ticket?"

Darcy bristled at the comment and would have let the man know what she thought, if Gil hadn't placed a hand on her arm.

"This is my betrothed. We would like three tickets, for the morning train." Gil took her hand and kissed it while the man looked stricken.

"Believe me you won't recognize her tomorrow." Gil winked at the man and took the tickets.

"What did you mean by that?" Darcy asked, looking back at the station agent.

"I mean we're going to get you done up like a real lady so Craven doesn't recognize you when you sit next to him on the train."

"N-n-next to him." Darcy looked up to see if he was still the man who professed his love to her. "You're going to put me on the train in a seat next to Craven?" She stopped and stared at him. This was a trick to get her to stay behind. "You don't want me along. Are you trying to scare me off?"

"No. You're going to work your charms on the old coot and get his confidence. Then you are going to ask him to join you at the back of the train to watch the sunset or something like that. Jeremy and I'll jump him, and we'll take him back to Galena all trussed up like a calf to be branded." Gil smiled like there wasn't a flaw to his plan.

"How are we going to get him back to Galena? We won't have any horses." She tapped her foot on the ground and waited for a response. His idea was not setting well with her. He'd left too many things undone.

Gil scratched his head and watched her. "We'll wait in the last car until we get to the next town. Then we'll rent a wagon and head back to Galena."

Darcy thought about his idea. It could work, as long as no one discovered them with Craven all trussed up.

"I wish he hadn't taken my badge. Then we would have looked official and not have to worry about someone trying to help him."

Gil took her hand. "Don't worry. I'll be right there in the car with you. When you get him to go with you to the back of the train, I'll follow."

"How are we getting me all fancied up?" Darcy asked when they joined Jeremy and the horses.

"Clay told me about a couple of ladies in town.

I'll tell them who we are and what we need. They'll take care of things."

Darcy looked at him. "What kind of ladies?"

"You'll like them."

Darcy spent the remainder of the day being bathed, pampered, and primped by the ladies. She'd nearly dropped her chin to the ground when Gil hauled her and Jeremy up the steps of a whorehouse.

He'd walked in as if he'd done that sort of thing every day of his life. She'd been introduced to two giggling women who immediately striped her and plopped her in a big tub full of bubbles and smelly soap.

She didn't mind trying on the different dresses for Gil. It was fun the way he sat sprawled in the large wooden chair and watched her step out from behind a screen. His gaze sought her face before skimming down the dress all the way to the floor. His eyes glinted with desire, and she knew his thoughts were about what lie under all the layers of cloth, making her cheeks burn.

"This one." Gil stood and extended his hand to her. Darcy put her hand in his, and he pulled her to him. He'd cleaned up and shaved while she was pampered. A sniff rewarded her with the smell of soap and bay rum. His new black suit accented his wide shoulders and slender hips. She thought of his taut muscle and smooth skin under the garment and itched to touch it. The women in the room twittered and backed out, closing the door quietly behind them.

Her body moved against him. She wanted to feel every contour. "Where's Jeremy?" she asked, sliding the jacket from his shoulders.

"At a friend's house." Gil unbuttoned the bodice of her dress.

Darcy pulled back. "A relation of the women here?"

"No. An old friend who moved cattle with me until he married."

"Oh. Good." His teeth scraped her neck. A shiver ran down her back and started a fire glowing in her center.

"Can we? Here?" she asked, unbuttoning his shirt and pulling the shirttail from his Levis.

"Yeah, I paid for the room for the night." He pushed the dress to the floor. The layers of linen and lace piled at her feet. She bent to pick it up. An arm caught her around the waist, lifting her off her feet.

"It'll keep." Gil carried her across to the bed, placing her on the silk cover.

Darcy moved her hand over the slippery surface. "I've never touched anything so fine."

"You deserve only the best. You look like an angel in the clouds." He leaned down and kissed the tip of her nose. "You are beautiful." He choked on the words as his lips softly touched hers.

Tears crept into her eyes; his gentleness and kind words overwhelmed her.

She opened her lips, encouraging him to take all he wanted. The kiss deepened as their hands roamed, memorizing the curves and rises of their bodies.

Gil pulled back. "I don't like this thing," he

said, thumping the corset the giggling twins had trussed her into. He smiled wickedly. "Though I do like the way it pushes you up." He kissed the mound of breast above the garment.

Darcy turned over, and he untied the contraption, sliding it down her hips and off the end of the bed. It landed with a thunk, and they both laughed.

"Much better," he said, taking a breast in each hand and kneading.

His touch vibrated her body with a need so blinding, her hips arched, and she battled with the fastenings on his Levi's.

"Whoa. I'm not going anywhere." He grabbed her hands, holding them over her head. She struggled to touch him, but gave in when he untied her chemise with his teeth. He pushed the cloth down with his face and nuzzled her breasts and belly.

"This isn't fair," she huffed in between pants of pleasure. His knee drew up between her legs. He rubbed against the juncture of her legs as he kissed her senseless one-minute and suckled her breasts the next.

"I like watching you take pleasure from me." He let her arms go and pulled her drawers down. She lay naked on the sensuous silk cover. The hair on his chest tickled her breasts as he slid his pants down and off. Her hands roamed over his muscular back and down to his tight bottom. He moaned as she squeezed the handful cheeks.

Giggling, she rolled him to his back and sat atop his stomach. His erection bumped her buttocks. Leaning forward, her breasts pressed into his hard chest as she kissed his chin and lips, and rubbed against his manhood.

He groaned and pushed her to her back, entering her with one quick movement. Darcy smiled slyly. This was what she wanted—him to take her like a man winning a prize, not like a porcelain doll.

She grabbed his bottom, pulling him deep as he thrust hard and kissed her with a fervor he hadn't shown before. The sensations came hard and fast just as their coupling. Wave after wave of light and scorching heat filled her body. Until a force, so strong it made her scream, sucked every ounce of life out of her when he thrust deep and let his seed spill.

Gil shook his head to clear the fog. He looked down at Darcy. Her dark hair splayed around her head and soft white shoulders like a halo. Heat radiated from her shimmering skin. A seductive smile played on her lips.

He reluctantly lifted his body from hers. In the brief moment air whisked between them, he grieved the loss of contact. Gil balanced on his forearms, his hands twined in her hair. The dark locks smelled of flowers and a spring day. He sniffed, and her eyes opened.

"That's what I've been waiting for," she said, smiling and licking her lips like a cat full of cream.

"What have you been waiting for?" He played with her hair and nipped at a pert nipple.

"You to take me like a woman and not a breakable object."

"Have I been?"

"Yes. I won't break. Lord knows I've had enough accidents to prove it." She put her arms around his neck and pulled her face up to his. "I want you to take me however and whenever you want. I am yours. Always."

"You are making us very happy."

"Us?"

Gil looked down at the erection that had grown with her words of commitment. Darcy looked down and laughed.

"I'm glad I could make you two happy."

A knock at the door stopped her laughter.

"Yes?" Gil called.

"There's a tray out here for the two of you." A giggle. "Sounds like you're gonna need some energy."

The footsteps departed, and he rolled out of bed. Gil crossed the room and opened the door. He grabbed the tray quickly, then closed and locked the door.

"What did they leave us? I forgot how hungry I was." Darcy sat up cross-legged on the bed. Her dark hair hung over her shoulder, curling around a breast. The flush on her cheeks and her swollen lips begged for more loving.

Gil's heart squeezed at the sight of her. He'd never thought loving someone could fill a person with such pride and fierce loyalty.

He cleared his throat and continued to the bed. "Looks like cold beef, rolls, strawberry preserves." He set the tray on the bed in front of her and sat on the opposite side.

Darcy took a piece of meat and bit into it. "Mmmm. Not bad." The lines of worry furrowing her brow meant she thought of something other than another round in the bed.

"What do I say to Craven tomorrow?" Her

worried eyes searched his face.

"Just sit by him and flirt a little. Ask him questions about himself. See if you can find out where he's headed." He took her hand. "I'll be in the same car watching everything. I won't let him touch you." He kissed her hand. "I promise."

"How will he not notice you?" She turned her hand entwining their fingers.

"I'll be dressed in business clothes. He's only seen me in my trail clothes. He won't think a gunslinger would be all dandied up." He smiled trying to make light of the situation. Craven was too self-centered to connect two well-dressed adults with either he or Darcy. But there was still the slight chance the man was brighter than he'd shown so far.

Darcy picked up a roll and smeared it with preserves. Gil shifted, bumping the cold tray into her legs. Darcy jumped, tossing the roll with preserves on Gil.

The look on her face as the roll slid down his chest told him she'd put tomorrow out of her thoughts. She giggled and covered her mouth. Gil arched his eyebrow and plucked the roll from his body.

Darcy leaned over the tray and ran her tongue up his chest, licking the preserves. He shoved the tray to the side, allowing her closer. Her small, soft tongue across his skin lit a bonfire in his belly. By the time she'd cleaned his chest, he was hard and hungry. Not for food. She lowered her head, giving his maleness the same attention she'd shown his torso.

Gil groaned and leaned back, allowing her all

the freedom she wanted.

When Darcy pushed her hair back from her face and looked at him, he knew she wanted more. She smiled wickedly and slithered up his body, making sure every inch of her touched his heated appendage.

Gil moaned in ecstasy as her small body slid over his. He'd bedded women before, but none had cared to make him crave them.

He wanted to throw her on her back and thrust so hard he touched her heart, but he could play her game. He would make her squirm and squeal with pleasure before he let himself go. His hands trailed over her body, kneading her here, barely touching there. His fingers danced across the hair at the juncture of her legs. Her breath sucked in. The curly hair grasped his fingers, urging him deeper. He found the nub he sought. Her body came alive under his knowledgeable fingers. She squirmed and arched. He lowered his head and tasted her.

Her breath became ragged as he tasted and kneaded her breasts.

"Oh! I can't take anymore. Please, do something." Her breathless plea nearly sent him over the edge. Spreading her legs wide, he knelt between them and raised her to him. With one thrust, he found the embrace he craved. He started slow, gradually thrusting harder and faster until her climax squeezed and pulled him deeper. He thrust once more, sending his love into her depths. Spent and filled with an aching tenderness for the woman beneath him, Gil pulled her limp body to his.

He had to find a way to keep her safe even at

the risk of making her mad.

## *Chapter 19*

In the morning, they dressed hurriedly. Gil tightened Darcy's corset and for a moment thought about using the strings to tie her to the bedpost. A large part of this depended on her, but he worried about her safety. He took her face in his hands and looked down at the small nose dusted with freck-les.

"Promise me if I tell you to run you will run. Don't look back."

She turned her head and kissed his palm. "Only if I know you're safe."

"No!" She had to listen to reason. Her life could depend on it. "If I tell you and Jeremy to 'get', you have to go. And know I will do what-ever necessary to get back to you. I couldn't bear to think you would be hurt trying to help me." He embraced her to his beating heart. She wound her arms around his neck. If only they could head to the ranch and forget about Craven and the stolen goods. They couldn't return to the ranch until he rounded up Pete.

He held her away and stared into her trusting, gray eyes before crushing his lips down on hers in a need to taste and feel her. There'd never be another woman move him as this accident-prone hell cat.

He pulled away from her lips and rested his forehead on hers. "Promise, you will do everything I tell you today. It could make the difference in how our lives turn out."

"I will." Her big eyes searched his face.

He tipped his head to kiss her, and she pulled back.

"You have to promise to be careful. I want to spend the rest of my life with you."

Nothing he'd ever heard sounded so sweet. "I promise." He held her in his arms and savored her sweet lips. Once they were at the train station they had to appear as strangers.

"We have to go," she said, pulling out of his arms. Gil rubbed a hand over his face and stared down at her. She was so strong and looked so fragile.

"You're right." He helped button her dress. As Darcy pinned a small hat with a large ribbon and three feathers onto her hair at a jaunty angle, Gil slipped his arms into a black, wool suit coat. He caught their reflection in the mirror as he took her arm. They looked like a young couple fresh from the pages of Sears and Roebuck. He smiled, plopped a bowler on his freshly cut hair, and escorted her out the door.

They had only a short amount of time to get Jeremy and get on the train before Craven showed up. Gil bought rolls at the bakery on their way to the station. He handed one to Jeremy and one to Darcy. He kissed her cheek and strolled up to the train and boarded. From a seat at the back of the car, he watched Jeremy climb up the steps of the last car.

The train whistle blew, and Craven hurried to the station lugging a carpetbag. When the porter tried to take it from him, he yelled at the man and climbed on board the train, dragging the bag up the stairs. Craven sat down, maneuvered the bag between his feet, and wiped the sweat from his brow.

The train moved slightly. Gil looked around for Darcy. She hadn't boarded. He started to get out of his seat when she bustled through the door, chattering like a magpie with the porter. He smiled as her voice bounced off the walls in a nasally twang.

"I never had such good service on a train before," Darcy found Gil in the last seat and winked at him as she patted the porter on the arm. "You just run the tidiest little operation." She smiled sweetly and batted her lashes. She'd spent the time alone on the station platform remembering some of the women she'd been around in the past. Eliza Hopkins was a woman in Portland who befriended her and Jeremy. It didn't take Darcy long to figure out the woman could out talk Jeremy, and that men, while finding her fetching to look at, would after a short period of time tune her out. She was hoping to have that effect on Craven.

She swished her skirts up the aisle and stopped by Craven.

"Sir, may I have the honor of sitting beside

you?" She didn't wait for an answer. Smoothing her skirt behind her bottom, she sat gracefully on the seat and situated her skirt. She looked over at him and smiled, batting her eyelashes just a bit, but not too much. Too much made you look like a ninny.

The train jerked, shushed steam along the sides, and moved forward.

"Is this your first trip on a train?" she asked, placing a hand on Craven's arm.

He looked down at the hand then back up at her smiling face. He smoothed his yellowed mustache with a plump hand and smiled back salaciously.

"No miss. I've traveled by train before. All the way back to Boston." He puffed out his chest.

"My, that is exciting!" she squealed and patted his arm again. "Did you go back to visit family? I have family in Atlanta and Saratoga." She hoped he didn't know those towns since she just threw them out there. She'd heard them mentioned in her travels, but didn't even know for sure what state or states they were in.

He smiled apologetically. "No. I've never had the pleasure of traveling in the south."

"That's too bad," she cooed and breathed a sigh of relief. She wouldn't have to lie her way through a conversation about the cities since he hadn't been there. "So tell me about Boston and what you do?" She leaned toward him just enough her bosoms peeked out at him. A sick feeling swirled in her stomach when he looked down and licked his lips. The lecherous gleam in his eyes had her wondering about Gil's idea. She didn't want the vulgar man to jump her, and Gil run to the rescue before they got Craven to the back of the train.

Craven cleared his throat and began a tale of his travels and how he was a large landowner in the growing town of Galena.

She listened intently over the chunk-a-chunk-a of the metal wheels on the iron rails as the train rolled along at a good speed and wondered what was in the bag he'd stashed between his feet. He had a hold of the strap with one hand as though he thought someone would snatch it from him.

When he stopped for air, she asked, "Where are you headed today?"

He looked at her suspiciously then pulled a cigar out of his pocket and bit off the end. She sat beside him demurely, acting as though the question a mere formality and he needn't answer if he didn't want to.

Lighting the cigar, he sucked in and puffed out a rancid stream of smoke. She refrained from waving the putrid smoke away with a gloved hand.

"I'm headed to Portland to find some financial backing for a stamp mill." He puffed on his cigar and smiled wickedly.

"Oh my, that sounds exciting. What is a stamp mill?" Darcy leaned closer, shifting enough to give him an eyeful and hope he would soon give her a lead-in to get him to the back of the train.

He nearly bloated with excitement as he told her about stamp mills and how he planned to make lots of money for investors. As he continued to talk, she formed a plan of her own.

"My daddy has dabbled in various moneymaking opportunities. And he has many friends who like to invest in opportunities that increase their finances." She could see the light coming on in Craven's head as he registered she could get him more backers.

He leaned closer. "I don't like to talk business with so many ears around." His beady eyes scanned the people in the train car. Her heart nearly stopped beating when his gaze lingered on Gil.

She touched Craven's arm and looked at him with what she hoped he read as interest. "We could go to the end car and step out on the platform. No one would hear us there." She held her breath as he mulled the idea over in his head. His eyes scanned the car once more, and a frown etched his forehead. She smiled reassuringly seeing his hesitation at whether or not she truly was a woman with a father looking to invest or a hussy out to milk him of his money.

He finally smiled and nodded his head. "Let's step to the rear of the train."

She smiled sweetly and hoped Gil noticed their departure. She'd been alone with Craven before and the idea of the same thing happening made her stomach pitch.

"Mr.—"

"Craven."

"Mr. Craven, you wouldn't make advances at me while we talk business would you?" She batted her lashes just briefly and hoped he had a whimsical comeback.

"Only if you wish me to," he said.

Darcy let forth a loud, tinny laugh and stood. She glanced toward the rear of the car and made eye contact with Gil.

Craven stood, shoved the carpetbag farther under his seat, and offered his arm. She placed her hand lightly on his coat sleeve and grabbed her skirt in the other hand, swinging it out of the way of the seats as they walked down the aisle. At the back of the car, she stumbled a little, grasping at the back of the seat in front of Gil. He mumbled and settled the hat down over his eyes, like he planned to take a nap. Her heart skipped when his lips curved into a smile.

He would be right behind them. She straightened and commented to Craven about men with big feet and always thinking they needed more space than the average person as they passed through the door and into the open air between the cars.

The clanking of the car connection and the metal wheels on iron tracks assaulted her ears and drew her gaze to the ground flashing by.

"We could just stand here?" Craven yelled.

"I'm fearful, I'll fall," she yelled back at him, yanking opened the door to the next car. Her heart beat faster when she saw Jeremy duck down in a seat about the middle of the car. Two men sat in the front of the car. Their legs stretched across the aisle way and their hats tipped down over their eyes like they were taking a nap. The hair on the back of Darcy's neck prickled. There was something familiar about one of them, but she wasn't sure, what it was. She stared at him a moment, and Craven applied pressure to her elbow, propelling her up the aisle. She lifted her skirt and stepped over the men's legs, making sure she didn't disturb them.

At the back of the train, they stepped out onto the platform. The wind whistled around them, making the ribbons on her bonnet, dance around her face. But other than the clack, clack of the steel wheels on the iron railing, they didn't have to yell at the top of their lungs to be heard.

"What's your daddy's name?" Craven asked, pulling out a cigar and lighting it. The smoke trailed off behind the train like a miniature smoke-stack.

Darcy watched it and licked her lips. She couldn't use her pa's name that would set him to thinking. Then she remembered the name of the rancher Gil worked for. "Jasper Chandler," she said, hoping he'd not had any dealings with the cattle rancher or her story would crumble around her.

"And what does he do?" Craven inched closer and his hand flexed, like he itched to touch her. Her skin crawled, and her knees turned to mush. When would Gil burst through the door?

"He's big in cattle trading," she said, biting the inside of her lip for telling a lie. She'd always believed in the truth or small white lies to keep food in their bellies, but she'd never flat out told stories of this proportion. It made her stomach queasy. The rocking of the last car didn't help either.

The man's eyes lit up, and he sidled a little closer. Darcy closed her eyes and gulped. Gil, where are you?

Just as she tried to formulate another lie, the door opened. Gil stepped out onto the platform. Craven turned to him. Darcy knew the minute he recognized Gil. His fat hand whipped out grasping her arm tightly. He pulled her to him and backed up to the railing.

"What are you doing here?" Craven growled, yanking her arm behind her. Darcy cried out in pain and glanced at Gil. Anger flashed in his eyes.

Gil clenched his teeth together and felt the muscle twitching in his jaw. His gaze ricocheted from Craven's face to Darcy's arm pinned behind her back. This was exactly what he hadn't wanted: Darcy in danger.

His hand slid to the gun slung low on his hip. Just the action made the tension in his jaw subside. He had to keep Craven busy worrying about him so the fat crook would loosen his hold on Darcy.

"I've got no problems with the lady, Craven." Gil let his gaze rest on Darcy's face. She was in pain, but pissed off. Good, that would give her the added strength she'd need to get loose.

"I don't either, but we'll keep her between us until you tell me why you keep following me." Craven eased up on her arm.

Good. Gil moved away from the door, making Craven back to the side of the platform. The gate was closed, but he saw Darcy glance at the latch on the gate. That's what he loved about her. She was already forming a plan to get away from Craven. Gil took a step forward to force the man against the gate.

Craven pulled Darcy closer. Darcy's face contorted in pain.  Rage flashed though Gil—hot and out of control. He didn't dare try to shoot. Even in this close of quarters he'd no guarantee he wouldn't hit Darcy. His hand lingered near the holster. Craven's eyes followed every movement he made.

The door opened.

Gil wasn't sure whether to be happy or up-set to see Pete and another man step out onto the crowded platform.

"What's going on here?" Pete asked, looking from Gil to Craven hiding behind Darcy.

Craven's face turned ash gray at the sight of his cohorts.

Gil would have burst out laughing if Craven didn't look so desperate. Desperate men were dangerous.

"Me and Craven were discussing the fact it would be wise for him to let the lady go," Gil said nonchalantly and placed his foot on the bottom rail of the railing around the platform.

Pete stepped up next to him and looked across at Craven and Darcy.

"You know she gets prettier each time I see her." Pete tipped his hat and grinned.

Gil used what little restraint he had left to keep from asking Pete how many times he'd seen Darcy.

Craven turned Darcy and stared at her.

Gil lunged forward. Pete moved at the same moment. Gil grabbed Darcy, yanking her away from Craven. Pete and the man with him grabbed Craven—one on either side.

Before Gil could check Darcy, the door opened and Jeremy stepped through dragging Craven's carpetbag.

"Hey!" Craven struggled against the men hold-ing him.

Gil had an idea about what the bag held. He

leaned over, grabbed the straps and pulled it to the edge of the platform. Fear and greed constricted Craven's pudgy face. His torment almost made up for the way he treated Darcy. Almost.

Gil shoved the bag over the edge.

"Jump," he ordered Jeremy and opened the gate. Jeremy looked at Darcy then Gil.

"She's coming right behind." Gil gave Jeremy a push. The boy remembered to curl up and roll. When Jeremy was safely on the ground, Gil kissed Darcy and turned her to the open gate.

"What about you," she asked, grasping his sleeve like a drowning person.

"I'll catch up. Jeremy knows what to do."

Craven broke loose and charged across the platform. Gil turned to keep the man away from Darcy. "Go." He pushed Darcy as Craven grabbed for her. "Roll when you hit the ground."

The tearing of cloth echoed in his ears. Craven held up a section of Darcy's skirt. Gil looked back to see her petticoats flying through the air as she rolled across the ground. She was safe.

Now he had three angry men to deal with.

# Chapter 20

Darcy remained on the ground and waited for the world to stop spinning. Dread entered as she reflected on the three men Gil had to battle alone. She sat up and stared down the tracks. The train appeared as a dot in the distance. She couldn't see Gil or the platform.

"Darcy, come on, we gotta head outta here." Jeremy grabbed her arm and started tugging.

"But Gil..." Her heart ached at the thought she may never see him again.

"He said we was to take this gold and get the rest back to Galena. Come on." He yanked on her arm. "We gotta follow orders and everything will turn out right."

She looked up into his young face. He believed in Gil. Jeremy had more faith in the man she loved than she did. Darcy sighed heavily and gulped down the fear lodged in her throat.

"Okay." She stood, winced at the sore muscles and bruises and took hold of one of the straps on the carpetbag. "Which way do we go?"

"Gil said to head away from the tracks, but keep heading south."

"When did he tell you this?" She hadn't seen Jeremy and Gil alone since they arrived in Baker City.

"When he came through the train following you and Craven. He told me to get the carpetbag under the fifth seat and come to the back of the train."

That was why it took him so long. He'd been planning while she fretted he wouldn't show up in time to help her.

"Did he stop and talk to anyone else in the train?" She hoped Pete and Skunk were on Gil's side. Though it put him in cahoots with thieves, it might keep him alive.

"Yeah. Them two that had a hold of Craven." Jeremy motioned to switch sides. They switched giving their other arms a rest and continued across the grassy expanse. "When Gil stopped and talked to me, they put their heads together. After I passed them, they stood." He looked over at her and shrugged with the shoulder not weighed down by the carpetbag. "I don't know if they were going to help or not."

A lump had crawled up her throat. Darcy swallowed. Her gut told her Pete wasn't to be trusted, but he had a bone to pick with Craven. Hopefully he wanted revenge on the old scoundrel worse than he wanted to harm Gil.

She wiped at the sweat beading her brow. All the layers of clothing not only made walking hard, but they were hot. She looked up at the clear sky and white-hot sun. It was going to get a whole lot hotter before they made it to any trees. She didn't know how far it was to the next town, or even where it was. They'd had some hard times in the last four years, but she'd never felt as deep a loss or helplessness as she did right now.

The carpetbag slid from her fingers. She dropped to her knees and covered her face with her hands. Tears she hadn't shed in years spilled forth, soaking her hands and the front of her dress. Her body shook as she thought of Gil facing the three men. The odds weren't in his favor. It didn't matter how far they lugged Craven's bag, it wouldn't help Gil.

A comforting arm circled her shoulders. She buried her face in Jeremy's shirt and wept. She should be the strong one. The one to make them get up and move forward. Her body was spent.

"It's okay. He'll find us." Jeremy smoothed her hair. "We gotta get this back to Galena. They think you were one of the robbers."

The words seeped through her sorrow. "What?"

"When you was missing right after the robbery, Craven said you were part of the gang that did it."

She pulled back and stared at her brother. He wasn't fooling. "They think I did it?" Blazes! She was a wanted woman. She wiped an arm under her nose and used a petticoat to rub the tears from her face. "Why didn't you tell me this before?"

"It didn't seem important." He smiled sheepishly.

"Didn't seem important! I'm a wanted bank

robber, and it didn't seem important!" She smacked him alongside the head and stood.

Jeremy grinned from ear to ear as he stood.

"You think it's funny I'm wanted?" She shook a fist at him and started to grin. "You scamp, you knew that would get me fired up." She grabbed him around the neck, knocked his hat off, and rubbed her knuckles back and forth across the top of his head.

"Hey, that smarts!" He struggled.

She opened her arm, and he traveled backward landing on his backside.

"Serves you right for letting me run around as a thief." She bent down to grab the straps on the bag. The sound of horse's hooves rumbled in the distance and grew in volume.

Darcy turned to the sound. Two riders approached fast. There was no place to hide either themselves or the bag. She plopped down on the bag, covering it with her petticoats. It was the first time in her life being dressed like a lady came in handy. Well, almost like a lady. A lady wouldn't be sitting in the middle of nowhere in a ripped bodice and her petticoats.

Jeremy sat down beside her looking anxious. His nervousness rubbed off. Biting her nails, she watched the men make a direct line for them. Who could be heading this exact direction? It wasn't a normal route. They hadn't come across any hoof prints or wagon tracks.

The horses slid to a stop about twenty feet away. When the dust cleared, Darcy looked up at a sight almost as wonderful as seeing Gil. Jeremy whooped, and they both jumped up and ran to the horses.

"How'd you find us Clay?" Jeremy asked as the two men dismounted.

Relief flowed through Darcy's body as she looked at the Halsey brothers. One was Clay and she reckoned the other must be the infamous Zeke.

"Soon as you three—" he looked around. "Where's Gil?"

"Still on the train." Darcy looked at the two men. She was glad to have them here to help, but the person who needed them most was on the train.

"No, he ain't," Zeke said, tipping his hat back and looking her over.

"He has to be. He shoved Jeremy and me off along with that carpet bag full of gold." The way they stared at her, she could tell they didn't believe her. "How do you know he wasn't on the train?"

"We were at the Powder train station waiting for the train, so we could help with Craven." Clay stared straight at her. "When Gil didn't get off we climbed on and walked the full length. He wasn't there."

Her knees buckled. Clay grabbed her about the middle, holding her up.

"Dang, does she do that often?" Zeke asked, looking at Jeremy.

"Only since her skirt caught on fire," Jeremy said, plopping down on the carpetbag.

"Let go of me." Darcy slapped at Clay's hands. He held on tight, but lowered her to the ground next to Jeremy.

"Zeke, get some jerky out of my saddle bag. We can't have our future sister, fainting from lack of food. Ethan'd have us fixing supper for a year." He winked at Jeremy. Gratitude warmed her heart as the two men sat quietly by and offered her water to wash the dry meat down with.

When she felt stronger, Darcy related all that happened on the train. "He was standing on the back platform with Craven, Pete, and Skunk, when he shoved me off." She looked at their faces. Neither one would give away what they thought or felt. It must be a Halsey trait. She frowned.

"We followed the tracks back from Powder. Saw the scuffle marks and your footprints, that's how we stumbled across the two of you." Zeke looked at his brother. "Let's take them to the mine. They can get a couple of horses, get the gold back to Galena, and we can set out looking for Gil."

Clay nodded.

"Why can't we go with you to find Gil?" Darcy didn't want to be separated from him. She'd become accustom to having him around to talk to and touch. Her body quivered thinking of the way he skimmed his fingers over her skin. That was something she wanted to feel for the rest of her life.

"You need to get that gold back and clear your name before you end up on a wanted poster." Clay tweaked her nose like she was a small child.

"Don't treat me like a child. I'm a woman, and I deserve to have some say in how we find the man I love." She stared defiantly at the men. Jeremy hid a giggle behind his hand. "What's so funny?" She asked, turning on her brother.

"It's kind of hard to think of you as a woman when you're sitting here cross-legged in your petticoats." He pointed to her hands clasping the toes of her kid slippers.

Embarrassment heated her cheeks as she glanced at the men sitting across from her. She hadn't thought about the position before. To sit on the ground in her petticoats this way was more intimate than proper. Many times she and Jeremy had sat around a fire just this way. But you were in pants. Her petticoats were tucked around her legs with her kid slippers sticking out.

While she told of their escape, she'd noticed their eyes stray to her chest, but then all men seemed to have their eyes drawn in that direction when they talked to women. She'd found it humorous dressed in her Pa's clothes, but sitting here in her unmentionables, she found it unnerving.

"You got a change of clothes with you?" she asked the men still gawking at her underclothes.

"You scared Gil's gonna find out you were traveling with us in just your petticoats?" Zeke grinned and waggled his eyebrows.

"No, I don't want to run across other randy men." They both had the decency to blush. "I don't think Jeremy or you need to fend off men that think I'm easy because I'm traveling in my underclothes like a common harlot."

They all flinched at her last comment. Zeke, the smaller of the two, went to his saddlebags. He came back and dropped a pair of Levis in her lap.

"They're gonna need to be tied on, but they'll be a spit more respectable than them white flashy drawers." He smiled. "Though I was having some really nice thoughts about how the two of us could run away and forget about my little brother."

Darcy glared at him. "You're too ugly for me."

Clay doubled over with laughter. Zeke just grinned as Jeremy slapped him on the back.

"Now that you've all had a good laugh, Jeremy, come stand in front of this horse." She crooked her finger at her brother. When he joined her, she untied the blanket on the back of Zeke's horse and held it out to Jeremy.

"Hold this so they can't see under." She walked to the opposite side of the horse and dropped the petticoats. With some degree of muscle she pulled the Levis up over the poofy drawers.

Zeke was right, the Levis were plenty big. It was a good thing or else she wouldn't have been able to stuff her chemise in them. She ripped a strip of fabric from a petticoat and tied it around her waist to hold the pants up.

"Okay," She stepped from behind the horse and watched the stunned looks on the men's faces.

"I know the kid slippers and dress bodice doesn't really go with large Levis, but at least I'm decently covered."

"I was going to say, no matter what you put on, you look adorable," Clay said, opening the carpetbag.

"Yeah, Gil's a lucky man," Zeke said wistfully.

Darcy couldn't believe two men other then Gil thought she was a catch. Had her uncle been so demented with vengeance he'd seen her as ugly when she wasn't? She looked at Clay and Zeke to see if they were fooling with her, but both men seemed embarrassed by what they'd just said.

"Let's split the gold between the horses since we have to carry Darcy and Jeremy," Clay said, handing a bag to each person. They carried the bags to the respective horses until the carpetbag was empty.

Clay and Zeke mounted their horses.

"Zeke, you take the boy," Clay said, leaning down to help Darcy swing up on behind him.

"Okay, but we'll switch off later. I want to visit with my new sister." Zeke winked and jabbed his heels into the horse's ribs.

Darcy wasn't sure she wanted to ride with Zeke and have him question her about his brother. Clay followed the other horse, and they were soon on a direct course toward the Elk Mountains. Contentment set in as they rode steadily toward the tree-topped mountains in the distance. Clay told her they would reach Sumpter by the following day if they didn't stop to sleep.

The thought of riding so many hours along with worrying about Gil had her nerves on edge. She was the first to spot riders coming up on their left. Darcy tugged on Clay's arm and pointed them out.

"Anybody you know?" he asked and whistled softly between his teeth to get Zeke's attention.

The silhouettes were of three men. One large, one small, and one tall. As they drew closer, she could make out large ears on the lead rider. She sucked in air and clenched the material of Clay's shirt.

"It's the rest of the gang that was on the train with Gil." Every nerve in her body tightened. "They know me as a dance hall girl."

Clay turned and looked at her. "I thought you said you were a marshal?"

"It's a long story, I'll tell you later." She squirmed as the men rode straight for them. "Act like you just picked me up out here wandering around. The way I look they should believe you."

"I'm not letting them take you. So don't go thinking you can go with them and find Gil." His voice was steady and carried a warning. He wouldn't be so easy to get around. He wasn't interested in her feminine wiles. And she wouldn't stoop that low to put him or herself in that position.

She unclenched her hand from his shirt and pasted a smile on her face as the horses circled then came to a stop.

"Where you headed boys?" Charles asked.

"Sumpter." Zeke said, moving his horse closer to Clay's.

"You're taking a dangerous route. Why aren't you going down the railroad and up the draw?" The other two nodded their heads.

Darcy snorted. Like they had enough brains to think of that themselves. Clay had kept her hidden, but when she snorted, Charles moved his horse so he could see her. She knew the minute he recognized her.

"You get around, girl," he said, sneering. "I thought you burned up in the cabin."

"I got out. These men found me wandering and were nice enough to give me a ride." She smiled back.

"Why it's that dancing girl," Red said, slapping his hat on his knee. "If Skunk was here we could finish our dance."

"Yeah, we could," she answered, thinking there

was no way she was dancing with any of them again.

"I'm glad you all got a chance to reminisce, but we need to get going. My brother's expecting us." Clay urged his horse forward.

Charles reached out and grabbed the horse's bridle. "I'm not through talking with the lady."

# Chapter 21

Darcy grimaced. She should have stayed hidden. Her impulsive nature may have put all their lives in danger.

"The lady's with us now and no concern of yours." Zeke moved in, putting himself, Jeremy, and their horse between her and the outlaws. Darcy looked over at Jeremy. His eyes were round and eager. He took the whole thing in like a theater play.

"Maybe I should decide who I want to ride with," she said, glancing from man to man. Clay and Zeke scowled while the not-so-bright bunch looked at her with sappy grins. Good looking, decent men or misfit thieves—sheesh, it was a tough choice.

She looked at Charles and his group. "Sorry boys, but I like where I'm headed just fine. It was good seeing you though." She grabbed the reins from Clay, turned the horse, and kicked it in the ribs. Clay slid sideways, but gained his seat and yanked the reins from her hands, as the horse bolted through the trees. Zeke and Jeremy crashed through the brush beside them.

She twisted her neck to see if the gang followed. The robber's horses circled one another as the men argued, flailing their arms in different directions. She laughed and hugged Clay.

"Tell me about how you met those men," he said, keeping the horse at a steady lope.

Darcy closed her eyes and thought back to the first time Gil made love to her. What a wondrous night it had been, until she crept out of his bed.

Leaving out the intimate parts, she explained ending up attached to a robber's horse, the pile of stolen goods in the cabin, the dancing, flying embers, and finally her abduction by Craven.

She finished her story. Her eyelids grew heavy, refusing to stay open no matter how hard she tried to hold them up. Clay's hearty laugh and Zeke's snorts didn't even raise her temper. She was too tired to care. Let them laugh at her expense. All she wanted was sleep. The horse had slowed to a walk some time before. The rhythm of the rocking horse and her rubbery neck, whipped her head back and forth.

"Lay your head against my back and wrap your arms around my waist. I'll grab you if you start to fall," Clay said when her forehead slammed into his back.

"Thanks, I don't know why I'm so tired." She rested her cheek against his scratchy wool shirt and dreamed Gil had his hand over her clasped hands.

"Damn it, Pete! I don't care what you do with your life, just let me loose." Gil struggled against the ropes binding his hands and feet as he glared at a man he'd once called a friend. A friend wouldn't truss you to farm implements. A shuffling noise swung his attention to his right. Craven was tied to a piece of farm equipment as well.

"I can't. Knowing you, you'd try to take Craven, and I have to keep him here until the boss shows up. We want to know what he," Pete pointed the knife he was using to clean his fingernails at Craven, "did with the gold."

"You idiot. I told you, the gold was in the carpetbag this cowboy tossed off the train with his girlfriend," Craven said, his face flushing a bright scarlet.

Gil thought the man might collapse from all the stress. He didn't like the idea of carting a dead man back to Galena. It would be hard to get him to confess to what he'd done.

"That wasn't the gold." Pete scoffed. "It would have needed more than one bag. You forget I helped load all the gold into that wagon?" Pete tapped Craven on the shoulder with his knife. "Don't be lying to me."

Craven's face puckered in indignation, proving he would rather die than tell where it was hidden. Gil knew where the rest of the gold was buried. He wasn't saying a word. He'd sent Jeremy to dig up the sacks and didn't want the robbers riding up on the boy and Darcy as they obeyed his orders.

"How do you know he didn't stash the gold in

a bank in Baker City?" Gil asked to take the conversation in a different direction.

"The boss and Al are checking on that." Pete pushed his hat back and looked at Gil. "Why do you want this guy so bad?"

"He told the town Darcy stole the money from the bank. I want to take him back to prove he was the thief, and she had nothing to do with it."

Craven flinched and looked at him with narrowed eyes. "That girl on the train was Marshal Duncan?"

"Yep, so was the harlot who kicked you." Gil grinned as the man's jaw dropped.

Pete chuckled and leaned toward Craven, taunting the man. "You mean that pint-size lady got the best of you?" Skunk and Pete whooped it up, harassing Craven and wiping the tears from their eyes.

Gil used the distraction to work on the rope bound around his wrists. He rubbed the hemp back and forth on the metal strap of the farm implement he was tied against.

Pete looked his way. He stilled his hands and wiped imaginary tears of mirth from his eyes with his shoulder. Hopefully, Darcy and Jeremy made it somewhere safe. The two of them lugging the carpetbag would be slow traveling. He'd told Jeremy to use a nugget to get horses at the first place they came to. He didn't think the town would mind the contents being used for a good cause—bringing their gold back.

All heads turned at the sound of horse's hooves. Pete stood and motioned for Skunk to check the door. Gil's headed pounded with urgency. He'd hoped to be loose and gone before the rest of the gang arrived. Getting Craven out of here with two men to overcome was hard enough. He didn't need more obstacles.

He worked harder at freeing his hands as the two men watched the door. Craven observed his movements and smiled slyly.

The man knew Gil wanted to take him back to Galena. Gil figured Craven thought he had a better chance talking his way around the good people of Galena than the robbers.

Gil's heart pounded as he vigorously rubbed the rope back and forth. The heat of the friction scorched his wrists. The muscles in his arms twitched and ached as he pulled his hands apart tightening the rope. The hemp fibers bit into his wrists, but he worked feverishly to get loose.

Craven cleared his throat and Gil stopped. Pete walked back from the door.

"Nobody important." He smiled and sat down on a keg of nails. "Skunk go round us up some grub."

The other man didn't appear happy to take orders from Pete. "Why me? Why can't you go look for some grub?" He stepped away from the door and faced Pete.

"'Cuz, I'm bigger and can shoot better." Pete stood, dropping his right hand to the butt of his pistol. His voice was noncommittal, but his stance issued a warning. "And if you see the boss, point him this direction."

Skunk stared at Pete's hand resting on the gun. The smaller man's feet shuffled a little as the air crackled with tension. Gil'd seen Pete face down wranglers before. If egged on, he rarely backed down. One thing Pete thrived on was proving his power, because his father always made him feel so insignificant.

If he could get the two fighting against one another, it could cut his odds.

"I'd do what he says. I've seen Pete. He's fast." Gil said, nodding his head solemnly.

"Who says I ain't fast?" Skunk squared up with Pete.

Gil looked at Craven. "What you want to bet Pete, here, downs Skunk in one shot?"

Craven grinned as he caught on to the ploy. "I think Skunk is tougher than he looks," Craven countered.

"Really?" Gil squinted and looked Skunk up and down. The man looked about ready to jump out of his skin. Gil had a feeling the robber had never really been in a gunfight. His pants shook from his knees knocking together. If he didn't need to get one of them out of the way, he would have found it all downright comical.

Before the bet could be made, Skunk opened the door, darting out at a run. Pete doubled over laughing, and Gil ripped the rope apart, lunging for Pete. Gil was at a disadvantage with his feet bound together, but determined to out wrestle his friend.

They rolled.

Gil's shoulder slammed into the point of a plow blade. Pain shot down his arm, but he didn't let go of Pete or take his eye off the gun in Pete's hand. Rolling about the dirt floor scattered hay and dust. Gil squint his eyes to keep from being blinded by the debris kicked up.

The door swung open.

Pete sneezed, and Gil wrenched the gun from his hand. More dust plumed around them as they struggled for possession of the weapon. Gil squinted to see through the dust and into the sunlight streaming through the open doorway.

"What the?"

Gil had never been so happy to hear his brother's voice.

"Over here." Gil stood, pulling Pete to his feet. The man sneezed and sneezed, rendering him helpless.

Hank walked into view as the dust settled in the building. Looking past him, Gil spotted Skunk trussed up like a calf about to be castrated.

"How'd you find me?" Gil asked, tying Pete's arms behind his back with the rope that once bound him.

"Followed your trail. These guys are easier to follow than a bunch of drunken miners." Hank clamped a hand on Gil's sore shoulder. Pain shot through him, making his knees buckle under this brother's touch.

"Sorry. Didn't know you were hurt."

"More pride than skin." Gil motioned to the corner. "Craven's over there. Let's leave these two and take him back to Galena."

Hank's face went blank. A sick sensation squeezed Gil's gut. He looked at the corner where Craven was tied and found rope with frayed ends piled on the floor.

"Damn!" Gil shoved Pete at his brother and ran to the door. In all the commotion the man had gotten away. If he caught Darcy and Jeremy taking

Darcy woke when the horse stopped.

"Wake up sleepy head." A male voice seeped into her dream. "The horse needs a rest and so do I."

She raised her head and wiped at the drool sliding down her chin. Whose back was she sleeping on? She looked down at the torn bodice and Levis covering her body. Gil? Where was Gil? She scanned the area. Zeke and Jeremy stood a few feet away. She pulled her arms from around Clay and placed her foot in the empty stirrup. Her groggy body moved sluggishly as she slid her leg over the horse's rump and dismounted.

"You were dead asleep," Clay said, dismounting and loosening the cinch. He pulled the saddle and blanket from his horse and tied the animal to a tree where it could reach tall clumps of grass.

"I didn't think I could sleep on a moving horse." She rubbed a hand over her face, trying to scrub the sleep away. "Do you think Gil's okay?"

Clay's face stayed rigid. "He's a smart man, I'm sure we'll see him soon."

"You don't look like you believe what you're saying." Her heart clenched. Would that brief, desperate kiss before he pushed her from the train be her last memory of him? Her heart hoped not, but her head said it was nearly impossible for him to get away from two ruthless men with guns. She knew Craven would never help him. He was a man only out to save his own skin.

"He seems to be able to land on his feet," Zeke

squeezed her shoulder. "I wouldn't worry about him."

"Why didn't you go find him when you saw Jeremy and I were safe?" She rammed her hands on her hips and stared at the two men settling down against their saddles like they didn't have a care.

"Gil made us promise to take care of you two no matter what happened to him." Clay motioned for her to sit. She shook her head. Jeremy was already fast asleep curled up in a ball on the horse blankets. How could he sleep when Gil was in danger? She cringed. She'd slept when exhaustion swallowed her.

"You mean a lot to Gil, and we aim to take care of you." Zeke yawned. "Even if you are a contrary woman."

"I take offense to that," she said, pacing back and forth.

"I figured you would, you take offense to most things a body says."

"Well!" She turned her back on the men and marched into the dark forest. They didn't really want her around. They were just keeping her because Gil asked them. She'd become a prisoner of the Halsey brothers. At least the robbers hadn't bad-mouthed her.

She sat down on a log. Gil where are you? Are you dead or alive? She didn't like the idea of the Halsey brothers watching over her. It would be nice to have a place to live and food. But she couldn't stay with them without Gil.

Her chest ached as loss crept into her heart. What if Gil was dead? She wrapped her arms around her body, trying to keep the sobs of despair contained. She would take the gold to Galena, but she wouldn't live with the Halsey's. Their resemblance to Gil would be too much for her to look at every day. If Jeremy wanted, he could live with them, but she'd stay in Galena. Where her wonderful memories of Gil were vivid.

A tear trickled down her cheek. A sob broke through her clenched jaw. As much as she wanted to believe Gil was alive and would return to her, she knew it would take a miracle to bring him back to her arms.

# Chapter 22

Darcy was drained and dry, when she heard the men saddling the horses. She straightened her clothes and patted her cheeks. They didn't need to know her despair. She pasted on a smile and walked back to the makeshift camp.

Jeremy watched her with a puzzled expression, but she ignored him. She didn't want to answer any of his hundred questions. She figured Zeke would like to have someone less vocal for the remainder of the trip.

"I'll ride with you this time," she said, walking over to where Zeke saddled his horse.

"Big brother get too randy with you?" he asked and was rewarded with a canteen hitting his back. "Ouch! I know better than that. You're too nice to hit on your brother's intended." He waggled his eyebrows and grabbed her around the waist, setting her in the saddle. He swung up behind her, putting his arms around her and his chin on her head.

"There, now you can see where we're going." His breath whispered through her hair.

She pinched his arm.

"Ouch!  What did you do that for?"

"If I'm sitting in front, I'm holding onto the reins, so get your arms back there where you're sitting." She took the reins and urged the horse forward. "I thought you were after some school teacher."

"I am, but that don't mean I can't see just how much you scratch and hiss."

Darcy chuckled in spite of herself. And she thought Gil was full of mischief.

"Tell me about your school teacher."

"Not much to tell. I'm interested. She ain't." She heard him sigh, making it easy to take pity on his situation.

"Maybe you're going about it all wrong. What have you done so far?" This was her chance to see someone else as happy as Gil made her.

"I've asked her to dance at the socials and asked her out to dinner." His voice lowered. "I even bought her a pretty hat." She felt him looking around. "But don't tell my brothers. I'll never hear the end of it."

"Why?"

"'Cuz, they'll think I have to buy her affections. I tell you I ain't never run up against such a stubborn woman."

"Why haven't you given up, if she's so against giving you her affections?" Darcy could almost feel his shoulders sag.

"Her hair's the color of a raven's wing. Her skin's as smooth as glass and white as cream. She's got clear blue eyes that deepen with her moods and a mouth that's just made for kissing."

Darcy turned in the saddle and looked into the dreamy gaze of Zeke. He was smitten. She didn't want to stand next to this goddess if Gil were around. It sounded like the woman would out-dazzle any other female.

"Okay, let's figure out what she doesn't like about you. You're not hard to look at. So it can't be that. You speak well. Can't be that." She sniffed. "Could use a bath, but so could I right about now." She shrugged. "I give up what is it she doesn't like about you?"

"I'm a miner."

"That's it?  All you gotta do is quit mining." Darcy glanced at him over her shoulder, giving him a look that said he was an idiot.

"I told her I'd quit, but she had a daddy that was always looking for the big strike. He died in a mine, and she's just now pulled herself up out of bad times. She's afraid I'd get the itch after we're married, and she'd be a widow or in the poorhouse again." He shook his head. "I can't seem to convince her otherwise."

Darcy mulled this over in her head as they rounded a corner. The Halsey cabin stood in the clearing all lit up by the bright early afternoon sun.

"It's about time you got back." Ethan dropped the ax he'd been using to chop wood. He crossed to the horse and lifted Darcy off like she weighed no more than a saddlebag. When her feet were on the ground, Ethan turned.

"Where's Gil?" he looked from one brother to the next. Finally his gaze landed on Darcy.

"Where'd you leave my brother?"

"It's a long story, and I'm thirsty and hungry. Can I tell you while we eat?" Darcy cringed as he turned an angry face to the others.

"Why haven't you fed this girl? Why are you all looking like mauled chickens?"

"Like Darcy said, we need some food, and we'll tell you all about it," Clay wrapped his reins around a tree limb and headed into the cabin.

Darcy's mouth started to water from the smell of fresh bread and roasted meat. They made sandwiches of the bread and meat while they all told pieces of what had happened.

"So Gil's out there by himself against three men?" Ethan ran a hand through his hair. "He's more of a fool than I gave him credit for."

Darcy felt her face flush with indignation. "He was trying to save me and Jeremy. If I don't take the gold back to Galena, my face will be on wanted posters." She looked at him through tear-blurred eyes. "I'd have done the same for him given the chance."

Ethan slapped a hand down on the table. "I'm not blaming anyone. We have to figure out where they could be and go help."

"That's the problem. They could be anywhere." Clay took a sip of the whiskey Zeke poured for everyone but Jeremy.

"Let's help Jeremy and Darcy get the gold back to Galena, then we can spread out different directions and look for Gil and the robbers." Zeke downed his whiskey in one gulp and wiped his mouth with the back of his hand. He grinned and winked at Darcy.

"Let's see you do that," he teased, eyeballing the full glass sitting in front of her.

Darcy didn't know what he was up to, but she wasn't going to be dared and not go through with it. She grabbed the glass, and Jeremy squirmed beside her.

"That's not a good idea, Darce," he warned.

She threw him a disgusted look and swallowed the entire contents. Her throat burned, and her eyes filled with tears as the liquid burned all the way to her stomach and smoldered.

"It really isn't a good idea," Jeremy counseled the grown men sitting around the table grinning from ear to ear.

"Why not?" Zeke asked, filling her glass and narrowing his eyes. "Bet you can't do that again."

Darcy narrowed her blurry eyes and scowled. "Watch me."

"Darce, No!" Jeremy grabbed her arm, spilling the contents all over her torn bodice.

"Jeremy! Look what you did. You ruined my dress." She looked down at the low-cut neckline, Levis, and kid slippers. The sight made tears burn in her eyes. She looked like a harlot, and she was sitting at a table with men drinking like a lush. What had happened to her? Where had she gone so far astray?

Hot salty tears rolled down her face and into the corners of her mouth. She couldn't stop them. Didn't even care to stop them. She let loose with her second good cry since Ma and Pa died.

When they lost their parents, she hadn't given herself the satisfaction of showing any emotion. Jeremy had to be looked after and she was the only one left to do it. Darcy studied her brother. He was a bit blurry. Her heart swelled with pride at the man he was becoming. She reached out, pulling him into her arms. She held him tight and cried.

"I told you," he said, patting her head and looking around the table at the men staring at her. "She does this every time she drinks anything harder than sarsaparilla."

Did she really? How did Jeremy know that? She wiped at the tears, but they wouldn't stop. "How, hic, do you, hic, know that?" she asked, leaning back to look at him.

"Once when Ma and Pa were still alive you found a bottle in the barn and drank some. They couldn't figure out what you were crying about when they found you. I found you first and put the bottle back. They never knew."

"Thank you Jeremy. Hic. You should be the older child. I'm no, hic, good at it."

He hugged her fiercely. "Darce, you're the best sister in the world."

She smiled and sniffed. A chair scraped the floor and feet shuffled. "Where're you going?" she asked, prying Jeremy's arms from around her.

"Get fresh horses so we can go get that gold and get your face off the wanted posters. The sooner we do that, the sooner we can get after Gil," Ethan turned to walk out. He stopped and turned back to the room. "We'll find him, and we'll take care of those that messed with him."

Darcy shivered. She didn't want to be Charles and his group when Ethan found them.

Several hours later they had the gold dug up and stored among the saddlebags. Darcy's stomach roiled and nearly spit the whiskey and food back up.

"I don't feel so good," she muttered and ran into the bushes. Bending over, she vomited on the base of a fir tree. She leaned her head against the tree, breathing in the clean scent. She willed the world to stop spinning and the sounds to stop ringing in her ears. When her stomach settled and the world no longer spun, she turned to head back to the group.

The men stood by the horses waiting. Out of the corner of her eye, she caught something moving slow through the trees to her right.

Before she could let out a warning cry, a hand clamped over her mouth and a pudgy arm pulled her against a round belly. If the body hadn't given him away the stench of cigar would have.

Darcy stomped and kicked her feet trying to break free. His grip tightened, and his voice hissed in her ear.

"Don't fight me and your beau will live."

He knew something about Gil. She stopped struggling and nodded her head. He removed his hand from her mouth, but before she could ask a question he shoved a handkerchief in and pulled her arms behind her back. Pain shot through her shoulders as he bound her wrists.

"Now we're going to quietly leave these men to their duties." Craven pulled her away from the scene as gunfire rang out. She struggled to look back to make sure Jeremy wasn't in the middle of things, but the man yanked her through the underbrush.

The sound of terrified horses and gun shots buckled her knees. Nothing could happen to the Halsey brothers. It would be her fault. She'd brought all this on them by masquerading as a marshal. And Jeremy. Please, let him live.

Craven threw her over his shoulder like a sack of potatoes and continued through the trees. She didn't care what happened to her. She deserved whatever fate for having so selfishly drawn good people into her catastrophic life.

The man could barely breathe when he reached a horse tied to a tree. He dropped her to her feet and held onto the stirrup as he wheezed and gasped for air.

"Girl, you are more trouble than any female I've ever come across, but I'll have my due. I'm taking you back to Galena. I'll tell the town folk all about you being the leader of the gang that robbed them of their life savings, and they'll be building the first ever gallows in Galena. I guarantee you that."

He draped her over the neck of his horse and climbed into the saddle, settling her across his legs. The thought of being hanged didn't set well with her. It was as unsavory as being flopped across Craven's lap. Surely the good people of Galena would know she wasn't a leader of a group of robbers. Nor would she steal from them.

Her only chance was if someone in town spoke up for her. She was sure Mrs. Danforth would, but would the respectable men of Galena believe a woman who ran a brothel? Blazes, if she wasn't stuck in a corner this time.

Where was Gil?

And please, Lord, keep Jeremy from harm where ever he is.

Gil lost Craven's tracks and headed straight toward the sound of gunfire and the clearing where Craven had stashed the gold. Following Craven, he'd crisscrossed three other sets of tracks. Hopefully, they weren't the robber's tracks or Craven just ran into an ambush.

Circling the area where Craven buried the gold, Gil listened to the shots and hoped it was the outlaws and Craven shooting it up and not Darcy and Jeremy. Given the time since he'd tossed the two off the train, the gold should have been recovered and the siblings headed to Galena.

He poked his head out between bushes. Ethan, Zeke, Clay, and Jeremy hid behind trees while three of Pete's gang wasted bullets. Why weren't they shooting back?

Gil stepped out behind the men on horseback and shot into the air three times. The horses jumped forward, unseating one robber and catching the attention of the others.

"What are you doing shooting at my brothers?" Gil asked, walking over to the man on the ground. He placed his foot in the middle of the man's back, holding him on the ground as he held his gun on the man with big ears.

"What the hell are you doing here?" The man looked around. "Where's Pete?"

"He's on his way to jail, just like you're going to be." Gil kept his gaze on the robbers as out of the corner of his eye, he watched his brother's sneak up behind the befuddled outlaws.

"Hey!" the big-eared man exclaimed as Ethan and Clay pulled the men off their horses. Gil grinned as they wrenched the robber's arms behind their backs and Zeke and Jeremy tied their hands.

"Where's Darcy?" Gil asked, looking back at the trees where his brothers came from.

"You didn't see her?" Ethan scowled and looked around the area.

Fear catapulted from the pit of Gil's stomach to his throat. He hadn't seen anything but Craven's tracks. And the greedy man now knew Darcy had duped him more than once.

"Darce! Darcy!" Jeremy called, running out through the trees.

"Why didn't you keep a closer eye on her?" Gil took his anger out on the man on the ground, yanking his arms behind him, paying no attention to the pain he caused.

"Take it easy." Clay pushed Gil away from the robber and finished the job.

"We put the last of the gold on the horses, and she hightailed it into the trees as pale as a new moon." Ethan put a hand on his shoulder. "She's probably under a tree sleeping."

"With all this noise?" Gil looked at his brother. There was something they weren't telling him. Why would she run off all white and then sleep through a gun fight?

He grabbed Zeke by the shirt front. "What did you do to Darcy?" His brother's eyes sparkled with mischief. The crooked grin was a sure sign they'd been up to something and it worried Gil.

"Nothin'. We was just sitting around the table discussing how you were bound to show up, even though that girl was thinking the worst had happened to you. We told her you always come back."

"Why would she run into the woods? A gunfight wouldn't scare her." Gil looked at Clay. He was always the most straight-forward of all the brothers.

"She was feelin' a little puny." Clay turned from Gil, nodding his head toward Ethan.

Gil looked at his oldest brother as Jeremy continued to call for Darcy. "What is going on?"

"We gave Darcy some whiskey to calm her nerves, only it made her shed so many tears we about drown. Then after the ride here, she didn't look too good and ducked into the trees. I bet she just got sick and then lay down to sleep it off."

Gil's fist shot through the air, before he even thought about who it was aimed at. It didn't matter it was his brother. He shouldn't have let Darcy go into the woods alone.

"She might be contrary, but she's not as tough as she tries to put on." Gil rubbed his knuckles as he looked down at Ethan sitting on his backside on the ground. "Since I can't depend on you to take care of the woman I love, then I'll do it myself." He strode away from the three startled men and mounted his horse. "Take these men back to Galena. I'm going to find Darcy."

*Chapter 23*

Darcy watched the town folk gather as Craven unceremoniously dumped her on her feet in the middle of town. Her legs nearly folded from lack of use. She leaned against the animal, grasping anything to keep her steady. Pain stung her arms like small needles. She winced and tried to catch hold of the stirrup to keep from falling face down in the dusty street. The merchant moved to help her, but Craven waved him back.

"You don't know how this woman made fun of us." Craven dismounted and tipped her head up for the gathering crowd to see.

Gasps as the people recognized her bolstered Darcy's confidence. If he'd just take the disgusting handkerchief out of her mouth she could tell them all he'd done to the town. He wouldn't though. He didn't want her spilling everything she knew about him. No one in town liked the mayor and would believe her over him.

Since she couldn't spew the truth, she glared

at Craven.

"Yes, this is the person we thought was a young man. A young man who courageously shot a bank robber."

Darcy nodded her head. Yes, she did pretend to be a young man, and she did courageously shoot the robber. Well, sort of.

"It was all a set-up. She wounded one of her own men, to make an impression on all you good people of Galena." The muttering in the crowd didn't instill confidence in her. They were swarming to Craven's lies like bees to honey. Only, she was the one about to be stung.

Where were the Halsey brothers? Surely they'd bested the fumbling robbers. And what about Gil? If Craven was alive and so were the robbers... Her heart lurched. Gil couldn't have made it off the train alive. Craven only threw out his comment to make her cooperate, she should have known better.

How could Gil be alive when it was three to one? The realization he was dead hit harder than her parents' death whom she'd loved for thirteen years. She'd known their end was coming. It showed in their eyes. But this... he was too young, too virile, and... Blazes. He'd captured her heart.

"This woman has made a mockery of your town. I believe we should make an example of her." Craven threw his hands in the air. "This woman should be hung!"

"No!" The shout shook Darcy from her path of self-pity. She'd known Mrs. Danforth would stand up for her.

The crowd mumbled and shuffled as the woman floated through them and straight up to Darcy. She pulled the dusty cloth from Darcy's mouth all the while glaring at Craven.

"What have you done to this woman?" she demanded, motioning for him to remove the rope.

"Nothing she doesn't deserve." Craven stuck a finger out as if to poke Mrs. Danforth's chest then dropped his hand like his finger caught on fire.

"What are the charges?" Mrs. Danforth crossed her arms and stared at the man. Darcy's fighting spirit swelled with the woman on her side.

"He doesn't have any charges, because I haven't done anything wrong. He's the one who should be thrown in jail."

The crowd looked from her to the mayor.

Craven didn't sputter or blink an eye. "This woman knows the robbers intimately, hid the gold, and was headed to the other side of the state by train."

"How do you know all this?" Mrs. Danforth asked, glaring at the man.

"I trailed them to a cabin where they were splitting up the money." Craven nodded his head as if affirming his words.

"I was setting the cabin on fire, I wasn't splitting up money." Darcy surveyed the crowd. Their faces looked doubtful as they tried to determine who told the truth. He had to talk himself into a hole, she'd done nothing wrong.

"I received word she and a couple of the robbers were seen in Baker City. I went there, and they tried to throw me off the train."

"We did no such thing."

"Then you were with the robbers?" The merchant, she'd thought of as her friend, asked.

"No, I was with my brother and Gil Halsey."

"He's one of the robbers," Craven quickly interjected. "Didn't you all see how he carried his gun?"

"I seen him talking to the young one who was asking a lot of questions about the man in jail," said Ted Haskell.

Darcy groaned. This wasn't working at all like it should. "I swear to you, I'm not friends with the robbers, and I didn't steal your money."

"Then why'd you disappear the night the bank was robbed?"

"Yeah, why didn't you get our post office back?" shouted another.

The crowd started toward her. Darcy ducked behind Mrs. Danforth's back as the woman turned to the crowd.

"When has any one of you believed anything Tobias Craven had to say?" The group continued forward.

"What's a woman of your reputation doing siding with an outlaw?" yelled someone.

"Yeah. Were you in on stealing us all blind, too?" yelled another. "Your fancied up women were at the party the night we was robbed."

Darcy said quietly, "Mrs. Danforth, save yourself. I've got nothing to live for. Gil was killed on the train, and Craven pulled me away from a gunfight. One my brother was in. I don't know if he's alive, wounded, or dead." Until she voiced what had banged around inside her head and heart since her abduction, she'd tried not to believe she was all alone. But the truth—there was no one to live for.

"Nonsense. Halsey wouldn't let anything stand between you and him. I saw the way he looked at you." Mrs. Danforth took a step closer to Craven. "If anything happens to this woman, you will never be able to set foot in this town again. I promise."

Craven sneered. "As long as she gets what's coming to her, I don't need this town." He waved one arm and gripped Darcy's arm so hard she squeaked. "Once this leader of the gang is hung the rest will stay away from here."

"Let's do it!" Came a shout from the back of the mob.

The tang of lead filled Darcy's mouth as fear gathered in her belly. They'd really hang her.

"I'm innocent. I'm not a robber. I tried to help this town." She struggled against the hold Craven had on her arm and dug in her feet.

"Let her go. She's an innocent woman." Mrs. Danforth grabbed her other arm.

Darcy was pulled like a sheet in a game of tug-o-war. Her shoulders ached and popped as the man and woman glared at one another.

"If you're so bent on making her pay, you should be able to convince a judge what she's done wrong," Mrs. Danforth said as sweat beaded her forehead.

Darcy's stomach churned from dread and pain. "Hang me if it will keep you from tearing me apart!" she shouted, causing the two to stop.

"I don't need a judge to tell me she needs hung." Craven pulled her away from Mrs. Danforth and started down the street. Darcy looked back at the woman. She stood in the street looking as befuddled as Darcy felt.

"Why are you doing this?" she asked as Craven stood her under a tree at the edge of town.

"You have been nothing but a thorn under my saddle since you got here. And you know too much." Craven turned her back to the people who followed them out of town.

"Get me a rope and a horse," he ordered, keeping a tight grip on her arm.

Darcy stared up the canyon. She'd made friends with the miners in that canyon. How could she have thought this was a good place to live? Blazes, the town folk were ready to string her up on the word of the worst crook in Galena.

The slow approach of a horse sounded like claps of thunder. When the sound stopped, strong arms lifted her up and she straddled a horse.

"This is ridiculous. As marshal did I ever do anything that made you think I was an outlaw?" She didn't speak to anyone in particular since her back was to the mob. Making this easier for them. Blazes! I'm not about to curl up. She twisted in the saddle, making the gawkers look at her.

"I've done nothing wrong. Craven is just silencing me, so he can steal more from you than he already has." She took a breath to start in on everything she knew about the man. He grabbed her by the hair, pulling her down to his level.

"You will not win this time," he said and crammed something into her mouth before he tied a bonnet backwards over her face.

The fabric was worn enough she had light, but couldn't see anything. She shook her head to dislodge the bonnet as her body was shoved back onto the saddle. The horse sidestepped and danced a little. Her heart raced. Should she jam her heels into the horse and hope she could stay on and not get knocked off by a tree limb? Thoughts banged and ricocheted in her head as loud as a hammer on metal.

What have I done to deserve to die this way? Tears trickled down her face. The only good thing to come of this would be to reunite with her family and Gil in the hereafter. She hadn't set foot in a church other than to ask for food since her parent's death. Maybe she wasn't going the same place as them. A shiver shook her body. She didn't want to die if she wasn't going to heaven.

Something moved in front of her face. She sniffed. The dry smell of hemp rope assaulted her nose. Something scratched her neck and tightened, poking like tiny pin pricks. She wiggled, but the movement only tightened the noose and dug the rope in deeper.

Panic squeezed her throat tighter than the rope.

I can't die.

Not until I set foot in church again. I want to see Gil.

"Hah!"

*Chapter 24*

Craven shouted and swat a horse on the rump as Gil and his brothers rode into town. The body attached to a rope in the tree wore kid slippers, Levis, and the top of a dress.

The bastard had strung up Darcy.

Gil yanked his rifle out of the scabbard. He took aim shot and cocked the lever, shooting until the rope halfway between Darcy and the tree limb ripped apart. Her body landed like a broken doll.

"Aaaiii!" Sorrow, and guilt collided inside as rage spurred him into action. Craven would die for stringing up Darcy. Touching his spurs to his horse, Gil raced after the plump man diving into the woods.

He caught the sorry excuse of a man cowering behind a pine.

"Get out here and take what you deserve." Gil leapt from his horse and yanked the fleshy coward from behind the tree.

"You murdered an innocent woman." Gil

punched the man in the face. "The woman I love." He punched Craven again. His knuckles meeting the fleshy face did little to diminish the loss squeezing his heart.

All the way to Galena, he'd envisioned reuniting with Darcy. And this lowlife had taken that chance away from him.

Forever.

Gil pulled his fist back to land another blow. A hand grabbed his arm as he started to let fly.

"No. This isn't the way." Ethan held his hand and searched his face.

"He needs to pay for killing Darcy." Gil wrestled his arm from his brother and landed another blow.

"No. Not this way. Darcy needs you." Ethan stepped in front of the bloody, unconscious man only standing due to Gil's firm hold on his jacket.

"Nobody can help her now." Gil's eyes burned with unshed tears. He should have made an honest woman of her. He'd planned to marry her as soon as Craven was behind bars. Now—Grief blurred his vision as he drew a fist back.

"Yes. You can. She isn't dead. Go to her. I'll take care of this rattlesnake." Ethan uncoiled Gil's fingers from Craven's jacket and shoved him back toward town. "Go on. Get on your horse and hightail it back to your woman."

Gil shook his head. Did Ethan say Darcy wasn't dead? The earnest look on his brother's face set his feet in action. He wouldn't put it passed his brother to tell him anything to keep him from killing the bastard Craven. But if there was a slight chance Darcy wasn't dead—he had to see for himself.

He mounted his horse and laid the spurs to the animal. He pulled up behind the cluster of people under the tree, covering them with a cloud of dust. The crowd opened up as he dismounted and hurried toward Jeremy, cradling his sister in his lap.

The look on the boy's face told him, she was alive. But by how much?

Gil dropped to his knees and gathered the small body into his arms. "Darcy, I'm here. Wake up. We've got a wedding to plan." He placed a kiss on her bluish lips.

They were cold.

His heart stopped. Maybe she was dead and it was only his and Jeremy's desire that made them think she was alive. He touched the red welt around her neck and shivered. A faint pulse vibrated under his fingers. If they'd been any later... he couldn't think about that.

"Come on, Sweetheart. I need your help. I can't have a wedding without you." He brushed the back of his knuckles across her white cheek and willed her to open her eyes.

"Get outta my way!" Lila pushed her way through the gathered crowd. "What that girl gone and done now?" she asked, staring at the limp body Gil held in his arms.

"She didn't do anything. That bastard Craven hung her." Gil glared back the direction Ethan came pushing Craven along in front of him.

"Well don't just sit there, pick her up and cart her up to Mrs. Danforth's. We got things ready to take care of her." She grabbed Gil's arm. "Come on, I know that bony gal ain't too heavy for ya."

Gil gathered Darcy in his arms and followed the broad backside of Lila down Main Street and up to the bath house. Jeremy dogged his heels all the way. He didn't blame the boy. If Jeremy were carrying her, he'd be right behind him.

At the house, Lila directed Gil to take Darcy upstairs. Two women stood by a room and waved him in. They sat Jeremy on a chair outside the door.

"Put her on the bed," one of the women said and pushed passed him to take off Darcy's kid slippers.

"Why isn't she waking up?" he asked, taking her limp hand.

"You'll have to ask Mrs. Dee. She's the only one with medicine knowledge." The woman didn't make him leave as she slipped the Levi's from Darcy's limp body.

He didn't care what anyone thought about him staying close while they undressed her. He wasn't leaving her side. Something hit the back of his knees, and he plopped down on a chair.

"You best sit. It could be a while." Lila's skirts swished as she moved to the opposite side of the bed and placed a wet rag over the ugly red welt on Darcy's neck. "I's seen men heavier than this thing dangle from a rope a lot longer, 'n' it didn't kill them."

Lila straightened. A tear glistened in her eye. She turned just as it slid down her cheek.

Gil swallowed the lump in his throat. Darcy had to live. It would take the two of them putting their heads together to figure out what he would do next. He couldn't go back to the ranch, not with

Pete Chandler going to go to trial for robbing and kidnapping.

Her fingers moved slightly in his hand. His heart thrummed with anticipation. Was she waking up? He squeezed her hand and leaned close.

"Darcy, it's me Gil. Wake up, Sweetheart."

Her translucent eyelids fluttered. "Come on. I'm waiting to ask you something." Her lips parted as her long lashes rose, revealing dilated, gray eyes.

His eyes burned with unshed tears as he looked down on the woman he loved. "I thought I'd lost you."

She reached up, touching his lips with shaky fingers. "Me, too," she croaked as a tear slid down the side of her head.

"Don't talk. It's bound to hurt." Gil kissed her hand. He'd always believed her fragile, but resilient. "I've been thinking, and as soon as you're well, we're getting married."

"Why?" she asked in a grating whisper.

"Why what?" He leaned down to hear her better and feel the warmth of her body. It reassured him.

"Why are you marrying me?" She winced as she forced the words out.

"Why wouldn't I?" What was going on in her head? Did the near hanging rattle her? She'd been all set to marry him before he threw her off the train. Was that it? Did she hold a grudge?

"I don't—" She swallowed painfully.

She loved him. He'd witnessed it in her eyes and her touch. He'd bring her around to marriage. If not today—soon.

"We don't have to talk now, you need to rest."

Mrs. Danforth entered the room. "How's she doing?"

"It's hard for her to talk." Gil held Darcy's small hand. "Her color's none to good either."

"The talking will have to wait. Her throat needs to heal. As for her color, I'm sure you can find a way to put some spark back into her." Mrs. Danforth smiled. "But for now, you need to leave. We want to get her into a nightdress and make her comfortable."

"I ain't leaving." Gil held onto Darcy's hand. He wasn't leaving her until she gave him the answer he wanted.

Mrs. Danforth turned to him looking like a mother cow with a newborn calf. "We aren't going to harm her, and we won't let anyone else in here other than you or her brother. Now, go take care of the men you brought to town all trussed up. And make sure Craven gets what he deserves."

Gil found himself dislodged from Darcy's hand and pushed out the door.

"How's she doing?" Jeremy asked, popping up from the chair by the door.

"She'll be fine. Just needs rest and no talking for a while." Gil put an arm around Jeremy's shoulders. "Come on, Mrs. Danforth will take good care of her, let's go make sure those outlaws and Craven are locked up."

"Thank you." Darcy winced. It hurt like a son-of-a-gun to push words out. If she wasn't feeling so darn puny, she'd go find Craven and…well, she'd do something that hurt as much as trying to talk.

"You're lucky Gil and his brothers came riding in when they did." Mrs. Danforth settled her against a pile of pillows. Between Mrs. Danforth and Sylvie they managed to get her out of the dirty, torn, and borrowed clothes and all washed up.

"I thought he was dead." She swallowed not only the pain of talking but the pain of the despair she'd felt believing he was gone. "With the outlaws and Craven being alive, I thought the worst for Gil." She bowed her head in shame and sipped the water Rose brought her. "I was ready to hang if it would have put me with my parents and Gil."

"We all want to be with our love ones when the end comes. But your end isn't even near." Mrs. Danforth smiled. "Your life is just beginning. I heard that man of yours ask you to marry him."

Darcy's heart fluttered. She wanted to spend the rest of her life with him, but, he'd yet to utter the words that she longed to hear. Words that would make anywhere they lived home.

"I think he's only asking," she rested her throat and continued, "'cuz he compromised me." The Halsey brothers hadn't come out and said anything against her, but she knew they planned on Gil marrying her because of his actions. She loved Gil, but refused to marry him if he didn't love her.

"That man is smitten with you." Mrs. Danforth looked at her as if dangling from a tree had addled her head.

"But is smitten and love the same thing?" Darcy wanted to believe he did love her, but until he came out and said it, she wouldn't marry him. She didn't want to be like the old women she'd met in her travels who found the man they loved looking elsewhere for things they should have been seeking at home.

"In my book they are." Mrs. Danforth stood. "I'll get you a cup of broth. You should be able to swallow that."

It didn't matter how many people she disappointed. Gil, Jeremy, the Halsey men, even Mrs. Danforth. She would refuse Gil until he said the words she needed to hear.

Gil smiled with satisfaction as he watched the outlaws and Craven bickering in the cell.

"If they keep this up, they'll have told us everything we need to get them thrown in a prison or hung," he said, turning to Ethan and Jeremy who were also taking in the spectacle.

"Someone should be writing all this down," Ethan said, looking around the room.

Jeremy found a paper and pencil in the desk drawer and handed it to Gil.

"Why me?" he asked, not sure if he wanted the job of sitting and writing down the prisoner's conversations when his mind was back at the brothel with Darcy.

"You're the logical choice for marshal now that everyone knows Darcy is a woman." Ethan patted him on the back.

"Me?" Gil looked at his brother and the boy, grinning beside him.

"Yeah, you."

"But I've got a job... Well, I probably won't have a job when Chandler learns his son is in jail for robbing and kidnapping due to me."

"There's no way you can go back there and work." Ethan slapped a hand on Gil's shoulder. "Besides, you'll have a family to provide for and from the way Darcy talks about this town, I think she wouldn't mind staying on."

"Yep, she likes Galena a lot," Jeremy chimed in, his eyes dancing with excitement.

"I think the town folk have to ask me. I can't just take over."

"Actually, brother," Hank walked into the room. "The town likes the idea of you taking over."

"How?"

"I guess you could say, we've been kind of spreading the word, you'd make a good marshal." Clay stepped through the door. The room overflowed with Halsey men.

One more body walked through the doorway. Jeremy's expression turned to pure hatred.

Gil stepped forward, "Can I help you?" he asked, blocking Jeremy from the view of the man.

"I'm Judge Lucas Duncan. I received a telegram to preside over a trial of a bank robber." He moved across the room and peered into the cell at the men still bickering.

Duncan. Could this be the uncle who... It had to be, the way Jeremy looked at the man.

"We've captured more of the gang making the trip worth your time." Gil studied the man. He had a cruel hook to his nose and dark, unwavering eyes.

"Ethan, why don't you and the boy go get something to eat," Gil said, making eye contact with his oldest sibling to make sure he understood to keep Jeremy away from this man. Ethan nodded his head and pushed Jeremy out of the room in front of him before the judge turned from the jail cell.

"Where do we set up for the trial?" he asked. "I'd like to get this over with today and head back to civilization."

"I'll find out for you." Gil started to head out the door.

"You'll find me in the saloon when you have things set up."

Gil nodded and motioned for Hank to stay with the prisoners. Darcy had to be told her uncle was the presiding judge. Damn. Would the man remain unbiased if Darcy took the stand? Could she control her hatred of the man?

Gil ran to the brothel expecting to find Darcy sleeping, instead he heard Jeremy's excited voice and Ethan trying to calm him.

"Darce, he's here!" Jeremy said, tugging on his sister's arm.

"I told you to get him something to eat," Gil said, rushing across the room to keep Darcy in bed.

"He bolted for here as soon as we crossed the street." Ethan said, running a hand over his face. "What is going on?"

Gil sat on the bed, holding Darcy under the covers. "Where do you think you're going?" he asked looking into her scared eyes.

"Out of here before he finds us." Darcy beat a fist on Gil's chest to no avail. They had to get away. She could tell by the look in Gil's eyes, he wasn't going to let them slip away like they'd done so often to stay one step ahead of the monster.

"He can't hurt you. I won't let him." Gil pulled

her into his arms. The safety of his embrace almost convinced her.

"He's a judge. He can hurt us anyway he wants." She looked at Jeremy, remembering how skinny and sick he'd looked when she stole him from her uncle.

"Not any more. You have us to help." Gil pulled her tighter against him. She wished she could believe him.

"You can't go in there!" Lila screamed as the formidable Judge Lucas Duncan strode into the room.

"I finally found you!" he bellowed, stalking across the room. Darcy cowered despite Gil standing and placing his body between her and her uncle.

"Who have you found?" Gil asked.

Darcy cringed as her uncle pointed a finger at her as she peeked around Gil.

"That harlot and her brother." Judge Duncan spun around, grabbing Jeremy by the collar. "You shouldn't have run away."

Ethan stepped up to the judge. "Take your hands off my little brother."

Jeremy's face lit up, and he yanked out of the judge's grip.

"What are you talking about?" The man sputtered and stared at Jeremy then Ethan.

"Jeremy is no longer a Duncan." The finality of Gil's words warmed Darcy's heart. "When I marry Darcy tomorrow, he'll be a Halsey, just like she will."

Darcy looked at Gil. The defiance shining in his eyes took her breath away. But was he only standing up for her to keep her out of her cruel uncle's hands?

"You plan to marry this harlot?" the incredulous look on her uncle's face made her feel filthy.

"No, I'm not marrying a harlot. I'm marrying the woman I love." Gil raised her hand and kissed her knuckles. The sincerity in his voice touched her heart and stirred her courage.

"And I'm marrying a true man. One who will never hurt me or anyone else who doesn't deserve it." Darcy glared at her uncle. "You got what you wanted, by telling our father you would take care of us. Money to buy your judge position." She motioned for Jeremy to come stand by her and Gil. "You can have the money, let us be. We have a new family."

The man opened his mouth, looked at Gil who stood by her side, holding her hand while his other hand rested on the handle of his pistol, then to Ethan standing with his arms crossed, glaring.

"Since you seem to have found a family, I'll leave you alone." He started to back out the door.

"One other thing." Gil stepped forward. "Darcy is the main witness for the trial your hearing. Since she's having trouble talking due to the bastard locked up in jail, the trial will have to wait until tomorrow."

The Judge started to open his mouth. Gil and Ethan both closed in on the man.

"And there'll be no prejudice against her when she testifies."

The judge looked at her than back at Gil and nodded his head, before hurrying out the door.

Darcy's heart stopped bouncing in her throat

as Gil sat down on the bed. Ethan grabbed Jeremy by the shoulder, moving him out the door and closing it.

"You really love me?" she asked, fearing he'd said the words only to convince her uncle he meant business.

"Let me prove it." Gil took her head in his hands. His lips brushed hers tenderly before he deepened the kiss, making her lightheaded and weak.

He drew his head back. "Now do you believe me?"

"Tell me again."

# Chapter 25

Darcy's heart brimmed over with happiness as she stood at the top of Mrs. Danforth's staircase dressed in a beautiful gown staring down at Gil Halsey, the man who would become her husband in a matter of minutes.

The appreciative grin and sparkling eyes took her breath away. He loved her enough to overlook her flaws and marry her. He'd stood up to her uncle and helped her through the trial. This was the man she wanted to spend the rest of her life with in good times and bad.

He held out his hand, and she started down the stairs, holding her skirt up so as not to trip and tumble down the stairs into his waiting arms. A relieved sigh escaped her lips, when her foot touched the rug at the bottom of the stairs. So far so good. The rest of the way was all flat.

"You look beautiful," Gil said, kissing the back of her hand.

"I'm thankful I made it down the steps without

falling."

"You know I'd catch you."

His words set her heart fluttering. The look in his eyes set her body on fire. He would always be there to catch her.

"Yes."

"Come on, the sooner you get hitched the sooner we can eat all that food Lila's got spread out in the kitchen," Jeremy hollered from the parlor door. An arm snaked out the door, pulling the boy back into the room.

"I guess we know what's important to him." Gil chuckled as he tucked her hand in the crook of his arm and headed toward the parlor.

Darcy couldn't think of a day she'd been any happier. The man she loved and who loved her was about to become her husband. Her brother had been brought into the Halsey fold as if they'd been born of the same parents. Nothing could spoil this day.

They stepped into the parlor. Her eyes lit on the man standing at the front of the room. She pulled back, but Gil wouldn't let her hand slip from his arm.

"Your uncle and I had a little talk." Gil tugged on her hand. "Come on, he's the only person around who can marry us legal. Otherwise we'd have to go to Baker City or wait for the preacher to come to town."

She stared at Gil and saw he wasn't about to wait. Waiting wasn't something she wanted to do either. Swallowing the lump of fear that lodge in her throat at the sight of her uncle, Darcy moved forward. Her foot caught in the hem of her dress.

Blazes. She made it down the stairs and couldn't even walk on flat ground. Gil caught her before she fell flat on her face. He smiled as he set her on her feet and took her hand, drawing her forward.

How had she been so lucky to find a man to love her unconditionally?

They stopped in front of Judge Duncan. She didn't look at the man who haunted her dreams and her travels. Her gaze remained on the face of the man saying he would take her for better or for worse.  Darcy never thought she'd ever hear a man say those words and mean it with the depth of emotion she saw in Gil's eyes.

"Sir, I'd like to add one thing," Gil said, never taking his gaze from her.

"Go ahead."

"Darcy Duncan, I will always love you and be by your side, but if you take up a rifle for any reason, you'll be paddled and never set foot outside our home again."

Those in attendance broke into laughter. Darcy laughed and threw her arms around Gil's neck, drawing him down to her level.

"I promise," she said and sealed the promise with a kiss.

# About the Author

All my work whether it's my romance or my mysteries have Western or Native American elements in them along with hints of humor and engaging characters. My husband and I raise alfalfa hay in rural eastern Oregon. Riding horses and battling rattlesnakes, I not only write the western lifestyle, I live it.

I love to hear from fans. You can find or contact me at:
patyjag@gmail.com
or my website – www.patyjager.net

Continue to the next page to find a listing of my historical western books or visit my website:
https://www.patyjager.net

**Historical Western Romance**
*Gambling on an Angel*
*Improper Pinkerton*
*For a Sister's Love*
*Christmas Redemption*

**Halsey Brother Series**
*Marshal in Petticoats – Gil's story*
*Outlaw in Petticoats – Zeke's story*
*Miner in Petticoats – Ethan's story*
*Doctor in Petticoats – Clay's story*
*Logger in Petticoats – Hank's story*

**Halsey Homecoming Trilogy**
*Laying Claim – Jeremy's Story*
*Staking Claim – Colin's Story*
*Claiming a Heart – Donny's Story*
*A Husband for Christmas - Shayla's Story*

**Letters of Fate Trilogy**
*Davis*
*Brody*
*Isaac*

**Silver Dollar Saloon**
*Savannah*
*Lottie Mae*
*Freedom*

**Contemporary Western Romance**
*Perfectly Good Nanny*
*Bridled Heart*

**Historical Paranormal Romance**
*Spirit of the Mountain*
*Spirit of the Lake*
*Spirit of the Sky*

Thank you for purchasing this Windtree Press publication. For other books of the heart, please visit our website at www. windtreepress.com.

For questions or more information contact us at info@ windtreepress.com.

Windtree Press
Hillsboro, OR

www.ingramcontent.com/pod-product-compliance
Lightning Source LLC
Chambersburg PA
CBHW060903190726
48286CB00002B/351